PERSONAL FOUL

BILLY TURNER

PERSONAL FOUL

A Novel

BILLY TURNER

PERSONAL FOUL

© 2015 Billy Turner

Edition ISBNs
Trade Paperback: 978-0-692-35155-0
E-book: 978-0-692-35156-7

First Edition 2015

This edition was prepared for printing by
The Editorial Department
7650 E. Broadway, #308
Tucson, Arizona 85710
www.editorialdepartment.com

Cover design by Kelly Leslie
Book interior design by Morgana Gallaway

In memory of Leviticus Monds, Evelyn Monds and Mamie Lucille Pinnock. Thank you for always believing in me.

PROLOGUE

Collingswood, Tennessee
Thirteen years ago

It was a hot, midsummer afternoon with enough breeze to make the temperature bearable on the basketball court and keep the pungent smell of weed from distracting thirteen-year-old Steven Lords as he crossed half court and eyed his next shot.

He stopped short of the faded three-point line and juked around a clumsy reach-in from an opponent. He was about to shoot when he noticed a police car turn the corner, just ten yards or so from the edge of the playground. The windows were down and he could see two white cops shaking their heads as a group of teens scattered from around the swing set, leaving the remnant of whatever they were smoking burning on the ground.

Drug-free school zone, my ass! Steven laughed to himself, passed the ball, and cut to the post, watching the cops head off in the opposite direction. They must have had bigger things to worry about in this neighborhood than some kids getting high in the parking lot.

Steven knew his mom would kill him if she knew he was playing ball over here, but at least he wasn't dumb enough to get involved in drugs and that kind of nonsense. It could get a little rough in this part of town, especially later in the day, but he actually liked playing ball on Mill Avenue every now and then. The cracks in the uneven concrete and double rims were a drag, but some of the "boys in the Wood" could really play. Plus you could always hear the newest jams playing out of somebody's car.

He nodded his head in time with "Ruff Ryder's Anthem" and glanced over to the far side of the playground. Some of the S. Avenue Crew were milling around outside the Crestlake Apartments, wearing their signature white do-rags and wife beaters and drinking out of paper bags. On the other side of the street, a couple of dreads in long T-shirts sat along the sidewalk on raggedy lawn chairs, watching the scene and trying to get a rap with some girls hanging around a decked-out Acura with its windows tinted black.

Steven was sweating like crazy and, as always, a little nervous there in his best friend Eddie's neighborhood, but that didn't stop him from leading his team to a twelve-point lead in a game of twenty-one. His teammates knew he was in the zone and kept the passes and assists coming. Steven didn't like to be a ball hog, but this was just one of those days. Sometimes he wondered if he didn't play better when he was a little on edge.

His team was one point away from their fourth win when he stopped at the top of the three-point line. For a moment everything seemed to move in slow motion. He could see every defender on the court and anticipate what each one was going to do. A picture formed in his mind—his move down the middle, then a quick shuffle to the left. A small jump, maybe half a foot at most, and then an easy swoosh for three without ever touching anything but air.

He faked a pass and then began executing. An effortless glide took him through his moves but before the calculated jump, he felt a jab on his back. The ball bounced off the double rim and then off the outreached hands of one his opponents on its way out of bounds.

"What gives, man?" Steven whipped around to see who had fouled him, only to stare into the wrinkled face of an old man who had wandered onto the court and stood unsteadily behind him. He held a fist full of crumpled-up dollar bills and wore a dingy Karl Kani sweatshirt and jeans that looked like they hadn't been washed in months.

"Watch where you're going, young buck!" the man said, then licked his ashy lips. "You damn chillens ain't got no respect."

"Sorry, man, my bad," Steven held up his hand to stop play until the man had a chance to stumble off the court.

"Hey, Stevie, you gonna stand there all day or are we gonna play some ball?" Eddie said. "Seriously . . . it's hot as bad breath out here."

Steven nodded and signaled for the inbound pass from Eddie, then began dribbling his way to shooting position. This time there'd be no stopping him.

A scrawny kid stepped up fast, arms up ready to block the shot, but Steven spun away. When another boy stabbed at the ball, Steven casually flipped it to his other hand. Then came a little head fake to throw off the bigger kids guarding the basket, and finally another calculated jump, everything as he had imagined it.

"That's game!" Steven wiped the sweat from his pimply forehead with his T-shirt, looked around, and saw his friends doubled over gasping for air. "Let's play another one!"

"Naw, man," Calvin said. "Damn that! It's hot and my cousin made a big-ass pitcher of Kool-Aid this morning. Let's hang this shit up and go get at it."

"Aw come on, just one more game?" Steven said. "We'll do three-on-three? It'll be me, Eddie, and Mark against you, Jason, and Devon."

"I'm wit' it," Eddie said and then looked over at Calvin. "But if we win, then you gots to hook me up wit' your cousin Michelle!"

"Fool! She don't want to have anything to do with your fat ass!" Calvin said. "She only dates ballers. Hell, Stevie has a better chance than you do, even with those skinny little legs he got."

Steven laughed. Skinny, maybe, but he'd grown seven inches in the past year. Each passing day felt like it brought him new skills. And more and more lately it was like he never really got tired like he used to. "Forget all that!" he said. "First team to twenty-one. Know who you got, fellas. Come on, let's ball!"

Steven stopped at the sound of Puff Daddy's "It's All About the Benjamins" booming from somebody's trunk and turned to see a white Cadillac Eldorado with gold trim and rims pull into the parking lot of a convenience store on the far side of the playground. The bass thumped loud enough to crack your teeth.

The game started, and after four easy baskets Steven had the attention of the car's passengers, the dreads sitting on the chairs, and a now couple of kids who had shown up out of nowhere and were standing on the baseline.

Might as well give them a little show!

A reverse lay-up here, a no-look pass there, a few three-pointers from way behind the arc . . . his shots were dropping like crazy and before long it was game point.

Time for the finale!

Steven stopped at the top of the three-point line, spread his legs, bent his knees, and placed the ball firmly at his hip. He grinned as a kid named Jason stepped up to guard him, saying, "You ain't got nothing, son!"

"I got fourteen of our twenty points." Steven faked a toss into his chest and then laughed. "Tell you what . . . I'll shoot it from right here, right in your face. I won't even watch it drop. That'll be game right there."

"So stop talking and show me what you got!"

Steven jab stepped him a few times and Jason backed off, opening the space he needed to get a clean shot. He turned his back toward the basket, knowing the five other boys were watching as the ball made its way to its target. If not for a slight summer breeze, it might have gone right in, but he knew the sound of a ball bouncing off the rim when he heard it.

Damn!

He turned around to see Calvin going for the rebound, while the biggest kid who'd been standing at the baseline got up in Calvin's' face with an arrogant sneer. One of his front teeth was half broken on a diagonal and one of his eyes drifted lazily to one side. "That's game, lil' niggas," he said. "Clear the court."

Calvin wasn't arguing, but the kid shoved him hard without waiting for an answer. Steven watched, frozen in panic. This was why you had to play early. Noontime was the best time to run because the thugs didn't take over the courts until later, when it got cooler.

While the kid who'd shoved Calvin dribbled the ball in

a circle, another boy pulled his shirt over his long dreads to reveal a lean, muscular, tattooed physique. A jagged scar ran across his chest, looking more like the result of a knife fight than an operating room. *Shit!*

Steven's adrenaline surged, but all the swagger and bravado of a few moments before was long gone. Now he was a scared thirteen-year-old kid about to get his ass kicked for no reason.

"Hey, you with them big-ass red shorts, come here!" the one with the ball said. Steven looked around at his friends, eyes wide. Nobody moved.

"That's *Jamal Jackson*," Calvin whispered. "I heard he broke some dude's jaw over at Lake Lytle last week."

Steven rubbed his cheek as he tried to summon the courage to walk over to Jamal. A lump hardened in his throat and shortened his breath, but he slowly advanced. He heard footsteps creeping up behind him, looked back and saw the same fear in Eddie's eyes that he felt. But something else, too—something wild. The two boys shared a nervous smirk and picked up their slow pace.

"What's your name, boy?"

The lump in Steven's throat felt like it doubled in size. They didn't ask Eddie his name. Why the sudden interest in him? He swallowed hard and said: "Steven . . . Steven Lords."

Jamal moved a little closer and Steven stood still, hoping no one noticed him grinding his teeth.

"Hey, man, get out of my boy's face!" It was Eddie, standing tall with his chest forward, stomach sucked in.

"Shut up, jitterbug." Jamal bumped Steven with his chest and stared at him. "Lords? You go to Kennedy, right?"

Steven closed his eyes and nodded.

"My lil' cousin quit basketball because of you," the boy said, tapping the top of Steven's head with his finger. "I recognized the crossover dribble and all that Globetrotter shit you was laying on them lil' punks."

Steven squinted hard but that didn't stop a tear that dripped down his eyelash and then his cheek.

"You made my cousin look all stupid in front of his moms, his sister, his boys, everybody!"

Steven shut his eyes even tighter. He knew Jamal kept talking, could feel the heat from Jamal's breath on his face but couldn't make out what he was saying. With his thundering heartbeat echoing in his ears, Steven couldn't hear anything.

"Look at me when I'm talking to you, punk!" Jamal spun him around by the shoulder, took the ball, and slammed it into Steven's chest. "So you think you got game? Huh? You think you can *play*?"

Steven stood motionless, clutching the ball.

"Come on, all-star! Man up. You hot shit when you got people watching, so let's go! You get the ball first." A hard shove sent Steven tumbling backward, away from the imposing shadow. He had his ball and he felt like he could make a speedy enough getaway, but he couldn't leave his friends hanging.

"So what's up, man? Let's do this!" Jamal said before he shoved Steven again.

"Hey, dawg, he ain't gonna play," someone else said from behind Steven. "Let's teach him a lesson!"

The thug's knuckles cracked as he balled up his fists. Steven tensed up when he looked into Jamal's yellow eyes, that seemed to glow against his dark complexion. Would the punch hit his face? It'd be hard to hide a black eye or bloody nose from his mom and even harder to explain a broken jaw. A blow to the stomach or chest would be a lot easier to cover up.

Steven closed his eyes. Best thing to do was run. He was faster than almost anyone out on the court and was pretty sure he could get away. Maybe they'd leave his friends alone.

"Aye, yo! What the hell is wrong with y'all?" a new voice shouted.

Steven opened his eyes and saw a tall, muscular man and his even bigger friend entering the park—the dudes from the white Cadillac.

The man took off his shades and got right up into Jamal's face. The white T-shirt he wore wrapped around his six-foot frame, while his gold necklace with a dangling Cadillac emblem rose and fell with every breath. He licked his lips as he sized up the boys, while his friend stood behind him and patted his fist.

"If you got a problem with lil' man, then you got a problem with me!" the stranger said, nostrils flaring. "If I was y'all I'd get the hell out of this park and make damn sure I never see you again, you feel me?"

Jamal clenched and unclenched his fist as he stared into the man's eyes. His friend stepped up and said. "Let's break out, man. This punk ain't worth it."

The boys grabbed their shirts off the ground and retreated across the street, heads hung low.

"And tell all your boys that lil' man is with me! If they want it with him, then they want it with me. You got that?"

Steven let out a long breath as the man walked over to him and laid a hand on his shoulder. "You okay, lil' man?"

Steven tried to wipe the tears from his eyes so he wouldn't look soft. Sniffling, he replied, "Yeah. I'm aight."

"You know, I was watching you from across the street, schooling your little partners over there. You got some game, man. I was impressed. So what's your name, anyway?"

"My name's Steven. Thanks for helping me, mister."

"My friends call me Dub. You know, I used to play ball at this park when I was a kid. I was a legend around here. I was in the newspapers and magazines by the time I was about your age."

"Word?"

"Word!" Dub replied. "After I put in work around here, I went on to play Division I ball on TV and all that."

"Is that where you got that scar on your chin? From playing basketball?"

As Dub smiled the sunlight reflected brilliantly off his gold tooth with a letter "*D*" cut out for the center. "Yeah, I got this scar from playing over at Lake Cole—a hard foul onto even harder pavement."

Steven nodded. He knew what that felt like. "Were you ever in the league?"

"Naw, never made it to the league. I played a little CBA ball though. But you got a lot of potential and I think I can help you realize it."

"I don't know. I just like to play, you know?"

"Hey, brother, don't doubt your skills. Don't ever doubt where skills like yours can take you! I've seen some great ballers and I've played against some great ballers and I'm telling you you're just as good as any of them. Let me help you. If you follow me and do like I tell you, the sky's the limit. You might even have what it takes to make the league one day."

Steven watched as Dub reached into the pocket of his baggy jeans and pulled out a wad of cash bound with a rubber band. He peeled off a few bills and pressed them in Steven's hand.

"If you do decide to let me help you, I promise you I can show you how to make more money in this game than you ever thought possible. I'll look out for you and who knows? Maybe one day you can look out for me."

Steven looked down at the wrinkled money. His mom would definitely tell him to say no. She'd say that taking money off the streets could lead to trouble, but this was basketball. What kind of trouble could come from hooping? Steven nodded his head. "Yeah, I'll work with you . . . if you really think you can help my game."

"No doubt! Meet me tomorrow after lunch up at Wells Gym." Dub said, "Me and you are gonna take this town by storm, and that's only the beginning, baby!"

CHAPTER 1

Miami, Florida
Present Day
Miami Coliseum
Eastern Conference Finals, Game 7

A in't that a bitch—Anthony just hit another jumper! Steven Lords looked at the shooting guard and gave him a wide-eyed grin. *Two minutes left in an elimination game and now he decides to get hot?*

Anthony could come off a screen better than any guard in the league. He'd hit his last four shots and gotten New York right back into this game. Steven shook his head as he took the inbound pass and dribbled up the floor. This series should've never gone to seven games. But now New York was riding a wave of momentum fueled by a nine-to-nothing run and it was going to be a dogfight the rest of the way. Where the hell did that ten-point lead go?

"How you love that?" Anthony said as he got back on defense. "I've got a lot more of it too."

There was no way Anthony and that watermelon smile of his was gonna win this series. There was still a minute left and a score right now could be a dagger in their chest.

Steven pumped his arms in the air, beckoning more crowd noise.

The seconds ticked away as Kyle, the point guard, made a bounce pass into the post to the power forward, Nate, who put up a shot that clanked off the side of the rim. Robert Miller, the team's center, snatched the rebound and fired it back to Kyle. Within seconds, a New York defender deflected a pass to Steven and charged toward the basket. A second later, New York had scored on a lay-up and Julian, Miami's small forward, had committed a costly foul. The ensuing free throw would put New York ahead. Miami promptly called a timeout.

The players huddled tightly, listening to Coach Hollis, who sat in the middle of the huddle drawing up a play. Steven draped a towel over his broad shoulders as he looked up at the scoreboard. 88-86, four seconds left, down by two. No big deal. This was definitely doable.

Coach Hollis had started drawing up a play, but there was no time to wait for something to develop. "Forget all that—just get me the ball," Steven said. "We got four seconds left. There's no way we're losing this game tonight. No way in hell, you hear me?"

Steven locked eyes with each of his four teammates in quick succession. "Seriously, everybody knows I'm getting the ball. So let's not mess around. Just get it in to me as fast as you can and I'll hit it, all right?"

Coach Hollis looked up at Steven with a knowing smile. "Okay, fellas. Here's what we're going to do . . ."

THE REF HANDED THE BALL TO JULIAN AND BLEW THE whistle. The crowd's noise dampened as they anticipated the next four seconds. The play unfolded as the coach had drawn it up. Steven got the jump on Anthony and caught Julian's pass.

4 seconds: Lords got the pass.

3 seconds: He took a hard dribble to the top of the three-point line.

2 seconds: A help defender met him at the line. He rose up for the shot.

1 second: He jumped a bit higher than his defender and got a decent look at the goal from three-point land. He released the shot. The ball rotated in a trajectory, heading straight for the backboard. As the ball made its flight Lords turned his back to the shot. He began to walk toward the bench when the ball hit its target with a satisfying *"swoosh!"*

In a situation that seemed desperate, true to form, Steven Lords had found a way to deliver.

CHAPTER 2

Miami Coliseum, 10:45 p.m.

Steven sat quietly in his locker stall with his cell phone in hand and looked out at the messy locker room. "They're waiting for you in the conference room, Steven," Dave Frasier, the team's Media Relations Director, called from the doorway.

Steven nodded and held up two fingers. "Give me just a couple of minutes, and I'll be right there, okay, D?"

"The sooner the better. There's quite a crowd in there."

Steven looked back to his phone. He'd missed fifteen calls already but not a single one from Karen, so the rest could all wait.

It had been an amazing night highlighted by the most meaningful shot of his entire career and the biggest win the city of Miami had seen in ages. He wanted so badly to feel the same elation his teammates did, but he was all but numb to it. He felt restless and hollow and was thankful for a few minutes alone.

He took a few deep, quick breaths to muster up the nerve to make the call and put the phone to his ear. Things had been more than a little tense with his wife the past few weeks, with his calls going unanswered and messages left with her parents going unreturned. But surely she wouldn't ruin this night for him, especially when all he wanted was to talk to his daughter.

"Hello?"

Steven's pulse raced at the sound of Karen's voice.

"H-Hey, baby. Did you see—"

"Goodbye," Karen said.

"I know you're upset, baby, but please just let me talk to Cass—"

It was too late. Karen had already hung up.

Steven leaned against the stall wall. Nothing had changed. Deep down he didn't expect it would, but there was always hope. After all, on a night like this, it seemed to the rest of the world he could do no wrong. But to Karen he couldn't do anything right.

"Lords, the room is getting restless. Are you ready?" Dave asked as he stuck his head through the doorway.

"Ready as I'm gonna be."

***

THE MURMURING OF THE MEDIA BEGAN TO BUILD AS Steven took a seat at the table. He looked out at the army of reporters jockeying for position in a room designed for far fewer attendees than were there. The high stakes of tonight's game had brought the media out in droves.

In anticipation of what he hoped would be the biggest win of his career, he'd taken his favorite cream-colored, four-button designer suit from his closet that morning and a coral dress shirt he'd gotten from his daughter the previous Father's Day. Some athletes wore sunglasses during press conferences, but Steven preferred to make eye contact with the reporters and cameramen. His agent, Allen Warner, always said eye contact showed sincerity. Sincerity paved the way to trust, and trust equaled millions in endorsements.

The room fell silent when Steven took a swig of water and slid his microphone closer, indicating he was ready to start. "So . . . did anyone catch the ending to the game tonight?" he said, offering a warm but practiced smile that had become a veritable trademark.

The crowd laughed and the press conference started in earnest. After nearly a half hour of answering questions about the final minutes, the last shot, and the team's preparations for the Finals, Steven was ready to get out of the stuffy room and join his teammates for the celebration. But he made the mistake of allowing one last question.

"Congratulations on a great win, Lord!" a reporter in the back of the room said.

That gravelly voice was familiar.

"Thanks, Pete," he said. "I was really hoping you wouldn't be here tonight." It would've been nice to go one night without hearing Peter Owens's voice or fielding any questions from that rag he wrote for.

"Aw come on, Lord, you know I wouldn't miss this night for the world. But what I did miss was seeing your wife and daughter in attendance tonight."

Steven bolted upright in his chair and took a few deep breaths to regain his composure. "Karen's out of town visiting relatives," he said, trying to keep his voice light. "I'll let her know you asked about her."

"I appreciate that, Lord, I really do." Pete was standing now and pointing a tape recorder at him. "But I actually haven't seen them at any of the games in, what, five or six weeks now, is that right?"

Steven narrowed his eyes. "I really wouldn't know about that, now would I?"

"Wouldn't know what?"

"About what you have or haven't seen. What I saw tonight was a good team busting its butt out there to bring this city the biggest win in recent memory. If you have a question about that I'd be happy to answer it, but otherwise—"

"That's just it," Pete said. "A big win in what's probably the biggest game of your career. I hate to bring it up but given the rumors—I'm sure we've all heard about certain . . . 'indiscretions' on your part—I just wanted to put the question we know everyone's asking straight to you and give you a chance to answer. So . . . is your marriage in trouble? Are you and your wife going through a separation?"

The room had gotten so quiet all you could hear was the hum of the A/C unit. Steven tugged on his tie as he stared out over the crowd, his adrenaline surging. "I . . . I don't see what that has to do with anything! And who do you think you are, asking me a question like that? Let me tell you something—"

He stopped when Dave Frasier grabbed the microphone. "Steven isn't here to answer questions about his personal life. He's only talking about the game. And on that note, let's wrap up this round of interviews."

Pete waved his hand in the air. "One more question! This won't—"

"Not gonna happen," Dave said. "The Lord shouldn't be expected to keep company with Judas."

Flashbulbs went off as Steven exited and beelined to the hallway back to the locker room, biting his lip so hard it could have gushed blood.

"Did you see what just happened, Al?" he said when he saw his agent approaching. "Did you see that shit? From now on I don't want to hear or see Owens, you got that? He doesn't talk to me!"

Allen put a hand on Steven's back and gently ushered him toward the locker room. "Let's get you out of here, all right?"

They had almost made it to the locker room when Steven heard a burst of commotion in the hallway behind him. Owens must have tried to follow him from the press room. Security had intervened, but he clearly wasn't giving up.

"Lord, I'm sorry, but it's my job." Owens called from behind him. "I get paid to ask the tough questions, man. You know it's nothing personal!"

Steven stepped toward him and pointed right into his face. "Nothing personal? You've been looking for dirt to dish on me since I was a rookie, and now you drag my wife and daughter into it?"

"I'm filing a restraining order against you, Owens," Allen said. "You can kiss your press pass goodbye for the Finals."

"Do what you want, but I'm not the one you need to be worried about, pal!" Pete shouted. "You've got bigger problems than me, I promise you."

STEVEN WASN'T A FIGHTER, BUT IT TOOK EVERY BIT OF self-restraint he had not to punch Peter Owens right in the mouth and teach the smug hater a lesson he wouldn't soon forget. It was a punk move to bring up someone's personal business like that in a press conference. And what the hell was this business about "bigger problems?"

A few more reporters were filing out of the press room, and the last thing Steven wanted to do was make any kind of scene in the vicinity of their cameras and microphones.

So he just turned and fell into step with Allen and Dave as they made their way toward the locker room.

He was just starting to settle down when he heard someone yelling and the sounds of a skirmish from around the corner opposite where Owens had been standing.

Christ, what now?

"I said, get yo goddamn hands off me!"

Steven stopped dead in his tracks and shot a worried look at Allen. That sounded like Eddie. And if he was as agitated as he sounded, arena security had their hands full.

Steven stepped around the corner and took in the scene. "Eddie, just let it go! You'll only make things worse!"

Eddie wasn't listening. He turned the corner and pointed down the hallway at Pete Owens with fire in his eyes like Steven had never seen.

"I'm about to bust my foot off in his ass," Eddie said.

"That's enough," Allen said, nodding at a second reporter who was pulling out a camera. "I need both of you in that locker room without another word. Now!"

It took a few moments to get Eddie settled down. He'd watched the streaming feed of the press conference on his iPhone and was almost as upset as Steven. "I'm telling you, you should've let me put these gators up that dude's ass!"

"I know," Steven said. "Truth is that I was tempted to

teach him a lesson myself. But you can't start a fight with everyone who has a problem with me. We ain't in the parks no more, bro. We gotta be smarter than that."

"Damn that," Eddie said. "What is it with that guy? Why he's always hating on you anyway?"

"I don't know," Steven said. "The problem is there were cameras everywhere tonight. I got an image to protect, you know?"

"And speaking of image, Steven, we have some business to discuss." Allen said, taking a seat in the locker stall between Eddie and Steven. "I got a call a few minutes before Eddie's little tantrum there and it looks like the people over at Nike can have the final version of your shoe in stores by game one. So they want you to shoot a spot right away."

"That's great, Al," Steven said, ignoring Eddie's sneer at Allen. "But I need to talk to Ed—"

"I also need you to stop by the suite before you leave and meet with a couple of guys from Kellogg's. I'm working on this deal to get you your own cereal. Limited edition 'Lord Flakes.' It's got little marshmallow crosses in it and every-thing. Kids will love it, and so will the Jesus freaks."

Steven sighed and leaned against the back of the locker stall. "Allen, can I get a minute to relax for a few? Eddie, what time is it anyway?"

"11:30."

Steven slouched lower in his stall. "Tell the Kellogg's guys

I'm sorry to keep them waiting but I'll be there as soon as I can."

AFTER ALLEN LEFT, EDDIE STOOD UP AND LEANED CLOSE to Steven. "Hey, man, I'm sorry if I was trippin' earlier. But check it—I ran into Julian and he told me about the party he's throwing at Roxie's tonight. Are you going?"

Steven said nothing.

"Well, are you? You may as well go. Ain't nobody waiting for you at home, right?"

"You got that right," Steven said, shaking his head at the thought. "I don't know what I'm gonna do. Why don't you just hang in the lounge with Al? I'll be there in a minute."

"How about if I just skip that and dip on over to the party?" Eddie said as he walked to the door. "Everybody's expecting you to come through. So don't be here all night."

Steven breathed deeply as he closed his eyes and ran his hand over his hair. *Finally, a little peace and quiet!*

CHAPTER 3

Roxie's Gentlemen's Club
Miami, Florida, 12:20 a.m.

Eddie strutted through the party with a tumbler of Captain and Coke in his hand and a smile on his face. Being Stevie's best friend always got him into good parties, and this was looking like it might be the best party yet.

He bobbed his head in time with the Latin dance music blaring through the speakers and savored the scene around him through the haze of weed and Cuban cigar smoke. This shit was seriously tip-top, first class all the way.

Julian knew how to throw a party, and he had pulled out all the stops in getting this jam together. In one corner of the room, some players dropped stacks of dollars bills on a couple of girls who kissed and pawed at each other like porn stars. Sexy, mostly naked women were getting down anywhere you looked, taking good care of about every player on Miami's roster. That was except for Steven, who hadn't made it yet, and a straightedge dude they called Rev, who Eddie never had much use for.

Having the party in the Grand VIP Room at Roxie's was a smart move. It kept all the haters and nosey-ass reporters out and let the boys be boys. Eddie had a killer buzz going already and he needed to find himself some company and see where the night might take him.

He looked around for someone to talk to and stopped when he noticed Nathan Randall leaning against a column and talking to a couple of tall Caribbean-looking ladies. "Nate, that was a nasty dunk you had in the third quarter, my brother."

Nate scowled as he looked Eddie up and down. "Thanks, man. I appreciate it," he said, then returned his attention to the girls.

"I know Steven gets a lot of props, but fo' real you throws it down, you know what I'm sayin'."

"Yeah, thanks, man."

"You know what I was thinking—"

"Look, brother, I don't mean no disrespect, but me and my teammates are trying to blow off a little steam after a big win, okay? I don't know how you got in here, but since you're here why don't you go and get up on one of these ladies and let me do my thing, all right?"

"Whatever, man."

Eddie checked himself over in one of the mirrored pillars next to the stage before going out and trying to mingle. His beard could've used a trim and his bald head looked a little ashy. But the black and gold silk Versace shirt and yellow diamond pinky ring screamed "boss player," and overall he was satisfied with what he saw.

He reached out and grabbed the arm of a pretty Latina girl walking past. "¿Que pasa, mama? Me llamo Eddie," he said with a smile on his face. "¿Quieres una fiesta conmigo?"

"Party with *you* when there are some real ballers in here? Please! You look like a broke-ass Rick Ross with your bald-ass head and nappy beard."

Eddie kept his smile as he moved closer to the girl. "You mean you don't remember me from the other week when we partied up at the Lexx that time? I'm 'The Lord's' boy."

"I remember Steven, but I don't remember you."

"Aw come on, mama! Remember when we all got down and—"

"Save it, sidekick! I don't get down with the help."

Fuck, what was with these people tonight? Nobody treated him like this when Steven was around.

Eddie smoothed the wrinkles out of his shirt and watched the girl storm off. His mood brightened when he saw a couple guys at a small corner table sniffing white lines off a mirror. He had started for the table when a bare-chested

Julian approached him with two diamond necklaces dangling from his neck and a girl under each arm.

"I see where you're heading, boy. You better know what you're about to get into," he said. "That's Tony Montana pure you're messing with. Not that nickel-bag shit you get down in Liberty City."

Eddie smiled. "I wouldn't expect anything less from you, man."

"Aight, that shit'll make you do something you'll regret." Julian said. "Don't blame me if you wake up in an alley and don't know how you got there."

"Don't worry about me. I can handle mines."

Eddie sat at the table, relieved by the warm reception and more than ready to take his buzz to the next level. Julian grinned as he sent one of his girls to sit next to Eddie and help him cut his lines.

Finally, a little respect. This was more like it!

THE GLOW FROM THE PINK NEON SIGNS LIT UP THE NIGHT sky as Steven pulled his silver Aston Martin to a stop in front of Roxie's front door to check out the scene. Julian's parties never disappointed, and this one was sure to be no exception.

"Congratulations on the win tonight, Mr. Lords," the valet said as he stepped out into the cool humid night. "They're all waiting for you in the Grand VIP Room."

Steven nodded and stepped out of the car. Stopping by

for a few drinks with the boys couldn't hurt. Then it'd be back home to try and get some sleep.

"Everybody's talking about that shot you hit," the valet continued. "Y'all gonna bring that trophy back to Miami, right?"

Steven smiled as he shook the man's hand. "Oh, you already know!" he said and then went inside.

Lil' Wayne's "Got Money" was blaring on the club's speakers when Steven stopped inside the doorway to survey the scene. An *Eastern Conference Champions* banner hung over the main stage. Red and black balloons representing the team's colors floated along the ceiling and a highlight reel from tonight's game was playing on all the plasma TVs. The party was jumping, but the more Steven thought about it, the worse he felt about being there.

He was about to try and slip out unnoticed, but the DJ must have seen him enter because the music came to an abrupt stop. Before the DJ could say a word, Eddie jumped up from a table at the back of the room and made his way toward Steven, if a bit unsteadily.

"Ladies and gentleman, the man of the hour!" Eddie proclaimed. "Our own personal Jesus and my dawg for life, Mr. Steven 'The Lord' Lords!"

Almost everyone in the room stood and applauded. Steven couldn't help but smile.

"It's about time you showed up!" Julian said. "We been at it for over an hour already."

He grabbed a bottle of champagne and handed it Steven. "Here's your bottle of Ace of Spades. Only the best for 'The Lord!'"

Steven grabbed the bottle and took a quick swig. "So what else you got goin' on up in here?"

"Come on, man, you know how I do! I got the United Nations of bitches in here. Food's over there and liquor is everywhere. I got fine hoes, lesbian shows, and freaks that will make you holla for a dolla."

"That's what I'm talking about!" Steven took another swig of champagne. He felt fingertips climbing up his back and a pinch on his ass. He looked down and smiled when he recognized a couple of familiar faces looking up from their sexy blond manes.

"I know what you like, boy!" Julian said. "I made sure Tanya and Heather were both here just for you. You remember them, right?"

Steven nodded and took a long drink from his bottle. Judging by the way Tanya was sucking on a finger and twirling a strand of curly blond hair, it wasn't hard to tell what her intentions were.

"Wazzup ladies? How y'all doing tonight?"

"Oooo, good, daddy, now that you're here," Heather said.

"Everybody's talking about the last basket you scored," Tanya said. "Why don't we all go to the back and congratulate you on your win?"

Steven took a deep breath as the girls guided him through

the room. He wanted nothing more than to kick back and enjoy this, but he couldn't shake thoughts of Peter Owens's questions. Maybe it was time to take things at home more seriously. This type of behavior was one reason Karen left in the first place, and if common sense was really common, that Aston Martin in the parking lot would be headed across the MacArthur Causeway.

But there was no resisting Tanya's advances—not with those soft, soft hands and hot-pink booty shorts.

"I see you over there, baby!" Eddie said as he pointed in Steven's direction. "'The Lord' is in the house!"

Eddie's half-drunken banter was all it took to get Steven's thinking onto a completely different track.

"Listen, man, please don't encourage this, all right?" He stopped and stared at Eddie, whose red eyes looked right back at him. "It sounds lame, I know, but I think I might need to take my ass home."

"Home? What the hell for? Ain't nobody home waiting, you should be out with your boys celebrating."

"I know, right? But I'm just trippin' on what happened earlier," Steven said. "If people are spreading rumors about me, then maybe I need to chill."

Surely Eddie could understand that. That's what friends did, right?

"Chill tomorrow!" Eddie said. "Tonight we celebrate. Plus, this is a safe place here. There's nobody here but your teammates, your boy, and some chicks who know how to keep their mouths shut." Eddie snuggled between two girls on the couch and threw his arms around them. "At least most of the time," he said with grin. " Seriously, man . . . I'm sorry 'bout what happened, but you gotta do you because I'm damn sure doing me."

As if on cue, Tanya and Heather walked over and steered Steven over to a red velvet couch. Steven let himself grin with anticipation and watched as the ladies slowly untied their bikini tops and let them fall to the floor.

His cell phone vibrated in his pocket, breaking the spell and giving him just the out he needed.

"Hold on, ladies—I need to take this call." Steven gently pushed Tanya off him, reached into his pocket, and rolled his eyes when he saw the number on the display. Damn girl had already called eight times tonight. Whatever it was had to be important enough to blow the phone up. Hopefully, it was something worth hearing.

"It's about damn time you answered your phone," an icy female voice said before he even had a chance to say hello. "I been calling you all night."

No greeting, no congratulations. Just an angry voice that had an edge to it he hadn't heard in a long time.

Steven pressed the phone tightly to his ear, looking in vain for a quiet corner where he might escape the blaring music. That wasn't going to happen, so he figured he'd get right to the point.

"Listen, it's been a crazy night and I can barely hear you. Did you handle that business like you said you would?"

"We need to talk about that."

"No we don't. We've already discussed it and we agreed that it's best if you—"

"I'm keeping it."

Steven pushed the phone harder to his ear. "Say what?"

"You heard me. I'm keeping it."

"Wait a minute, we agreed—"

"No, you agreed! And you know what? That two hundred grand? I'm keeping that too."

"Michelle, wait . . . you can't do that!"

"I can do whatever the hell I want to do."

Steven felt his adrenaline surge, hard, pulsing the same way it had a few hours ago. It took every bit of restraint in him not to throw his phone at the wall and watch it shatter.

"Where are you right now?"

"My room at the Murcielago. You know the number."

"I'm on my way."

CHAPTER 4

Biscayne Boulevard
Miami, Florida, 1:37 a.m.

Eddie wasn't happy about having to leave the party, but something bad must have happened to get Steven so upset.

"Where the hell we goin' anyway?" Eddie asked as he divided his attention between the road and his silent passenger. Steven had told him to head downtown but not much else.

"Murcielago Hotel."

"Why? Wazzup?"

"It's goddamn Michelle again," Steven said. "She called me at the club, says she's not gonna have the abortion."

"Say what?" Eddie heard a car horn, looked up, realized he'd drifted into the oncoming lane, and jerked the Aston Martin back to his side of the road. Julian wasn't lying when he said that coke was potent. Eddie's brain was on overdrive, and though he'd only had a few drinks he was really feeling them. But he had to stay focused.

"Pay attention, would you? I need some time to think and that shit ain't helping!"

Eddie sat up straight and gripped the wheel tighter with both hands.

"She changed her mind. She wants to have the baby," Steven continued. "If she goes through with it, there's no telling where the damage stops. But you can be damn sure Karen will file for divorce and try for custody of Cassie. And if word gets out as to why, I can kiss my endorsements goodbye."

Eddie shook his head. "I told you that bitch was no god-damn good. Been telling you that since way back in high school. So what you gonna do now?"

"That's what I'm trying to figure out," Steven said. "At the end of the day I can't *make* her do anything." He let out a long sigh and stared through the windshield. "All I know to do is go to the hotel and try to reason with her, you know?

"Look here, man, you've talked to her, you've reasoned with her, you've even tried to pay her ass off to the tune of almost a quarter mil," Eddie said. "Ain't nothing work. All she want to do is blow up your spot and get whatever she can get."

"I don't know about that. Maybe she just wants to keep the baby."

"You can't be too sure."

"What do you mean?"

Eddie narrowed his eyes and shook his head. "Nothing, man . . . I just don't trust that girl is all."

That seemed to satisfy Steven. "If you got any better ideas, I'm all ears."

Eddie thought for a minute. His brain felt like it was starting to throb. Something about Michelle had always bothered him, and lately she'd shown a new set of horns. He didn't want to upset Steven but this was serious trouble.

"You've got too much goin' on—and a whole lot of other shit happening if you win the championship—to let Michelle mess it all up," Eddie said. "You need to stop this shit and I'm talking once and for all."

An awkward silence enveloped the car.

When Steven didn't say anything, Eddie continued, "Seriously, man. I know a few guys that put in some work. Now it'll cost a little piece of change, but it'll be one hell of a lot less than that greedy bitch is gonna cost you if you don't handle this. All I gotta do is make one phone call and all this becomes a memory."

Eddie glanced nervously at the frown on Steven's face.

His blood was boiling from cocaine and rum, and crazy as it was to be having a discussion like this, the idea made a world of sense to him. But Steven hadn't said a word and Eddie couldn't read his expression.

"Man, I was just fucking with you!" Eddie said with a sudden burst of laughter to cut the tension.

Steven sighed. "You sure? You're fucked up, you know that? That was seriously fucked up. I thought you were for real."

"What? Were *you* serious? You want me to make a call?" Eddie asked. "You know I keep the heat on me. Just say the word and I'll handle it. You know my man Jimmy works in the hotel and—"

"Oh, hell no, man! I don't like that dude, I don't trust that dude, and I don't want him around me."

"Jimmy's good people. Plus, he's a huge fan of yours. If you say the word—"

"Your boy ain't wrapped too tight," Steven said. If you can't see that then maybe Allen's right?"

Eddied stiffened in his seat. "Right about what?"

"Come on man, all this weed and coke and whatever the hell else you've gotten into lately . . . that shit ain't good for you. And after that craziness you just said to me, I think he might—"

"Al needs to mind his own damn business," Eddie said. "Anything he says and you just run with it."

"You know it ain't like that. He's just concerned, that's all. Honestly, I can't say I blame him."

Eddie shook his head. "Concerned my ass. He ain't concerned about nothing but trying to get me out of the way."

"I'm not so sure that's it, bro. You've changed. You're talking all crazy. You're hanging out with these shady-ass people—like hotel Jimmy—and saying stupid things. I'm starting to worry about you a little bit."

"Don't worry about nothin'. I've got everything under control. Besides, I'm your boy. You know if you need somethin', I got you."

"Yeah, I know, man." Steven said, still gazing out the window. "I just can't stop thinking about how I coulda got myself into this."

Eddie nodded, relieved with the change in subject. "So, what are we gonna do about this?"

"I don't know, man. I'm starting to think maybe I don't have the right to tell her what to do with the baby. It's not like she wasn't pregnant before." Steven said as he shrugged his shoulders. "I fucked up and there's no reason why this kid should have to pay for my mistake."

Eddie whipped his head in Steven's direction. "Are you fucking high or something?" he said with a scowl. "You honestly believe letting her keep this baby is gonna solve your problem?"

"I don't know what else I can do. I know what's at stake and the risks involved, but what else is there? I mean, I love Cassie with all my heart. That little girl is my world. Do I really have the right to take that joy away from Michelle?"

"Let me tell you something, bro. This ain't about being happy to have a kid or whatever you're trying to make this out to be. I see how happy you and Karen are with Cassie, but it ain't like that for Michelle. I can guarantee that—"

"But Ed, I—"

"Let me finish. This kid is sho' nuff a lottery ticket for her. It's a way to stay in your damn pockets for the rest of her life. Michelle is a straight-up gold digger and she's been that way since high school.

"Whatever," Steven said, but Eddie could tell his point was sinking in.

"Let's not forget that girl's from Ivy Green. You remember what Ivy Green is like. That place is crazy. Did you ever think . . .?"

"Ever think what?" Steven said.

Eddie looked at his friend and decided against saying anything more. "Nothing, man. Here we are anyway. Just don't underestimate this chick's greed, okay."

They pulled into the circular, palm-lined hotel driveway and stopped at the lobby. Steven sat in the passenger seat, pulling on the door handle and staring at the hotel's automatic doors.

Eddie sighed. "Go on up and do what you need to do. I'll wait in the parking lot."

"Thanks, man." Steven said as he opened the car door. "Hey, let's keep this visit between us, okay? This is our business—we clear?"

"Hey, we were never here, bro!" Eddie said. "But just know that whatever you need, I'm right here."

CHAPTER 5

Murcielago Hotel, 9:13 a.m.
Five days before the Finals

Marta Arroyo hummed to herself as she slowly pushed an overloaded housekeeping cart down the burgundy-plush-carpeted hallway of the Murcielago. She liked working the quieter VIP floors at the top of the hotel. She was heading to her first room of the day when she noticed a cobweb gathering on one of the frosted glass sconces on the corridor's wall. She took a moment to wipe it down, made sure none of the others needed the same attention, and then knocked on the dark wooden door of one of the hotel's premier suites.

"Housekeeping," she said. When no one answered she slid her access card into the door and gently pushed it open. "Housekeeping!" she said, louder. Again, no one answered.

Still humming to herself, she took her cloths and spray bottles from the cart and went to work. She started with the giant picture windows overlooking the bay and then carefully dusted the fragile stone sculptures on each end table of the plush leather couch.

The living room didn't look like it had seen much use, but she still took her time, making sure everything was wiped down and cleaned properly. After a careful vacuuming of the marble floor, she took some fresh beige bed linens from the cart in the hallway and started for the bedroom. She stopped short when she saw a woman lying on the floor.

"My god, you nearly scared me to death," Marta said, rubbing her chest and taking a few deep breaths. It wasn't all that strange to find a guest passed out in a room, even up here in the penthouse suites. Truth was, you never knew what to expect cleaning up after Miami's rich and famous, and there was talk all over the hotel of some big game that had the city celebrating last night.

Marta moved in closer to the woman, figuring she should probably try and wake her up and at least get her into bed. The poor girl was laid out flat on the cold floor without a sheet or blanket. Her face was turned away so Marta couldn't see her eyes, but something didn't look right.

She watched for a moment and realized the woman was lying perfectly still, with no signs of breathing. Marta's jaw dropped when she walked around the bed. She got a full view of the blank stare in the woman's brown eyes and the blue-and-red bruising on her neck. The girl wasn't drunk—she was dead.

DETECTIVE RUSSELL HOWARD OF THE MIAMI-DADE Police Department arrived at the hotel shortly after the first-responding officers. He'd been out all night, having arrived home only an hour or so before sunrise. All he knew was a woman was dead at the Murcielago and there was no sign of forced entry.

Less than a half hour after getting the call he ducked under the yellow crime-scene tape across the elevator door and walked down the hall to suite 2205.

"What a dump, huh?" he said to one of the uniforms standing at the open door of the luxuriously appointed suite. "Anyone else been in here besides you guys?"

The young cop laughed and shook his head. "Far as I know, just the maid. And it don't sound like she stayed too long."

Russell sniffed the air and noted a lemony aroma. Maid must have polished the furniture, and who knows what else. That wasn't good. "She the one who found the body?"

"That's right," the patrolman said, pulling out his notepad. "Name's Marta Arroyo. Started making her rounds about nine this morning, and this was the first suite she started cleaning. I asked her what time she found the body and she couldn't say exactly. But she alerted her supervisor right away, and that's when the call hit 911."

"Where's she now?"

"On her way to the ER. Manager says she completely freaked once she realized the lady was dead. She has heart problems so they sent her to University Medical to get checked out."

"Were you able to get anything from her? Was she able to talk?"

"Sorry. Didn't have much time and she didn't have a lot to say except she left the body just like she found it."

"And where was that?"

"On the floor in the bedroom," the officer replied. "Right this way."

Russell glanced at the doorjamb and then followed the cop down the hallway into a bedroom that was easily the size of his whole apartment. He couldn't see the body at first, and his breath caught in his throat when he walked around the bed and found her.

He hadn't been in homicide long, and seeing dead bodies still got to him. To make matters worse, this girl was stone-cold gorgeous. Tall, thin, flawless toffee-colored skin and coffee-brown eyes that might have been her best asset, had they been shining with life.

He crouched next to her and leaned in close. No way this was a robbery, not with the diamond pendant necklace lying over some nasty bruising on her throat. Maybe she was there with someone to begin with? Her black nightgown looked a little too sexy for her to be sleeping alone.

"What do we know about her?" Russell asked.

"Name is Michelle Tibbs," The officer said. "Out-of-towner. Arrived four days ago."

"Did you go through her things? Did you touch anything?"

The officer shook his head. "The manager met me in the lobby and gave me all the info he could as we were coming upstairs."

"Good." Russell nodded then leaned closer to the victim and moved her head slightly. She'd clearly been roughed up a bit—had dried blood on the corner of her mouth. He didn't have much to go on, but Russell would have bet a week's pay that the killer was male and probably knew her biblically.

He stood when he heard his supervisor's voice in the living room. A moment later, Detective Sergeant Arturo Morales walked into the bedroom followed by some techs from the crime-scene lab. He stopped when he saw Russell and gave him a quizzical look. "I'm surprised to see you in here, Detective. Did you process the scene first or go straight to the body?"

Russell said nothing but quietly sighed. *At least he didn't call me Junior.* One thing about being a rookie detective was the privilege of having your superiors check up on you.

Russell had every intention of going back to look more carefully at the suite but wanted to see what he was dealing with first. Given the lack of signs of forced entry, the necklace, and the nightgown, this had all the signs of a romantic tryst gone wrong, some kind of jealousy thing or maybe an unlucky wife caught cheating.

Rather than trying to explain, Russell gave Morales a rundown of what had happened with the maid. "Looks like she did a lot of cleaning before she found the victim, I'm afraid. Bet you two-to-one the scene's been compromised."

"No suckers' bets for me, Junior," Morales said. Then he grabbed hold of Russell's tie and gave it a jerk to straighten it. "Christ, what'd you do, sleep in your suit or something?"

Russell grimaced when he took a look in the mirror. His skin looked pale and his eyes were red and puffy with fatigue. He hadn't actually slept in his dark-blue suit but might as well have for how wrinkled it looked. He tried to smooth his sandy-brown hair that looked like a mess of straw and hay, but there was nothing he could do about the five o' clock shadow.

"Sorry, Sarge. I was out pretty late at a poker tournament at The Hard Rock," he said. No need for Morales to know the full extent—that Russell had taken a beating when the four aces and a king he was holding got beat by a straight flush. He had managed to make some of his money back at the tables. But he was still down over $250.

"You're a detective now, Junior. So buy yourself an iron

and clean up your act, all right? I've got a feeling about this case. You're gonna be needing your A-game."

"Right," Russell said. He didn't see the correlation between how a detective dressed and how he did his job, but there was no harm in the suggestion. Then again, Art's khaki pants were always pressed and he'd been on the force so long his thick black beard had flecks of gray in it.

"So what was she anyway?" Morales moved in to have a closer look at the body. "Escort? Call girl?"

"Not with all this luggage." Russell said as he began going through one of the suitcases he'd noticed in the closet. "Quality stuff too. Lots of designer labels."

On the night table he found her wallet in a Gucci purse that smelled like it was brand new and checked her ID. A scan of recent calls in her Blackberry revealed eight calls to someone named Steven the previous night. Russell dialed the local number but only got a generic voicemail greeting. He noted the number on his pad and moved on to the rest of the items in her purse.

He found a bottle of folic acid tablets and a date book, but with no appointments listed for the four days she'd been in town.

Damn! They could find out who Steven was easily enough but it'd be good to know whom she'd been here to see. The folic acid worried him, too.

After finding nothing more of interest in her luggage he headed to the living room and watched the CSI team meticulously combing for fingerprints, hair samples, and whatever else. Looking for clues in a room that had already been cleaned seemed like a waste of time. "Any chance of getting you guys into the bedroom?" he said. "The maid was cleaning in here before she found the body in the other room. Might not be anything usable."

"My boys are thorough," said Davis, a lead investigator with CSI whom Russell had only met once. "It'll take some time, but if there's anything here we'll find it." Then he turned back to Morales. "So did you watch the whole game? Did you see 'The Lord's' last shot?"

"'The Lord'," Russell said. "What a joke."

"Maybe, but I didn't see anyone in New York laughing last night. Y'know my kid camped out at the mall three hours before it opened just to buy a pair of his shoes? It's crazy," Davis said.

"You're crazy." Russell said. "The guy's a total fraud."

"So what's with you? You don't like sports or something?"

"Russell prefers games of chance." Morales said.

"That's right," Russell said as he reached into his pocket. He took out his wallet and held up a hundred dollar bill. "I bet your boys don't find a single thing in this room. You have five guys working? I'll give you five-to-one odds we don't get one usable clue."

"I'll take that bet," Davis said. Surely he knew even better than Russell that hotels were notoriously tough to pull viable prints and DNA from because there were so many people coming and going. But that was Davis's problem. And this was one bet Russell wouldn't mind losing if it helped him find the killer.

RUSSELL WAS GETTING READY TO HEAD OUT AND TRY TO get a statement from Marta Arroyo when one of the cops at the door said the manager wanted to see him. The man looked anything but managerial, five foot five at best with thick glasses and skin that looked as pale as beach sand against his dark suit. Watching all those detectives dusting in his hotel must have shaken him.

"Are you okay, Mr. . . . ?"

"Whitmore. I'm the general manager," he said, still glancing nervously at the investigators in the hall. "I'm sorry I couldn't get back up here sooner. This is a terrible tragedy, and frankly it's got some of our other guests in a bit of a state."

"I can imagine." Russell nodded affably. The guy sounded slightly effeminate, but that wasn't a big deal. His jitters were bound to make his guests more anxious than anything MDPD could do. Russell reached into his jacket pocket for his pad and pen. "So . . . was this room registered in the name Michelle Tibbs?"

"I have all the information right here," Whitmore said, flipping through some notes on a clipboard. "Ms. Tibbs did in fact reserve this room. She had a four-night reservation and was due to check out tomorrow."

He laughed nervously, then looked at Russell apologetically. "Sorry, Detective—that probably wasn't the best choice of words."

"Was anyone traveling with her?

"Not to my knowledge. She's a return visitor. I checked the database and it looks like she always makes the same reservation—for a single luxury suite."

"Any idea who she came to visit or what her business was?"

"No, sir."

"How'd she pay for the room?"

"Credit card."

"Well this is all very helpful, Mr. Whitmore. Thank you. Is anyone from your night staff still here?"

"Sorry, third shift leaves at seven in the morning. They were long gone before anyone realized what had happened."

"Then I'll need to see the work schedule and phone numbers for the night shift. The concierge, bellboys, parking attendants. I also need to know if she ordered anything from room service. You think you can get that together for me?"

"Of course—I'll have my assistant get on that right away."

"Great. Are there any security cameras on this floor?"

"Not many, I'm afraid. All rooms above the twentieth floor are generally reserved for our more exclusive guests who require a great deal of privacy. So there's not much surveillance on these floors."

"Still, I'll need access to whatever footage you do have. Getting off the elevator, I know I saw at least one camera. I'll also need to talk to the guests in the two adjacent rooms. Just to see if they heard anything."

Davis, looking for Russell, came out into the hallway. "Sorry to interrupt, Detective—the ME wants to talk to you."

Russell nodded and handed his card to the manager. "Thanks again, Mr. Whitmore. My fax number is on the card there when your assistant has that info for me. And please don't hesitate to call my office if you find out anything that might help us."

"Of course," Mr. Whitmore said. He paused for a moment, then looked at Russell sheepishly. "Detective, do you have any idea when we'll be able to use this room again? It's one of our most popular—"

"A woman is dead," Russell said. "Have some respect, would you?"

CHAPTER 6

"So what'd you find out?" Russell asked the medical examiner as he walked into the bedroom.

"Right now I'd say death by strangulation. There's trauma to the larynx and the trachea. Bruising around her throat indicates somebody very strong did this. But that's just preliminary, of course. I'll have to get her back to the morgue for a full autopsy."

"Time of death?"

"Sometime between two and four a.m.," the ME said. "You can take that to the bank."

Russell walked back over to Michelle's handbag. "I found folic acid pills in her purse," he said, holding up the bottle. "Any idea why she'd be using these?"

The ME shook his head somberly. "At her age, there's only one thing I can think of."

"Pregnancy?"

"I'm afraid so. We'll find out for sure, but I'm guessing she was either pregnant or trying to get pregnant."

All they could do was hope for the latter.

Russell headed for the lobby, hoping to talk to somebody with hotel security before heading out to talk to the maid. A small group of reporters and a camera crew had gathered in the foyer and several uniformed police officers were now on scene as well. Now the fun would begin. It didn't take long for word of a murder in one of Miami's swanky hotels to bring out the jackals.

Russell followed signs to the security office and found Whitmore standing at the door, talking to one of the cops from upstairs. Judging by the redness in his face and the extra shrill in his voice, he was steamed about something.

"I just don't see why we need uniformed police officers harassing our other guests," he was saying as Russell approached. "We've had three guests check out already, and—"

"Excuse me a minute . . . Detective?" the officer said.

Russell nodded sympathetically.

"Thought you should know I just got done talking to James and Brittany Davenport, a couple from Boston. She was fast asleep but he says he heard some pretty heated arguing around two-thirty this morning."

"They were right across the hall!" Whitmore said. "They might have heard the whole thing."

"You sure about the time?" Russell asked.

"That's what they said, two-thirty. They also said they were going to move to a different hotel, but I've got their cell phone number if you want to talk to them."

"Did any other guests hear anything? What about the guests next door?"

The officer flipped through his notepad. "Mosley, the guest in 2210, said he'd been out partying all night," he said. "I believe him too. The guy looked hammered. There are still a couple guys knocking on doors trying to get statements."

"See? That's just it!" Whitmore said. "A murder is bad enough. I know you gentlemen have a job to do, but can't this be handled more discreetly?"

Russell rolled his eyes, but smiled as affably as he could manage and suggested they go inside the security office. "Listen," he said after closing the door behind them. "I know how badly you want us out of here. We've got some work to do still, and the more cooperative you and your staff are, the faster this goes, okay?"

Whitmore nodded.

"Now I'm gonna need you to get me a complete list of all the guests staying in the hotel, and it would be a big help if you could highlight the guests that stayed on that floor last night. Do you have the security footage ready?"

"Ah, yes," Whitmore said, expression brightening. "We've got last night's video cued and waiting."

He led Russell to a small, hot room full of cheap

black-and-white video monitors. A small metal fan, which generated more noise than cool air, blew from a corner of the table into the face of the lone tech on duty. Russell nodded as he flashed a crooked smile. This guy couldn't get laid at a Star Trek convention. In his dark-brown uniform that seemed two sizes too small, he looked liked biscuits busting out of their container. Russell pulled up a chair and sat down.

There were live feeds from the public areas of the hotel going to all the monitors except for a separate playback unit on the desk in front of the tech. There, a still image of a darker hotel lobby was frozen on screen, the time stamp reading 12:58 a.m.

"Is someone in here watching those live feeds 24/7?" Russell asked.

The tech looked uncomfortably at Whitmore for a moment, and then said, "Not exactly."

"Is someone *ever* watching these feeds in real time?"

The tech shook his head. "Honestly, that's how the system was meant to work. But the A/C doesn't work so good in here. So it's rarely manned unless there's a problem. But any footage gathered is saved for forty-eight hours so we can review it in the event of an incident."

"It's a perfectly viable system for our needs, I assure you," Whitmore said.

"Apparently," Russell said as he scanned the feeds' sources, mostly the lobby, restaurant, bar, and swimming pool. The tech explained that while feeds from the lower floors were available, there was only the one camera on the VIP floors.

"Okay, let's see what we've got, then," Russell said.

The tech hit play and the three of them watched foot traffic coming and going through the hotel lobby to the main elevators. They saw nothing of interest until Russell finally noticed someone headed for a single VIP elevator on the other side of the lobby instead of the bank of main elevators. The time stamp read 1:44 a.m.

Russell inched closer to the screen. The guy was big—easily over six feet—but more lean than bulky, and there was something familiar about him. He was obviously in a rush, and with all the people looking at him in the lobby he must've been somebody important. But who was it?

Russell took a deep breath. The camera angle made it difficult to place the face until the guy looked directly at the lens while using his key card for the elevator. Steven Lords.

"Now that's interesting," Russell said, backing away from the monitor. "Is Mr. Lords here a registered hotel guest?"

"No, he isn't a guest. I would've known if he was," Whitmore said.

"You're sure he didn't use a fake name to register?"

"Positive. Ever since 9/11 we have to ID all guests upon registration. He might be visiting a guest, or even staying with one, but I can assure you he's not the one who booked a room here."

Lords had won the biggest game of his career, and he wound up at a hotel in the dead of night? It didn't make much sense. He should've been out celebrating or something, but instead he'd come here.

"Do you know if he was visiting anyone? His wife maybe? Anyone at all?"

"Sorry, Detective, but how could I possibly know that? I can see if there's anyone with the last name Lords registered, but beyond that—"

"That'd be fine, Mr. Whitmore, thanks." Russell turned his attention back to the monitor. The odds of this panning out to anything were slim. But with eight outgoing calls to someone named Steven on the victim's cell phone, he didn't want to miss anything. And some alone time with the tech might be helpful.

After Whitmore left, Russell asked to see the footage from the top floor. The tech pressed a few keys and the images on the monitor changed. "There you go. Penthouse floor, 1:45 a.m."

Russell watched as the footage rolled at 2x speed. The view was from the camera he'd noticed, framing the elevator door from the far opposite wall of the hallway. The picture quality was crap but it would still provide a decent enough look at anyone getting off the elevator. But no one came or went down that hallway, and there was no sign of Steven Lords.

"Rewind it and slow it down a notch will you?" he asked.

The image seemed to remain completely unchanged as the tech backed it up and let it play.

"Rewind it again," Russell asked as he moved closer to the screen. It appeared as if nothing changed; it was like looking at a photograph. Something was suspicious about the footage.

"Play it forward, normal speed please."

"Is there something you're looking for, Detective?" The tech asked. "You're not going to see any changes if no one gets off the—"

"I know that, "Russell said, trying to keep the impatience out of his voice. "There's something wrong with this video."

He pointed at a lamp on the wall as he sat back in his chair. "That light flickers every three seconds." Russell said. "Light bulbs that go out don't normally flicker in a pattern like that."

The tech looked closer, his nose almost touching the screen of the little monitor. The door opened behind them and Whitmore joined them in the cramped office but said nothing.

"Wow, that is weird," the tech said. "Let me see if I could pull up the time-coded footage."

He fiddled with a few buttons until he found the video he sought. Russell leaned forward and stared at the screen. The only noticeable difference was the series of numbers on the bottom of the screen, and those had obviously been altered.

"Why does that time stamp on the bottom keep displaying the same time?" he asked. "Is it possible someone could have tampered with this video?"

"Absolutely not!" Whitmore said from behind them, his tone indignant. "No one's allowed in here but our staff, and I can assure you no employee of the hotel would do something like that. Also, I just checked and our records don't show anyone named Lords registered as a guest here."

Whitmore handed Russell a sheet of paper. "This is the list of the guests."

Russell took the list and looked down at the security tech, who was looking down at the floor. Russell sat on the desk, in front of the monitors. He leaned toward the tech, who deliberately avoided eye contact.

"I'll ask you then," Russell said to him. "What do *you* think happened?"

A long, awkward pause. "Yeah. Someone could have messed with the video. It's not that hard to loop a static image to the servers. Not even the first time it's happened, actually."

Russell heard Whitmore bristle behind him but kept his eyes steady on the tech.

"What do you mean?"

"Well . . . just that we've had some thefts in the hotel is all."

"Thefts? What kind of thefts?"

"Jewelry, watches, iPods, stuff like that. Things people can fit in their pockets."

"Has this ever been reported?"

"Detective Russell," Whitmore said. "This hotel has an image to maintain. We certainly don't want people thinking they aren't safe or their valuables can't be protected. I'm sure you can understand our policy to handle these sorts of incidents—which I assure you are very rare—in-house."

Russell had about had it with Whitmore. But he told himself to keep his cool. "How does that happen?" he said after a moment. "How does a place like this have such piss-poor surveillance?"

"We went for the lowest bid on the security system, that's how," the tech said before Whitmore could speak. "The truth is there are glitches all over the network, which makes it very hard for us to do our job. Sometimes the cameras and key-card logging systems stall or go down altogether. Before you came in, I tried to pull up a record of when the room was accessed last night and I couldn't find that information."

"That's enough, Mr. Roberts," Whitmore said.

"No that's not enough," Russell said, standing and glaring at Whitmore. "We have a woman and quite possibly her unborn child dead here . . . and a security system with some obvious limitations. So I'd suggest you stop worrying about this hotel's reputation and let your staff tell me what I need to know."

He turned to Roberts and nodded encouragingly. "Has that ever happened before? Have you ever had a glitch in video and room access at the same time?"

"Not that I know of, but I suppose anything's possible. "

"Who was on duty last night?

The tech glanced at a clipboard. "That'd be James Cooper. He's not here now, but it looks like he's scheduled for the same shift tonight."

Russell turned to Whitmore. "I need a phone number and an address for Mr. Cooper. Also a list of anyone with access to this office. And for God's sake, if you or any of your people have knowledge about vulnerabilities in the system or who might know how to hack it, I want to know."

Whitmore nodded. "Of course."

Russell turned back to Roberts. "What's your full name?"

"Chris Roberts."

"Well thanks, Chris. You've been a big help," he said and handed him a card. "If you think of anything else I ought to know, give me a call. And do me a favor and call me if Mr. Whitmore here or anyone else gives you any flack about what you told me, you understand?"

CHAPTER 7

Miami Coliseum, 9:23 a.m.

The scoreboard read 88-86 and there were four seconds on the clock. The lights blazed and crowd noise filled the arena. The court was as glossy as it had ever been, as the players took their places. The defense was ready and set up perfectly. Both benches stood in anticipation of Steven's last-second shot. This time there would be no surprises.

Eddie watched as a production assistant sprayed Steven in the face and arms to make it look like he was sweating. Eddie's sunglasses hid his eyes from the glare of the bright lights but did little to ease the throbbing in his head. He hadn't talked to Al yet, but he was sure he'd be pissed Steven had gone to the hotel.

Calling Allen ahead of time and letting him know Stevie wanted to go see Michelle would've been best, but there just hadn't been time. Allen might be mad, but there was no denying the visit with Michelle had done Stevie a world of good. That had to count for something.

Now, if he could only do something about this headache! He'd had worse mornings lately, but Eddie's wrists and hands were sore as hell and he had no recollection why. There was plenty about last night he didn't remember, but at least he hadn't totally blacked out again. Julian wasn't lying about that coke being potent, and he had no idea how much he'd had to drink.

Eddie was reaching for a bottled water when he felt Steven's phone vibrating in his pocket. He stroked his mouth and chin and thought about whether or not to answer when he saw it was Michelle calling. Probably best to let the call go to voicemail.

"CUT!" THE DIRECTOR YELLED. "THAT WAS PERFECT, everybody! Absolutely perfect."

"You sure you got what you need?" Steven said. "I can do it again if you like."

"Not necessary, I assure you. I know it doesn't look like much now, but once we get it into post-production and put it together with live clips from last night, it'll look just like it happened in the actual game."

"All right then. Hope the spot comes out great."

Steven smiled as he untucked his jersey and headed for the locker room. He stopped when he saw Allen and Dave standing next to Eddie, who'd been acting strange all morning and looked just terrible. Maybe Al was right and it was time to get Eddie some help before he hurt himself or somebody else.

"Keep that jersey on," Dave said. "Let's run down the interview schedule. We've got some kids from the children's hospital in the locker room. They want to take a few pictures with you, get some autographs signed—you know the deal."

"Not a problem. I invited them over this morning to watch the commercial shoot, so I was expecting that," Steven said.

"Also, Heather Shaw from *Miami in Style* wants to interview you on your pregame routines and how you stay in shape. That'll be out on the practice court."

"Sounds good. Anything else?"

"You kidding? We've got media people from Italy that want to interview you, and then we need to schedule some league promos for the Finals. That's not pressing, but we might as well get it out of the way. And the season ticket holders' luncheon is today. The team and the coaches need to be there. It's mandatory, so please don't forget."

***

Steven was headed toward the locker room when he felt a tug on his arm from behind. "Shit's about to hit the fan, bro," Eddie said.

"What are you talking about?"

"Michelle called."

"Really?"

"Did you talk to her?" Steven asked. "What'd she want?"

Eddie glanced at Allen and shrugged his shoulders. "Hell if I know. I let it go to voicemail but she ain't leave no message."

Steven sighed. "Okay, I'll give her a call then. Where's my phone—"

"Wait wait wait!" Allen said. "I thought we agreed that you weren't going to have any more contact with her. Didn't we say you were going to stay away and let me deal with her from now on?"

"Sorry, man. The stakes have gone up," Steven looked around to make sure no one else was in earshot. "I went to see her after the game last night. She wants to keep the baby."

"You mean you went to her hotel?" Allen asked.

"That's right."

Allen ran his fingers through his blond hair and looked at the ceiling. "Let me make sure I heard you correctly," he said, trying to restrain his frustration. "You talked to Michelle about actually keeping this baby? That has to be the most asinine thing I've ever heard."

"Since when is doing the right thing asinine?"

"Right thing?" Allen scoffed. "How is giving her carte blanche to use you as her own personal ATM for the next eighteen years doing the right thing?"

"Sorry, but I'm doing what I should've done in the first place," Steven said " It was your idea for her to have the abortion. After talking to her more, I didn't see any reason why we couldn't reach some sort of an arrangement to take care of the baby and still keep it on the hush. That way everyone wins."

"So what was her response to this miracle solution of yours?"

Steven shook his head. "It was strange. She gave me some kind of dry smile and laughed," he said. "She said she'd think about it. After that I just lost it. I mean, what kind of shit was that?"

"A colossal waste of time if you ask me," Allen said. "I wish you would've talked to me before you went off half-cocked and started making deals that could damage your brand."

"Hold on a second, Al," Steven said. "Since when do I need to get your permission to talk to somebody about my own goddamn business?"

"Let's not go there, okay? You have an image to maintain and—"

"I don't want to hear it. I got myself into this whole situation and I can get myself out of it, so let me deal with it!"

Allen put a hand on Steven's shoulder and gave him firm shake. "Steven, you've got to listen to me. This isn't some trivial personal matter. This is me trying to protect you from a person who can singlehandedly ruin you. Do you want to lose fifty million a year in endorsements over this?" Allen asked. "If you just stick to our agreement and let me handle things—"

"That's not going to happen!" Steven pushed Allen's hand off his shoulder. "This doesn't involve you. Me and Michelle have history and if you just stay out of my way I can fix this, I promise."

Allen stepped back and nodded his head. "Fine with me," he said. "Just remember that if you blow it and Karen splits, she's gonna take half your assets with her. The tabloids will have a field day desecrating your image, and before you know it all your fans will forget about 'The Lord' and start thinking of you just another asshole athlete who can't keep his dick in his pants."

"Maybe. But I'm the one who puts the ball in the basket. I'm the one—"

"Who constantly jeopardizes a lot of hard work with a lot of questionable choices!" Allen leaned in and dropped his voice to a whisper. "If Michelle was the only one, that'd be one thing. But let's talk about facts for a minute. When the *Star* had those pictures of you and that chick Amber or whoever, who made that go away? Could you handle that yourself? How about Abella, Kim, Jodi, Rebecca? And we damn sure can't forget about Natalia, who almost sued you for paternity before. Who took care of all that?"

"I hear you," Steven said. "But you need to understand—"

"No, *you* need to understand that you've stepped into some shit that's deeper than you thought and it ain't gonna just wash off those one hundred-and-fifty-dollar sneakers I negotiated for you."

Steven stared at the ground. None of this was Allen's fault, and it was stupid to be yelling at him. But the idea of sending his agent into fight for him on something like this made him feel like a punk. And what the hell was he thinking getting himself into this situation in the first place?

His conjured up memories of a bedroom, making quiet love to Karen with their daughter down the hall. It'd been ages since that had happened, and when it did he felt secure and happy. But in the darkest recesses of his mind, sex with Karen bored him in a way he could never admit to her.

Sex with Michelle was rarely anywhere close to a bedroom and as wild and unpredictable as it was with anyone he'd ever been with. There was no denying the thrill and the pleasure of what she could do for him. Nor the crushing sense of guilt he had after it ended. But then that would fade and he'd be back, and the cycle would start all over again. What the fuck was wrong with him anyway?

Steven shook his head to clear the confusing wash of emotions and looked at Allen.

"Sorry, man," he said. "I can't just sit around and do

nothing. Nobody knows Michelle better than me. Let me keep trying to talk to her. That's all I'm saying. Give me one more shot to convince her to change her mind."

"You've done the best you can. You made her an offer and it sounds to me like she pretty much laughed in your face. If you want to continue to try to explore some way the two of you can pacify this situation, be my guest. But let me just say you can talk all you want . . . I'm afraid she's no longer listening."

Steven thought about that. She hadn't budged an inch last night. If anything she'd seemed to take pleasure in taunting him with her refusal, rubbing it in his face because there wasn't a damn thing he could do about it.

"So what do I do?"

"Just stay focused on your game and let me deal with Michelle. I need you to stay as far away from her as you can. I don't care how much she calls—do not go and see her, Steven!" Allen rubbed his forehead. He gave Eddie a cold stare and continued. "I've got too much invested in building your brand and I'll be damned if some glorified groupie is gonna wreck it."

Eddie put his arm around Steven. "Ain't nobody gonna tear down what we done took time to build! So what happens—"

"What *we* built?" Allen said. "Really, Eddie?"

Steven was about to say something but Allen just kept talking. "Okay, we're going to have to go into damage control. When the media asks—and they *will* ask—let's just say you were having a late dinner in the hotel," Allen said. "We know people at the Murcielago that will corroborate that story."

"I don't know," Steven said. "I don't like it, but I'll play it your way."

"Playing it my way has kept a lot of stuff out of the papers and off TMZ. I'm going back to the hotel. I have some calls to make. I need you to stay focused. Win the championship. I've got a busy summer lined up for you, but I need you to relax and keep your eyes on the prize, okay?"

Steven watched Allen disappear around the corner.

"Give me the phone," he said to Eddie. "Let me call her before I go into the locker room and talk to these kids. Allen may be right, but there's at least a chance she's come to her senses, right?"

"But you told Al you wasn't gonna talk to her." Eddie reached into his pocket and hesitantly took out Steven's phone.

"I don't give a damn. If I don't do something to get this whole situation under control, I'm gonna go crazy."

Steven's fingers trembled as he dialed her number. He held his breath in anticipation as the phone began to ring. His nervousness waned when the call went to voicemail.

"Hey, it's me. I'm sorry about last night. Things got a little heated and well . . . anyway, I saw your missed call and I'm hoping you've decided to live up to your end of our deal. Get at me when you get this message. I'll talk to you later."

Steven pressed the end button and gave the phone to Eddie. "If she calls back give me the phone," he said. "I don't care what I'm doing. Get me the phone."

CHAPTER 8

WLDM Channel 67, 11:13 a.m.

Miami station WLDM bustled with preproduction activity as Peter Owens got ready to tape *The Stat Line*. He could barely feel the feathery strokes of his makeup artist Gloria as she applied foundation and deftly erased the wrinkles that thirty-five years of sports journalism had left on his face.

It wasn't all that long ago that he had a head of thick, dark brown hair. He'd had his ups and downs since starting out as a club reporter covering a minor league baseball team in upstate New York, but he was long overdue in the effort to take things to the next stage of his career. The modest ratings on his show were already dropping, and with each day he felt a sense of opportunity slipping away. What he needed more than anything was to break a real story, something that would make his colleagues in the sports world notice, maybe buy him a ticket out of the shitty life he'd somehow managed to settle for. And now it looked like he had it, as Miami was ready to take center stage in the sports universe.

"You think I should maybe start dying my hair?"

"What for?" Gloria said with a snarky smile. "It's so thin on top, you barely need to worry." She showed Peter the brush to emphasize her point. He grimaced at the tangle of salt-and-pepper hair clinging to its bristles.

"If you ask me, you'd be better off leaving your hair alone and trying to lose a few pounds," she said with a laugh.

He closed his eyes and imagined what he'd look like setting behind a desk at ESPN, cameras rolling, or maybe behind the mic on his own national radio show. There had to be something out there for him better than this.

FIVE MINUTES LATER HE WAS HEADED TO THE SET WHEN his producer, Roger Willis, hurried up to him excitedly with a sheet of paper in his hand.

"What's happening, Roger?"

"A dead woman at the Murcielago Hotel last night," Roger said. "That's what's happening. And you'll never guess who she was."

Peter looked at him impatiently. "Maybe you can save me the trouble?"

"According to you, mistress of the world's biggest basketball star."

Peter's breath caught in his throat. "Michelle Tibbs?"

Roger nodded. "Affirmative—and this totally changes the focus of our show today! Christ, we could actually be breaking the biggest story in the country for once," he said. "Pete, you're absolutely sure this Tibbs woman was sleeping with Lords, right? I mean, we need to have our facts straight."

Peter glanced at the clock and led Roger into a vacant office saved for an intern the station never seemed to be able to afford. He sat on the edge of a battered, gray desk, ran his fingers through his hair, and thought before saying anything. What in God's name happened at that hotel last night? Lords had to be in one hell of a dire situation, sure, but could he really be capable of murder?

"Hey, Pete, you okay?"

"Yeah, I'm fine," Peter said. "This whole thing just comes as a total surprise, you know?"

"So what—did you know her on a personal level or something?"

"Let's just say I've made her acquaintance," Peter said. "But I know for a fact she's the reason Lords was at the Murcielago last night."

Roger sat. "Why don't you back up and start from the beginning?"

Peter let out a long breath. "Okay, about a year or so ago,

I was in Denver doing a story on the Robert Miller, some human-interest bullshit about how this guy finds God, turns his life around, and becomes our starting center. So I'm waiting in the lobby to meet him for the interview and I see this woman walk into the hotel. I don't really think much of it because you see lots of good-looking women in hotels."

"But?"

"Well for one thing, she's drop-dead gorgeous. I'm talking a girl who can stop traffic, you know? She had this big Gucci handbag, a bunch of flashy jewelry, and these oversized Chanel sunglasses. It's eleven o'clock at night and we're in the lobby of the Four Seasons—you don't need sunglasses."

"She had a little money, so what?"

Peter leaned in. "Now fast-forward a few months to New Orleans. I'm walking through The Ritz-Carlton and guess who I see? Same girl. Then it happens again a few months after that, this time in Houston. By this point I'm getting really curious because she's obviously involved with someone on the team. So I walk up and introduce myself. I tell her I'm Peter Owens and I work for *The Miami Post*. I ask her if she's a model or something because I know some photographers who would love to shoot her sometime."

Roger chuckled. "That sounds pretty sleazy, Pete."

"Let me finish. She says no, so I chat her up a bit and she tells me her name is Michelle Tibbs. I apologize for bothering her and I leave her my card. Later, I did some digging and found out that she and Steven Lords were high-school sweethearts."

Roger sat up in his seat. "I'm not sure I'm following. It sounds like Lords was getting some on the side while his team was out on the road. Wouldn't be the first time or the last."

Peter shook his head tersely. "Would you just listen? By this point I know how to find her, and a few months later I 'bump into her' in The Grove. Ten minutes later we're drinking coffee at The Cheesecake Factory and for whatever reason she starts totally dishing the dirt on Lords."

"What kind of dirt?"

"It was all off the record, but she was mad as hell at him. Said that Lords had broken off their little fling because his wife spotted her at a game and recognized her. Then she went on to tell me about all these other women he'd supposedly been with. I mean she really gave up the goods."

"Too bad it was all off the record."

"I know, right? I swear it's the story of my life."

"So what about last night then? You don't think Lords killed her, do you?"

"Let's think about this for a second," Peter said as he stood and started pacing the office. "His marriage is in trouble. We know that Tibbs and Lords were having an affair, and I have visual proof that puts him at the scene last night—"

"Wait a minute—earlier you mentioned having some

exclusive video of Lords leaving the hotel. How did you come get it?"

Peter stopped in his tracks. "How did I get the video?"

"Yeah, exactly. It must have been awfully late. Come to think of it, how'd you know Lords was even at the hotel to begin with?"

Peter looked around the office as he loosened his collar then took his cell out of his pocket. "I got a call on my cell."

"An anonymous call?"

Peter pretended to scroll through the numbers in his phone. "What's the local number to the Murcielago?" he asked.

Roger whipped out his iPhone and looked up the number. "786-555-6292."

"That's the same number and three-digit exchange. Probably somebody at the hotel," Peter said. "I've given my card to a lot of the staff at a few of the swankier hotels just in case they happen to see anything newsworthy. I actually got into it with some jerk parking attendant who tried to make me move my car."

Roger looked puzzled. "Say what?"

"I parked in the valet lot because that's where I could get the best view of Lords. The damn attendant got all up in arms because I didn't have a ticket, so I had to get out of my car and set him straight."

Peter sat on the desk and leaned closer to Roger. "But listen, Rog, I think you're right. We are sitting on the story of the year right now. Follow my lead and we'll break this thing wide open."

Roger slowly nodded as he smiled. "Count me in! What's our next move?"

Peter thought for a minute. "I think I should call the police, let them know I've got some vital information about this case."

He picked up a phone, dialed the receptionist's desk, and waited anxiously while she connected him to the Miami-Dade Police Department. Sad though it was, there was no denying that a dead girlfriend was a much better story than a cheating husband. Providing the police with exclusive information would put him at the center of the investigation and in prime position to cover it.

"Miami-Dade Police Department. How can I help you?"

"Hi, my name's Peter Owens of *The Stat Line* and I have some information about the murder at the Murcielago hotel last night. Who's the detective in charge of that investigation?"

There was a pause and then the sound of papers shuffling. "That'd be Detective Russell Howard."

"May I speak to him, please?"

"Sorry, he's not in. Why don't you give me your number and I'll have him call you?"

"I like this," Roger said after Pete hung up. "I like where this is going. This could be just the shot in the arm this place needs."

Peter brushed the lint off his coat and straightened his tie. "We have footage no one else has of him leaving the same hotel the night of a homicide. The victim of that homicide was a girlfriend of his. The beauty is, whether he did it or whether he didn't do it doesn't even matter. But if he does turn out to be a suspect, all the better. We'll be in on the ground floor."

"I think I need to get some promos together for the second broadcast later this evening," Roger said. "We've got to make sure that everyone tunes in tonight."

"That's what I'm talking about, Rog," Peter said. "When a story like this comes around, you have to go with it."

Roger stood and headed down the hallway, clearly energized by the conversation.

"Look out, America," Peter said to no one in particular. "I think I'm finally on my way!"

CHAPTER 9

Russell walked through the lobby of police headquarters. With any luck Tibbs's personal effects had already been delivered. A little more examination might shed light on whether Steven Lords was the Steven she called last night. Maybe even give up a clue as to whether he went to see her.

"Russ, you had a call from a Peter Owens who said he has some information about the Murcielago murder," the station secretary said as he walked past. "Said he works for the *Post* and he does a sports show on Channel 21 television that you should check out at today at 1:00."

Russell thought it highly doubtful this Owens guy had

anything important to contribute to the investigation, but it couldn't hurt to check out his show. Then maybe he'd call.

He smiled when he saw Michelle's belongings waiting for him on his desk. He sat down right away, tore open the sealed evidence bag, and scattered the contents over his desk. He was sifting through a pile of makeup, grooming items, and breath mints when he noticed a red light flashing on Tibbs's cell phone. He checked the display and saw a single inbound call from "Steven," presumably the same one she'd called so many times the previous night.

The fact that he'd called her back suggested Lords wasn't his man. Lords was certainly a cheater, but cheaters weren't necessarily killers. Still, what if Lords was both? The press would have a field day with that one. It'd serve the philandering bastard right.

"Any luck with the maid?"

Russell looked up to see Art Morales nearly on top of him. The dude was like a cat sometimes, showing up out of nowhere.

"I talked to her but she didn't have much to add to her initial statement," Russell said. "Sounded to me like she cleaned the living room pretty carefully before even looking at the bedroom. Says her supervisor is a real hard-ass, especially in those upper suites. She felt terrible that she might have cleaned up clues but the poor lady was just doing her job, of course."

Morales pursed his lips thoughtfully. "Nothing else to offer? Nothing seemed out of place or odd to her when she first got there?"

"Not that she can remember. Just that it didn't look like the living room had been used much. No glasses out, nothing missing from the minibar. So the odds are against a friendly date or something."

"You think this might have been random then? An intruder rather than someone she knew?"

"Hard to say. It looked to me like she was expecting someone. I mean, who wears a sexy nightgown like that if you're not expecting a little company?"

"Search me," Morales said. "Everything I saw hanging in the closet looked pretty nice. Maybe that's just how she rolls, you know?"

"You mean rolled," Russell said. "But at least I won my bet, right?"

"Not so fast, Junior. Davis just called and told me that his boys did manage to pull something useful from the room."

"Really? What did he get?"

"Fingerprints off of the victim's throat," Art said. "So Davis said he'll be seeing you on payday."

Russell threw his hands in the air. "No way. That doesn't count. The bet was for pulling something off of the room, not the body," Russell said. "He can't be serious."

"He sounded pretty serious to me. And if you ask me, you should be thanking your lucky stars because fingerprints off skin are not easy to get. We get a match on those prints, and this thing could be a slam dunk!"

Morales was right, but something told Russell that wasn't going to happen.

"So run down what we have so far."

Russell sighed. "Let's see. I've got a dead girl in a luxury hotel suite. I've got no witnesses and no activity on that floor around the time of her death according to security video—which, by the way, was obviously tampered with. I've got a compromised crime scene and phone records for the room saying she didn't make any calls, but that's no surprise because who the hell's going to use a landline in a hotel these days?"

"So other than a possible print match, it sounds to me like a handful of shit and nowhere to fling it," Art said, nodding sympathetically. "But something will break. It always does. How about the cell phone?"

"Just a bunch of calls to a guy named Steven, who probably isn't our guy because he called her back early this morning."

"You trace the number?"

"Waiting to hear back from Verizon. For all I know 'Steven' could be Steven Lords, if you can believe that. The one thing I know for sure is he was at the hotel last night, cheating bastard."

"Easy, Junior. Unless he's taking a play from O.J.'s playbook, I'd say the odds of him being the killer are pretty slim."

Russell nodded. It was hard to believe a guy would kill his mistress hours after taking his team to the Finals. But you never knew.

"The press is going to be all over this if Lords has any kind of involvement," Morales was saying. "So I need you to be really careful, all right?"

Russell agreed and filled Morales in the message from some reporter at the Post.

"Did he sound serious? You think he might have something?"

"Fuck if I know," Russell said.

Morales went back to his office, leaving Russell at his desk contemplating Tibbs's personal effects.

"Nice purse, Russell," a pretty Latina officer said as she passed by his desk, headed for the break room.

"Hey, Torres, what kind of makeup do you use?"

"Revlon. Why?"

"Here, take a look at these," Russell said.

"What about them?" she asked.

"Is this stuff any good?"

She picked up a tortoise-shell compact. "It's pretty high end. It's really expensive—the kind of stuff you get at specialty department stores. What else you got over there?"

"Body sprays, makeup case, all kinds of stuff. Take a look."

She sifted through the cosmetics on Russell's desk. "Yeah, this girl had some good taste, that's for sure. That Chanel makeup case alone will set you back at least four bills. This stuff belonged to that dead girl from the Murcielago I heard about this morning?"

"Yup," Russell said. "Won't do her much good now. Thanks for your time, officer." She winked at him and went her way.

His gut told him Michelle Tibbs had a sugar daddy, but that was an assumption. There were no business items of any kind in the suite, no briefcase or laptop or even appointments in her book. But he still wanted to know what she did for a living.

He reached into his desk for his pack of playing cards and shuffled the deck. Michelle had a lot of expensive stuff. Exactly what was she into? He picked up her cell phone and scrolled through the numbers again. He saw an entry that read "Sis" and realized it was time he contacted the family.

CHAPTER 10

"Hello, this is Detective Russell Howard of the Miami-Dade Police Department. May I speak with the sister of Michelle Tibbs?"

"This her sister Rhonda, who you say this is?"

Russell hesitated before responding. Making calls like this was like removing a Band-Aid; it went easiest if you ripped it right off.

"Miss Tibbs, I'm very sorry to disturb you. My name is Detective Russell Howard. I'm calling from Miami and I'm afraid I have some bad news."

"Please don't tell me 'Chelle done went and got herself in some mess."

If only it were that simple. "I'm sorry, Miss Tibbs. I'm calling because your sister Michelle was found dead in a hotel here in Miami this morning."

"*What?*" It came out as a strained whisper, so quiet Russell could barely hear it.

He hadn't been working homicide long, but he'd been at it long along enough to know how these things generally played out. The first reaction was almost always surprise, disbelief, a sense of utter shock and amazement. Then came silence. Then came anger or anguish, and he'd take anger any day of the week.

But Rhonda Tibbs didn't say a word. He heard the phone crash to the floor and the sound of muffled sobbing in the background.

Russell put the receiver on his desk, then tightened and relaxed a fist a few times while he waited. There was nothing he could do to make this process easier. His job was to catch the killer, and he felt his resolve strengthening with each moment he listened.

"Hello? Hello? Who this is?"

Russell scrambled to pick up the receiver when he heard the voice. He gave his name again and asked who he was speaking with.

"This is Calvin, Calvin Williams. I'm Rhonda's cousin. What she cryin' 'bout? Is Chelle aight?"

Russell repeated the grim news in a steady monotone. Calvin was obviously shaken but he managed to keep it together and ask some coherent questions. Russell saw no harm in being honest about the fact that Michelle's death was definitely a homicide.

"Murder? That don't make no kind of sense, man. But you did get the son of a bitch that did it, right?"

"Not yet," Russell said. "I'm heading up the investigation, and some information about Michelle would actually be very helpful. Were you two close?"

"Yeah, we came up together. She was my cousin. We was more like brother and sister, you know what I'm sayin'? Damn, this is messed up."

Russell could tell by the labored breathing that accompanied Calvin's words the grief was taking hold. Redirection was the key and he had to keep him talking.

"Mr. Williams, I don't know if you know this but the Murcielago is a very upscale hotel here in Miami, and your cousin was found with a lot of very expensive clothing and makeup in her baggage. You mind telling me what she did for a living?"

He heard a sigh on the other end of the phone. "Michelle wasn't never the one to hold down a real nine-to-five, you know? She had a part-time hustle at a few temp jobs, but nothing serious."

Russell made a few notes on his pad. "Do you know if she had any other sources of income then? The hotel she was staying in can run up to fifteen hundred a night."

A pause followed. That last question had struck a nerve. It sounded like Calvin had something to say but then thought better of it. "Sorry, I don't know what else to tell you. Like I say, work wasn't really her thing."

"Maybe you can tell me about Steven Lords then," Russell said. "Did your cousin have some sort of a relationship with him?"

"Stevie?" Calvin asked. "Her and Stevie used to kick it back in the day but . . . hold on a second."

Russell heard some shuffling as he scribbled the name "Stevie Lords" on his notepad and circled it. The connection was established and it made some sense. Lords certainly could've been bankrolling this woman, who could've been extorting him with a pregnancy. It sounded like a long shot, but even long shots paid out every once in a while.

"It was Stevie, wasn't it?"

Rhonda was back on the line, her voice hot with rage. "That goddamn Stevie killed my sister, didn't he? That son of a bitch! Have you checked his ass out? I bet he had something to do with it!"

She was screaming so loud Russell nearly dropped his pen as be bolted upright in his chair. "By Stevie, do you mean Steven Lords?" he asked.

"Yeah, that's exactly who I'm talkin' 'bout!" Rhonda replied.

"What makes you think Lords had anything to do with your sister's death?" he said. "Did you talk to her last night? Did she tell you she was meeting him or something?"

"I ain't talked to her in a few days," Rhonda said. "I don't know if she saw him last night or not. But I *do* know she was still messing around him. They had a thing back in high school, you know, and . . ."

Russell could almost hear the wheels turning as Rhonda contemplated what to say next.

"Miss Tibbs, if your sister and Steven Lords had some sort of relationship, it's important you tell me what you know."

He heard Rhonda blow her nose and then take a few deep breaths. "Yeah, they had a thing going. Stevie was messing with her on the side. You know, treating Chelle like some sort of jump-off. But I don't think she saw it like that."

"Lords is married, right?"

"He married, but you know how these goddamn athletes are. He probably got chicks every damn where. I bet his wife ain't got no clue how sleazy his ass really is."

Russell picked up his pen and resumed taking notes. "Getting back to Lords and your sister—"

"He broke up with Chelle back when he was in college, right after she lost their first child . . . if you can believe that." The sadness in Rhonda's voice was still there, but it had hardened into bitterness. "A real man don't do that kind of shit, Mr. Russell!"

Russell waited for a polite moment. "I found some folic acid pills in your sister's purse. Is there any chance she might have been pregnant again?"

Rhonda sighed. "I was with her the day she found out, maybe four or five weeks ago. I don't think I ever seen her so happy. She knew it was Stevie's and she just carried on and on about how she wanted to have his baby and how everything was gonna be okay now. Damn, she was so stupid."

"So the plan was to keep the baby?"

"*Her* plan was, but Stevie had other ideas. Kept talking about how he had too much on the line, his marriage and his image . . . said she needed to have an abortion."

"But she didn't want that?"

"That Stevie don't have much sense but he got plenty of money, and so next thing Michelle knows, he's trying to pay her off to do what he wanted."

"You're sure about this? Do you know how much?"

"Hell yeah I'm sure. I don't know how much but I know it was a lot. That's the reason she went to Miami in the first place. I don't know what the arrangement was but you can be damn sure she wasn't going to give up on having that baby, no matter how much money he threw at her."

Russell sat back and let the reality settle in. There was one hell of a motive emerging and it was better than the theory he'd had.

"Miss Tibbs, are you sure Michelle took money from Steven for an abortion she had no intention of getting?"

"Listen, I didn't agree with everything my sister did," Rhonda said. "I know how it must look to you, but she wasn't some gold digger trying to get over. She just wanted a baby is all . . . and a life for it. She never said so outright, but I always felt like she hoped Stevie might change his mind about staying with Karen."

"What about you? You think that was a possibility?"

"Hell naw! Don't get me wrong—Steve and my sister had a thing for each other like you wouldn't believe. But he only wanted one thing from Michelle, and believe me it wasn't a house and a white picket fence. And it damn sure wasn't no baby."

"Was he ever violent with her? Did they ever fight physically?"

"Not that I saw, but he ain't stupid enough to do anything like that in public," Rhonda said. "Chelle knew I didn't like him so I'm not even sure she'd tell me if he had. But I'll tell you one thing."

"What's that?"

"What you see is *not* what you get with Steven Lords. He been a cheater and a liar all his life."

They talked a few more minutes, then Russell hung up the phone and ran his fingers through his hair. At least Lords's visit to the hotel made a lot more sense. The trick now was to prove he'd been in Michelle's suite. Russell shook his head. Things had gotten a lot worse.

A fax had come in from the Murcielago—eight pages long and listing nearly 175 employees who had access to the security office. That wasn't exactly a dead end, but figuring out who might have been responsible for tampering with the video would be like looking for an ice cube at the gates of hell. Might have to be done, but that was a lower priority at that point.

Russell shuffled the playing cards into his palm a few times and slumped back into his chair. Lords looked like an obvious suspect. He had the motive and the opportunity, but killers didn't usually place calls to their dead victims unless they were trying to establish an alibi. And if he were trying to do that, why leave a voicemail?

"Hey, Russ, we just got a hit on that phone number from Michelle Tibbs's phone." Once again, Art Morales had appeared seemingly out of nowhere. "You'll never guess who it belongs to."

"Bet you twenty bucks it's Steven Lords."

Morales sat in the chair next to Russell's desk and pulled a sandwich from a white paper bag he'd been holding. "How the heck did you know that?"

Russell pulled a few napkins from his drawer, set them on the desk, and filled him on what he'd learned from Rhonda Tibbs. By the time he finished, Morales's disposition had brightened considerably and half his sandwich was gone.

"So all you have to do is place Lords in the hotel last night and you have your first suspect. That's one hell of a suspect, too, I might add."

"I can already place him. I overheard a couple of bellboys saying they saw him at the hotel after the game. We've also got him on the lobby surveillance cameras. But what I don't have is footage of him on the victim's floor or anywhere near her room. And thanks to the maid, there's no physical evidence to put him at the scene."

"Still, that'd be some coincidence if he wasn't in there," Morales said.

"There's something else bothering me," Russell said. "Michelle's phone shows an inbound call from Lords this morning. You think maybe he's trying to give himself an alibi?"

Morales took another bite of his sandwich and nodded. He brushed the crumbs off his shirt and onto Russell's desk. "Could be. Reminds me of this case I worked about nine or ten years ago. Remember when the dot-com bubble burst and all the tech stocks shat the bed all at once?"

Russell rolled his eyes. Here we go! Class is in session at the Art Morales School of Police Work. "Yeah, I remember, but it didn't affect me. I was at Fort Benning doing PT. What's that got to do with anything? I really don't have time for these strolls down memory lane."

"La experiencia es algo que no se tiene hasta poco después de que se necesita," Art said with a smirk.

Russell sat puzzled. Art sounded like the Dos Equis guy mixed with Juan Valdez. He always liked to go to some kind of Spanish proverb to get a point across. He thought it made him seem witty or wise. It was annoying as hell.

Art shook his head. "Christ, you live in Miami. Learn to speak some Spanish, will you?" he said. "It means 'experience is something you don't get until after you need it.'"

"Yeah, yeah, yeah," Russell said. "Can you please get to the point?"

"I'm getting to it. So this guy puts a ton of money into some Spanish search engine or something like that. Well, the market falls and the guy loses big. Now he needs money. He took out a huge insurance policy on his wife when they first got married. I think it's around two million or something and he wants to cash it in. Long story short, he sets up this whole deal and kills his wife. Then the bastard has the nerve to call her the next day as if everything's okay . . . leaves some message about being sure to get dog food on her way home.

"We found out soon enough it was bullshit, just an effort to throw suspicion off himself, but you should have heard how convincing he was on his message—all 'hi honey this, I love you that,' you know? Lords could've been doing the same thing. What did he say on his message?"

"Just an apology about what happened last night. He said things got a little heated and he hopes she lives up to her end of their deal," Russell said. "He's also expecting her to call him back."

They sat in contemplative silence. There was no doubt it was a clever move on Lords's part to try and make it look like he thought Michelle was still alive. But was he actually expecting a return call?

"You know, this has me thinking," Morales said. I don't suppose you saw the postgame press conference last night?"

"Please tell me you're kidding," Russell replied while rubbing his hands over his face. "I had better things to do than watch a phony like Lords."

"Oh yeah, your card game," Morales said. "Well, you missed some local reporter grilling Lords about his wife not being at the game. I didn't think much of it at the time, but looking at it now, Lords got really upset. I guess there was something to that after all."

"Was the reporter named Peter Owens?"

"That's right—why?"

Russell scrambled around his desk looking for the message. "That's the guy I was telling you about who called from the Post. Said I should watch his show today, actually."

Morales looked at his watch. "You mean *The Stat Line*? That started twenty minutes ago. Why aren't you watching?"

Without waiting for an answer, Morales got up and headed for the break room. This was probably a big waste of time, but Russell had no choice but to follow.

Two outdated television sets were mounted to a shelf, and it only took a second to find Owens's show, just back from a commercial break. The camera panned wide to show Owens standing on the set next to giant image of Lords on a video screen.

"Welcome back to *The Stat Line*. We all know Steven Lords has had a remarkable career. From playground prodigy to basketball icon to Madison Avenue pitchman, he's done it all. We've seen him hit a lot of big shots in games, and last night's shot may have been the biggest. But how does he celebrate those moments?

"I know one thing 'The Lord of South Beach' does. He frequents upscale hotels during late-night hours," Owens said as he signaled the producers to roll footage: a grainy yet discernible video of Steven Lords leaving the Murcielago Hotel.

"What you're seeing here is footage I personally shot late last night when I saw Lords leaving the Murcielago. Now, for those of you who don't know, what's strange about this is that the Murcielago was also the scene of a murder. The victim, who was found strangled to death this morning in one of the hotel's penthouse suites, was a woman named Michelle Tibbs, who just happens to be a very close—" he stopped and made air quotes with his fingers—"*friend* of Steven Lords.

"I'm not saying he did it—that's for the police to determine. I can only hope police do a thorough investigation and our hero, South Beach's savior himself, had nothing to do with this heinous crime."

Owens continued talking about his exclusive coverage and encouraging viewers to tune in regularly, so Russell turned down the volume and looked at his boss in amazement.

"Get to that studio and talk to Owens right away," Morales said. "Find out everything he knows and how the hell he got the vic's name before it was released to the media."

Russell patted his jacket to confirm he had his keys. Morales might be right. This case could get very big very quickly.

CHAPTER 11

The Condos at The Murano, 1:15 p.m.

Allen Warner walked across the cool marble floor of his spacious Coconut Grove condo and took a moment to savor the view of the calm, blue water of Key Biscayne. He'd moved in a few weeks ago and hadn't had much time to decorate.

He went to the wet bar and poured himself a Johnnie Walker Blue, neat with a splash of water. After years of working with low-level journeyman players, it felt good to be representing a bona fide superstar. Some agents spent their entire careers never getting to negotiate anything more than a few ten-day contracts. Representing Steve was a whole different animal. These commissions on nine-figure contracts and multimillion-dollar endorsements were easy to get used to.

But somehow the more money he made, the more money he needed to support the lifestyle he'd aspired to all his life. With the condo he'd just bought here for nearly three million, a four-bedroom beachfront saltbox on Martha's Vineyard, and a closing pending for a cottage in Malibu, it was more important than ever to keep the gravy train rolling.

Steven represented the sole epicenter of Allen's earnings potential, which worried him. On one hand, he was without a doubt the most talented player in a sport surging in popularity. But on the other hand he had piss-poor judgment when it came to protecting his own image. Steven was a genuinely good kid, but he was so naive when it came to women and what they could do to him. It was a relief that he'd acquiesced when it came to this latest problem with Michelle, but they clearly weren't out of the woods. Allen Warner knew the value of hedging his bets and wasn't about to leave anything to chance.

Rather than worry about it, he held his glass of scotch to the sky and silently toasted Steven Lords, the cornerstone and future of Allen Warner Sports Management. The future looked bright indeed, and bringing home the championship to Miami would be the icing on the cake.

He turned on the TV with the volume low and headed for the couch with a contract proposal in hand; some company in China wanted to put Steven's picture on a line of backpacks. The basic terms looked decent, but the numbers were way off.

As he sat back and considered a counterproposal, something he heard caught his attention. He bolted up, rewound the TiVo, and turned the volume up on his eighty-inch plasma television. What the hell did Owens just say? Allen watched again, barely noticing as the baccarat crystal glass he was drinking from fell to the floor and shattered.

AT STEVEN'S INSISTENCE, EDDIE HAD DECIDED TO TAG along to a team function for the season ticket holders at the Mayfair Hotel. Stevie could be a sadistic bastard. He knew a brother wasn't up to par after a wild night, but he'd kept right on bitching about coming to this damn luncheon.

Eddie sat alone at an empty table drinking from a pitcher of water, trying to hydrate and deal with his cotton mouth. His eyes still burned from lack of sleep the previous night, and even after three Advil, his nose still hurt and his head still pounded.

While Steven was busy smiling, shaking hands, and signing autographs, a few of his teammates looked beaten. Eddie nodded at Kyle, who hid behind dark sunglasses, looking every bit the wreck. He was trying to play it off with his arm draped around his girlfriend, talking to a few fans, but he was clearly using that girl as a crutch.

But that damn Julian was a stud. The ringleader of the party, and he looked about as fresh as Stevie did. Eddie poured himself another glass of water as he watched Steven and Julian pose for photos. Whatever that guy had should be put into cans!

The music of Jay-Z accompanied a buzzing from Eddie's hip pocket. Hopefully it was Jimmy calling back with something to take this edge off. Eddie took out his phone and sighed when he saw Allen's name on the display. This call had been bound to happen. Based on the agent's earlier cold stare, Eddie could tell that Allen wasn't too happy with him taking Steven to the Murcielago. But so what? His best friend needed him and it was his job to help him. Allen should've been grateful.

Eddie got up from the table and walked into the hallway. He didn't feel like talking, but it was best to get this over with.

"Wassup, Al?"

"My question exactly, Eddie!" Allen said. "The Murcielago hotel last night . . . why don't you tell me what really happened?"

Eddie began pacing in the hallway. "It was just like Stevie said. Michelle called him and he went over there to talk to her. That's all."

"Then why is Michelle lying in the county morgue and that douchebag Peter Owens is broadcasting exclusive video of Steven leaving the hotel?"

Eddie's legs suddenly felt wobbly. He stumbled into an empty conference room across the hall and barely made it to a nearby chair. He tried to respond but his throat was so tight he couldn't find the words. A lot of last night's details were still sketchy, even to him.

"I don't have time for your nonsense, Eddie! I need you to tell me what the hell happened! Didn't I tell you to make sure you kept Steven away from her? How could you possibly screw that up?"

"What the hell was I gonna do, man? He wanted to go and see her, so I took him, aight? I thought maybe I could talk him out of it on the way."

"So what happened when you got to the hotel? Don't leave anything out either."

Eddie loosened the top button on his shirt and took another deep breath.

"Stevie was freaked out, Al. The man was scared. He didn't know what to do. He couldn't handle this shit alone."

"I'm not interested in your excuses. Just tell me what the hell happened."

"I parked the car and waited for Stevie. He was taking way too long, so I just went up there to take care of shit, you know?"

"Christ, Eddie! You really are a moron, you know that? How'd you even get up on a VIP floor?"

Eddie wasn't about to answer that question. He wasn't a dealer or anything like that but he did favors for people sometimes to help pay for his own habit, including a couple of buddies who worked at the Murcielago. Getting to Michelle's room was not a problem.

"That don't even matter, Al. All you need to know is Stevie had done already gone when I went up to see Michelle. She said he'd just left. I could tell she was mad as hell about something so I asked her what happened, and that's when we got into it."

"Into what?" Allen asked.

"I don't remember everything she was saying. She was talking all crazy and laughing and shit like that. The girl was getting on my damn nerves with all that—"

"Christ, Eddie, I don't care about what she said. I want to know what *you* did. Can you just tell me that?"

Eddie scrunched his eyes and thought back to the dizzying blur of coke-fueled rage and the crushing sense of anxiety he felt as he snuck down in the service elevator to get Stevie's Aston Martin. "Truth is, man," he said after a moment, "I don't quite know what happened. But I thought she was breathing when I left."

"You *thought*—fuck, you truly are worthless, you know that? I'll tell you what happened: You were up there all fucked up and lost your mind and choked a pregnant woman to death. That's what goddamned happened!"

The truth of the matter was Eddie didn't remember shit about what had happened after Michelle opened the door and started laying into him. But the fresh scratches on side of his neck had him worried.

"And now the guy you say you were trying to protect is headed for the shitstorm of a lifetime," Allen said, "because you were stupid enough to pull this shit right when he's still there on the premises."

Eddie got out of the chair and started pacing. "How should I know somebody would have a camera on him that time of night?"

"Are you kidding me? He's Steven fucking Lords! There are always cameras on him. There are always people watching him. Dammit Eddie! What the hell were you on anyway?"

"Naw, man, I was cool. We'd been to Julian's party, but only for a little while."

"Enough bullshit, Eddie." Allen said. "I have half a mind to turn you over to the authorities."

"Come on, man, I was just trying to help the situation," Eddie said. "But you said Michelle needed to be dealt with—"

"And she would've been! But you really screwed things up. You didn't help anything. Michelle's baby wasn't the only issue on the table, remember?" Allen said. "I just got that business taken care of, but now you've gone and made things worse."

"Look, Al, I'm sorry. I didn't mean to hurt Stevie. I'm his main dawg, you know? He's like a brother to me."

"And that's the only thing keeping me from turning you in. His mind's going to be damn near in the tank now as it is."

Eddie fell silent. He knew Allen had never had much respect for him. As far as he was concerned, Eddie was nothing but a "homeboy" looking for a free ride. Eddie dropped his head. This was a chance to show Al he wasn't the only one who knew how to take care of business. When the shit hit the fan, somebody else besides him could step up, hold shit down, and cover the bases in the process.

Eddie raised his head as he sat back in his chair. "Well, I did cover my tracks," Eddie said.

"Oh yeah?" Allen asked. "Enlighten me on how exactly you did that."

"I know those kinds of hotels have security all up in that bitch. But you remember Jimmy—I mean James Cooper—right? The hotel security guy?"

"You mean that wannabe thug you hang out with and probably get your fix from?" Allen said. "Is he mixed up in this too?"

"I thought this'd be a good chance to fix everything, so I told him Stevie was in a jam and he offered to help out. I gave him a lil' piece of change to watch my back. And he broke off a lil' something for the parking guy at the front . . . and some dude who carries the bags off . . . so it's like we was never there," Eddie said. "I thought it was the smart thing to do, you feel me?"

"You thought that was smart? Steven was still there. Owens still has him on video. People still saw him! Hell, if you really wanted to be helpful, you could've left yourself in the video and left Steven out. Now he may be suspect number one. Plus, you created a loose end that we need to tie down."

"It was late. There wasn't nobody walking around. Plus, my people don't snitch, man. Dude is from a place where snitches wind up in ditches. Don't worry. It's gonna be okay."

"Your people are gonna get you killed," Allen said. "I'm sorry I don't share your optimistic view of your friends. Bottom line, Eddie—your friend needs to be taken care of. I'll be damned if I let Steven take the fall for a mess you made."

"Okay, Al, I'll handle the loose end."

"No! You will not do another thing, do you understand?"

"Okay, I got it."

"Do you understand? I've already given you way too much leeway as it is."

"I ain't no goddamn kid! I don't appreciate you talking to me like one."

Allen scoffed, "Eddie, I don't have time for your petty sensibilities. I really don't. What I need for you to do is go and fetch Steven like the good 'dawg' you said you are.

Don't tell him anything. Just get him out of there and let me handle everything from here."

"Fine," Eddie said.

STEVEN HAD BEEN SIGNING AUTOGRAPHS AND POSING FOR pictures with his fans for nearly a half hour when he felt a nudge in his side. He turned to see Eddie standing next to him, face long and eyes sad.

"Wassup, Eddie? Everything okay?"

"It's Allen," Eddie nodded toward the cell phone he was handing to Steve. "You need to talk to him right away."

Eddie wasn't one to let his emotions get to him, but his eyes were red and a little moist.

"You're going to need to sit down for this," Eddie said after they reached the solitude of an empty ballroom across the hall from the autograph session.

Steven sat.

Eddie watched with somber eyes as Steven put the phone to his ear. "What's going on, Allen? Why is Eddie crying?"

"Are you somewhere private?" Allen's voice was as strained as he'd ever heard it.

"Why, what's going on?"

"It's Michelle . . . she was found dead in her hotel room this morning."

"What? Quit playing," Steven laughed nervously and

glanced at Eddie, who was wiping his eyes and staring at the ground.

"I'm serious, Steven. She's dead," Allen said.

"I don't understand . . . she just called me a few hours ago. She can't be dead, Allen. That doesn't make any sense. This has to be some kind of joke—"

"It's no joke, Steven." Allen kept talking but Steve wasn't listening. This couldn't be right. There was no way Michelle could be dead.

Eddie walked over, tears trickling down his face, and patted Steven on the back.

"This isn't possible!" Steven screamed, interrupting whatever Allen was saying. "She called me this morning, Al. There's no way."

His hands shook as he tore the phone away from his ear and looked across the room. His breath became heavier as memories of Michelle seeped into his mind. Her laugh resonated in his ears. Eddie wrapped his arm around his shoulders and Steven leaned toward him, his heart churning with sadness and disbelief.

THE PHONE HAD DROPPED TO THE FLOOR, SO EDDIE PICKED it up and put it to his ear. "Al, you still there?"

"Yeah, I'm here. How's Steven?"

Steven was slumped in a chair, head in his hands, looking

absolutely devastated. His lips moved like he was mutter-
ing something but Eddie couldn't make out the words.

"Not good, Al. He's in pretty bad shape. What do you
need me to do?"

"Someone needs to tell him about Owens's video of him
from the hotel—and that Owens has gone public with
what he knows about Steven's relationship with Michelle."

"Now? You sure now's the time to tell him?" Eddie whispered into the phone.

"Christ, I don't know . . . tell you what, first thing you
need to do is get him out of there, just in case someone saw
the show. He's in no shape to answer any questions. Take
him home and stay there until practice tomorrow. Don't
answer any calls, especially from Michelle's phone, as it's
likely to be the police. If they saw the show, they're going
to want to talk to Steven."

"I got it, Al. No calls unless it's you."

"And let's wait to say anything about Owens's show,"
Allen said. "Don't say a word about it. Just get him the hell
out of there and give me a call when you make it home."

"Okay, Al. We're leaving right now." Eddie ended the call
and turned his attention to Steven, whose face was still bur-
ied in his hands.

"Stevie. It's gonna be all right," Eddie said. "We're gonna
get through this."

Steven's face slowly emerged from his hands, his eyes red
and puffy from crying. "I was so stupid. I treated her so

bad. After everything we went through. I treated her so bad," he said. "What about the baby? This is so fucked up!"

"We can't worry about that right now, and this ain't the time to be hard on yourself, man. You didn't do anything wrong. She knew what she was doing. She knew what she was getting into. You did more than you should have. You took care of her. You know that."

"What happened? Do the police have any suspects? Do they have any kind of leads? Do they know anything?"

"We need to talk about that."

Steven turned and looked at Eddie. "What? What about it?"

Eddie hesitated before answering. Fuck it, he thought. This was something Stevie needed to know.

"I don't know too much about it, but Allen said this afternoon Peter Owens aired some kind of video of you leaving the hotel last night."

"He *what*?"

"I know, right? I don't know where he got the video. But Al said he showed a tape of you leaving the hotel last night. He also connected you to Michelle."

"Why would he say that? Where would he get a video? Is he following us or something?"

"I don't know. But Allen wants us out of here before people start asking questions. You're a mess," Eddie helped Steven to his feet. "Put your shades on, and let's get you home."

"I know, man, I know. Shit's fucked up! Who'd wanna do something like that to Michelle?"

"I don't know. It doesn't make no sense," Eddie said. "But we can't think about that right now. Let's get you back to your house so we can plan our next move."

"Okay. Let me go find Coach and let him know I'm leaving," Steven said, heading for the door.

"No. You go get your car and head straight home. I'll let the team know what's going on and then I'll meet you at your house in a few. Al said he'll check in with you a little later."

Steven doubled back to give Eddie a hug. "Thanks for being here, man. I appreciate it."

"You don't need to thank me, dawg. I'm your boy. You know I'll hold you down. Don't worry about it. Don't worry about a thing. I'll catch up with you at your house."

CHAPTER 12

Miami-Dade Police Department, 3:30 p.m.

By 3:30 that afternoon, a long line of news vans had jammed the street in front of the Miami-Dade Police Department. The close proximity to downtown made it easy for local networks to dispatch news crews. Reporters gathered around the stairs and palm trees that surrounded the four-story, red brick-and-stucco building, hoping to get an update on what was already being dubbed the Murcielago Murder.

Russell had been at his desk for all of two minutes, reviewing his notes from his meeting with Peter Owens, when Art Morales showed up, his face tight with tension. Art had been around too long to let the stress of that place get to him, so things must've amped up since that morning.

"I hope that smile on your face means you got something useful," Morales said.

"Oh, he gave me something useful," Russell replied. "Laid it all out for me in fact."

"Okay, out with it. Captain's waiting for an update."

"Maybe I should give it to him directly?"

"I don't think so," Morales said. "Just tell me what you found out."

"Okay . . . turns out this whole thing started way back when Lords and Tibbs were dating in high school, up somewhere in Tennessee. Sounds to me like they broke up for a while, but Lords still had a thing for her and at some point started sleeping with her behind his wife's back. Not long after getting married, actually."

"So we've got a connection to the victim—that's good," Morales said. "But how the hell did Owens get the video?"

"Said he got a call from an unknown number around two o'clock. The guy on the other end told him if he wanted a story, he should get over to the Murcielago Hotel pronto because—and I'm quoting here—'the Lord moves in mysterious ways.'"

"Clever."

"Right, but before Owens could ask if he meant Steven Lords, the caller hung up," Russell said. "So Owens figured he'd head over to the Murcielago, getting to the hotel at about two thirty. Not long after he pulled up, he saw Lords getting into his car and driving off. His crew was off duty so Owens used one of those flip cameras to get the video. His production guys are sending over a copy of the show."

Morales leaned back in his chair. "So he had no idea who called him?"

"None at all. Just chalked it up to an anonymous tip."

Art shook his head. "That sounds shady at best, but it's not the worst account I've heard over the years. I wonder how someone would get his cell number in the first place, though."

"I asked the same thing," Russell said. "He leaves his business cards at different hotels around town, hoping for something like this to happen."

"So anyone could have called him?"

"I guess, if you look at it like that. What are you trying to get at, Art?"

"I'm not getting at anything. It's just the whole thing sounds sketchy. You're talking about going after the most famous basketball player on the planet, and that's not going to sit too well with the brass. They love their superstars, especially when they're about to bring a championship to the city of Miami. I don't think that's enough to build an investigation on, given the importance of your prime suspect."

Russell rolled his eyes. "Well how about this: We have Lords at the scene. We know he was having a secret relationship with the victim. Plus he has a motive."

"Run it down for me, Junior. Let's hear the motive."

Russell leaned across his desk. "Rumor has it that Lords's marriage is on the rocks. Then his girlfriend, Michelle Tibbs, gets pregnant with his child . . . he has to get rid of her or else risk losing everything." Russell reared back in his chair. "You've seen his commercials. The guy comes off like he's the goddamn pope. I know for a fact there's no way he's that fucking clean."

"Oh yeah? How do you know that?"

"Well . . . in this day and age, who is?" Russell said. "But I'll lay odds that he damn sure isn't. I'll bet a week's pay on it."

"No gastar su dinero antes de tener que. Never spend your money before you have it," Morales said as he tapped his index finger against the desk. "We don't have time for your bets, Junior. This case could go high priority any minute now, so you need to plan your next move."

"I think I need go and talk to Lords himself. I want to get his side of the story and find out what's going on," Russell said. "Let's see what his alibi is on the night in question."

"Wrong! You aren't ready to talk to Steven Lords yet."

"Why not?" Russell said, shrugging. "If this was some Liberty City thug we'd be crawling up his ass right now and sweating a confession out of him. Lords isn't anything special."

Morales shook his head tersely. "Let me tell you how this works, Junior. By this time tomorrow, the big suits will be coming in here and sticking their noses where they don't belong. We need to get our ducks lined up first. If you're going to go after a Steven Lords, then you'd better be sure your case is ironclad. The last thing you want is to have some pencil pusher looking over your shoulder at every move you make, waiting for an opportunity to reassign you."

"Okay then," Russell said. "What do you think I should do?"

"Go home and get cleaned up a little. You're going to have a long night tonight. You should interview everyone who was on duty last night. Find out if anyone saw Lords on Tibbs's floor last night. Get us something solid and concrete to go on and we'll take it from there."

"Okay. I'll do that. But I'm telling you it's all there. Just let me talk to him. I'll go over to his house and talk to him."

"You want to question him about the murder of his girl-friend at his house without his lawyer present? Muy loco," Morales tapped Russell's forehead. "Use your head, Junior. You're smarter than that."

"If this punk is innocent, he won't need a lawyer."

Morales chuckled. "Man, what is with you and this guy? What'd he do, fuck your girlfriend or something?"

"I'm just not fooled by all the commercials and every-thing. The whole city treats him like he's God. If you let me talk to him, I'll show you he's no better than—"

"Give it time. He's Steven Lords! Where's he gonna go?"

CHAPTER 13

Miami-Dade Police Headquarters, 7:00 a.m.
Four days until the Finals

Ed Stones waited outside the police department, checking his camera equipment and making sure he was ready to roll when the press conference began. He watched as reporters paced the sidewalks, trying to get police officers to go on record with what they knew about the murder of Michelle Tibbs.

Casual onlookers littered the sidewalks. As Ed took his camera from the truck, a spectator approached him.

"Hey, man, what's going on out here this morning?"

"Big press conference," Ed replied. "Looks like every news outlet in the country is here."

"Is it about that girl Steven Lords killed over at that hotel?"

"We don't know if he killed her or not, but police are going to tell us what they know in about fifteen minutes."

The man shook his head. "He did that shit! And that girl was pregnant too? Damn!"

Ed laughed it off. "Well let's just wait and see what the police have to say."

JUST AS MORALES PREDICTED, THE CASE HAD GONE HIGH priority. The high-ranking brass of the Miami-Dade Police Department had ordered major shift changes and suspension of other open cases for the duration of the Murcielago investigation. They also requested that Russell brief them on his investigation before the press conference began.

The good news was that now Russell had backup at the hotel, interviewing employees and trying to figure out who might have tampered with the footage. The bad news was now everyone would be watching him like hawks.

Russell sat at his desk, reviewing his reports before his meeting. There was queasiness in his stomach as he struggled to make sure he knew the merits of his case inside and out. Could he honestly expect to go into this meeting with Steven Lords as his prime suspect and be taken seriously? As he continued to turn the pages, they started to cling to his sweaty hands. This was useless. The Chief of Police was waiting to be briefed and Russell had no idea what he was going to say.

"They're waiting for you in the conference room," Morales said as he approached Russell's desk. "Come on and let me have a look at you."

Russell wiped his hands on his pants and gathered his notes. He took a deep breath to calm himself and stood.

"For crying out loud, Junior, this is the big time. You couldn't iron that shirt?"

"I did iron it. Used spray starch and everything."

"Here's another piece of free advice: Get yourself a good dry cleaner. Stop taking your suits to the machines in your building." Morales straightened Russell's collar, looked him over, and nodded. "Okay, we don't want to keep everyone waiting."

Morales escorted Russell through the station and to the conference room. With each step, Russell's heartbeat quickened. He loosened his collar to ease the tension building in his neck.

"You look nervous," Morales said.

"I am. Wouldn't you be?" Russell replied. "I'm about to go present my case to the Chief of Police."

"Relax—Chief Cavanaugh's a good man. He's a cop just like us. He's not like those dicks in city hall. He cares about real cops and real police work. Be calm. When you tell him what you have, be convincing. If he thinks you believe in your investigation, he'll believe in your investigation."

"Well that's good to know."

"But you'll want to watch out for Deputy Chief Garcia," Morales said. "He's a former Internal Affairs stooge and word is he's been snaking around all morning asking questions about you and the investigation. Garcia's all about politics, so don't let him rattle you. You just convince the old man and you'll be okay."

As they arrived at the conference room door, Morales placed his hand on Russell's shoulder. "I'll be here when you're done," he said as opened the door.

Russell let out a deep breath before he walked in the room.

CHAPTER 14

Russell sat at the far end of the table, tapping his fingers against the glossy brown surface. There was nothing more intimidating for a rookie detective than being in a room full of superiors on a high-priority case.

Officials from city hall sat on both sides of the table but Russell kept his eyes on Chief Cavanaugh, who sat on the opposite side, whispering to a subordinate. The chief looked a bit like Jack Nicholson in *A Few Good Men*. He had more gray hair than Jack but that same look in his eye—like he could either start laughing any minute or rip your lungs out on a whim.

Cavanaugh caught Russell's eye and gave him an almost imperceptible nod, but before saying anything he got up from his chair and looked out the window at the growing throng of reporters that had gathered to cover the upcoming news conference.

"Well, gentlemen, we have ourselves quite a crowd this morning, so let's make this quick. Detective Howard, I'm told you're a smart young detective with a bright future. Your captain speaks very highly of you. So why don't you rundown what you've uncovered so far?"

Russell could feel everyone's eyes on him as he stood to present his findings. He cleared his throat and said, "The victim's name is Michelle Tibbs and—"

"Speak up, son. This isn't a library."

Russell nodded and continued his rundown of his morning at the Murcielago. He didn't know who the guys in suits around the table were, but they all looked bored with what they were hearing until he mentioned checking Tibbs's cell phone log and finding calls to Steven Lords.

"How do you know it's Lords's number?" one of the men asked.

"It was listed in her contacts only as 'Steven,' but we've since gotten conformation from the wireless provider that the account for that number is in Lords's name. She placed several calls to him on the night in question, and there are hundreds more during the past few months, incoming and outgoing. So it's clear—"

"But why would you even think that this 'Steven' whose name you saw on her cell was our own Steven Lords?" another asked, face tight with hostility.

"I didn't at first," Russell said evenly. "It wasn't until I saw surveillance footage from the hotel that I learned that

Lords was there that night and, as it turns out, right about the same time the ME confirmed time of death."

"So what?" someone said. "How do you know he wasn't there visiting someone else or maybe having a late dinner after the big win?"

"We canvassed the place thoroughly, with uniformed officers talking to employees and guests. None of the wait-staff at any of the restaurants recall seeing him."

Russell took a long swallow of water. "I also thought he might've been there to see his wife, because it's been reported they're having marital problems. But Karen Lords wasn't registered there and no one on duty recognized a picture of her, so it's unlikely she was anywhere close to the hotel last night."

"So you don't know why he was there or who he was seeing?" a thin man with a thin mustache and a receding hairline seated next to Cavanaugh said. "All you *know* is he was at the hotel about the same time this woman died."

"She didn't just die," Russell said. "She was murdered. We know that for a fact. We also know Lords was at the hotel right about the same time she was killed and, by the sound of reports from a few of the bellboys, he was uncharacteristically agitated and in quite a rush. And we now know he had a relationship—"

"You didn't answer the question, Detective. How do you know he was there to see the victim?"

"Truthfully, sir, I can't rule out the possibility of his being at the hotel for another reason. But what I was about to say is we now know that he was in an extramarital relationship with the victim, that the victim was pregnant, and that according to the victim's own sister, Steven Lords is the father. So until we find any evidence to the contrary, I think it's more than reasonable to assume Lords was at the hotel to see the victim."

"That doesn't mean he killed her."

This statement got nods all around. From everyone but Cavanaugh, that was.

"Of course it doesn't, "Russell said. "But we can't rule him out as a possible suspect either. Especially since there are no other leads at the moment."

The thin man glared at Russell and shuffled some papers in front of him. "You have Lords on video at the hotel, but in statements you and other officers took, no one remembered seeing him—"

"I said earlier that two bellboys—"

"Said someone *saw* him. But no one talked to him. No one saw him with anyone, and I'm gathering that if you had security footage of him going to the victim's room you would have shared that with us."

"I have good reason to believe the surveillance cameras have been tampered with."

"That's exactly my point," the skinny man said. "You said in your report the security video may have been altered. If that's the case, why wouldn't you consider the person who altered the video a suspect . . . or at least a credible lead?"

Russell stood in silence. He hadn't considered the video tech a suspect. Why would he? A connection had been made between Lords and Tibbs, so to pursue any other leads would have been a waste.

"Are you *gambling* on the notion that Lords killed that woman?"

With his head tilted to one side, Russell stared at the thin man, who seemed to be sneering at him. This was supposed to be a review of the evidence against Lords, not an indictment against the guy leading the investigation.

"Exactly what are you trying to get at?" Russell asked cautiously.

"What I'm getting at, Detective, is that according to some of your colleagues, you have a penchant for betting."

"Legal gambling," Russell said. "And I don't see how that has any bearing on what we're talking about here."

"Well I do," The skinny man turned to Chief Cavanaugh. "This investigation is too important to be conducted by a rookie detective with a vice. If the press gets wind of this it could compromise the investigation and give a black eye to the city and this department."

"Hold on for a minute, Mr.—"

"It's Deputy Chief Luis Garcia. And let me add something else. I've known gamblers to be reckless and irrational. Naming Steven Lords a suspect with circumstantial evidence looks to me like recklessness. Particularly since you've given no thought to whoever tampered with the security footage."

As the men seated around the table nodded in agreement, Russell shook his head. It felt like somebody had come and taken a dump all over the investigation—and that somebody was the pencil-pushing prick sitting next to the chief. Deputy Chief Garcia leaned over and whispered into Chief Cavanaugh's ear. He sure got a lot of pleasure out of busting a cop's balls.

"I'm curious, Detective. I considered your account of the interview you conducted with Peter Owens, and let me see if I got this straight," Cavanaugh said. "Your theory of the crime is Lords killed Michelle Tibbs because she's having his child?"

Russell paused. It made a lot of sense to him. Was there something he was missing, or had Garcia torpedoed the only other person in the room who might've believed in this investigation?

"You are aware you're talking about *the* Steven Lords?" Cavanaugh added.

Russell looked at the faces staring back at him.

"Yes, sir. I'm fully aware of who I'm talking about . . . and what he means to the city," Russell said. "But with all due respect, this is a murder investigation, and there's no room to worry about Steven Lords's celebrity. With his marriage at stake and possibly millions of dollars in endorsements on the line, I think there's a plausible motive here. And we certainly have opportunity."

Whispers filled the air as the men shared their thoughts with one another. The churning in Russell's stomach had slowed as he watched his superiors nod at one another in discussion.

"Detective Howard," Cavanaugh said.

"Yes, sir?"

"It probably won't surprise you to hear I came here this morning with my own thoughts of turning this case over to a more experienced detective. But now I'm finding myself inclined to trust your captain's confidence in your abilities to handle this investigation."

"Thank you very much, sir."

"But I can't ignore—nor can you—that this is a very delicate situation, given Mr. Lords's standing in the community. I did some checking of my own, and he's been a model citizen—not so much as a parking ticket since coming to our fair city. You understand that?"

"Of course."

"He's also something of a role model. So no matter how damning the circumstantial evidence may be against him, I feel like he's earned the benefit of the doubt. Don't you agree?"

Russell didn't, but he wasn't about to object. He nodded.

"Good. Here's my decision. You seem to have enough evidence to warrant a further investigation, so I'm going to give you forty-eight hours to build your case against Lords," Chief Cavanaugh said. "If you can't find anything substantial in that period of time, then I want you to drop it. Let the man go and bring this city a championship."

"Yes, sir," Russell said.

"Don't make us all look like a bunch of dicks, Detective. You do your job and you do it carefully. Everyone will be watching."

"I'll make sure to do my due diligence, sir."

"So what's your next move, then?"

"I'd like to go and talk to Lords and get his version of what happened last night. ESPN reported the team would be practicing this morning and I think it'd be best to speak to him as soon as possible."

"Well good luck, Detective. Make sure you keep your captain abreast of your investigation."

Deputy Chief Garcia considered Russell though narrowed eyes.

"Thank you, sir," Russell said as he gathered his reports. "You won't regret this."

CHAPTER 15

Miami Coliseum, 10:25 a.m.
Three days until the Finals

Russell squeezed through the legion of reporters and cameramen that had started to gather on the concrete walkway outside the coliseum. Security was surprisingly strict that morning; Russell quickly found out that was because of a press conference scheduled for later that afternoon. The steady influx of reporters must've been gathering to cover whatever hand job the team was ready to give to Miami's faithful. He flashed his badge to a man in a blue uniform, who nodded and reported Russell's arrival into a radio clipped to his shirt.

"Please wait here, sir," the guard said as he directed Russell out of the path of the incoming media crowd.

Puzzled, Russell stood next to the guard. Who had this guy called? Russell glanced at the receptionist, who seemed to be playing with her cell phone behind a window across the room, and then looked back at the guard. Maybe building security procedures called for the guard to announce visitors, but then what was that receptionist's job? Russell nodded as he stroked his chin. *Someone's expecting me.*

A perky, bespectacled man with short, dark hair walked out of the open double doors where reporters had been entering. The reporters had seemed to part and make way for him, so he must've been both well-known and important. The man approached Russell with an affable smile and his hand extended, like he was welcoming guests aboard a cruise ship.

"Detective Howard?"

Russell nodded. "That would be me. And you are?"

"I'm Dave Frasier, the team's director of media relations. Deputy Chief Luis Garcia called me a few minutes ago and said you might be on your way. I understand you have some questions for Steven Lords?"

So much for the element of surprise. This whole thing was starting to feel like a set-up.

"Steven's still in practice," Dave said without waiting for an answer. "But if you'll follow me, I'll show you where you can wait for him."

Russell looked at Dave as they walked side by side

through the corridor. He was on the short side, probably about five seven, but with an athletic build. He walked upright and purposefully, with no discernible rhythm to his stride. Dave noticed a piece of lint on his shoulder and brushed it away. His khaki pants were ironed to a crease and his white polo shirt was tucked in tightly. No doubt this guy played by the book.

They walked down a long, drab hallway somewhere within the bowels of the arena. Over the sound of their footsteps echoing throughout the corridor, Russell could hear the sound of a motor running and something beeping in the distance. His eyes followed the endless pipes and wires that ran along the building's walls and ceiling.

"So would you like a little tour of the facilities here?" Dave asked. "We've got a few minutes to kill before practice wraps up."

Russell considered Dave through narrow eyes and shook his head decisively. "I'm afraid this isn't a social visit, Mr. Frasier. Just show me where I can talk to Lords."

"There's a lounge in the team's locker room. It's at the end of this hall."

To fortify his resolve, Russell remembered the bruises on Michelle's neck and the cries from her sister Rhonda. Lords had a lot to answer for, but as much as he hated to admit it, Morales had a point. Lords wasn't some Liberty City thug. He was a superstar at the top of his game, who was about to play in a series that had this whole city buzzing. So Russell knew he couldn't go in like the Gestapo, no matter what he thought of Lords.

An open entryway gave Russell a glimpse of the basketball court. He figured it must have recently emptied, if that was where the team practiced.

"Hold on a sec," Russell said as he walked through the entrance and into the heart of the arena. Russell, with Dave following, approached the edge of the basketball court. The lights were dimmer than they were for games but still bright enough to show off the luster of the floor that had been waxed a few hours prior.

"Okay to walk on it?"

Dave extended an arm forward. "Sure, go right ahead. The team's at the practice facility next door, so it's all yours."

Russell stepped onto the court. The echoes of his footsteps filled the empty arena as he made his way to the basket. He looked into the rafters and saw the enormous scoreboard and rows of empty red seats rising three levels.

He walked until he was directly under the basket and reached up. Even on his tiptoes he was several feet short of reaching the rim.

"Seemed a little lower in the park when I was a kid."

"These rims are ten feet. Some playground rims are between eight and nine feet," Dave said.

Russell stepped back and looked at the rim and again at the ground. "You a betting man, Dave?"

"Depends on what the bet is."

"I bet you I can reach the rim with my vertical jump."

Dave smiled. "You're about what, five nine or five ten?"

"Five ten and a half and I'm wearing loafers. So what do you say?

Dave nodded. "Okay, what's the bet?"

Russell grabbed his ankle and stretched his leg back. "If I can touch that rim, you get me two lower bowl tickets and a parking pass for game one."

"What's in it for me if you can't?"

"You tell me," Russell said. "What can I do for you?"

Dave thought before answering. He looked nervous, conspiratorial almost.

"How about this, and feel free to stop me if I'm over the line, okay? But I've got this nephew—a good kid, you know—but I found out from my brother that he got pulled over and ended up getting arrested for having a little pot. He wasn't driving or anything, said he was just holding it for his friend. But now he's got a court date in a couple weeks and I was wondering . . ."

"You were wondering?"

"You know," he said, face sheepish. "Maybe you could talk to the arresting officer. Let him know he's studying Sports Administration at St. Thomas University and a conviction might really mess up his future."

Russell raised an eyebrow. He hadn't figured Dave for the type to ask him to fix a drug charge. Good to know he wasn't so straight-laced after all.

He let the question hang for a moment. The odds of any-one actually pushing for a conviction of a misdemeanor possession in a case like that was less than remote, but why tip his hand? "Say no more," Russell said. "It's a bet."

Russell took off his jacket and handed it to Dave, who draped it over his arm. He then bent his knees a few times to loosen them and stepped back. It had been a while since he'd tried this, but he was pretty sure he could do it. The trick was not to pull something.

He took a big step, bended his knees and leapt off the floor, reaching for the orange hoop. His outstretched hand barely grazed the rim before he came down and almost slipped on the court in his loafers.

Yes!

"I believe that's two lower bowl seats you owe me," he said as he breathed heavily. "Plus a parking pass."

"I can't believe you did it," Dave said as he handed Russell his jacket. "I'll have your tickets waiting for you at will-call on the night of the game. All you'll need is your ID to claim them."

"All right. Don't leave me hanging, though. I'd hate to have to issue a warrant for your arrest."

"Don't worry—I always pay my debts. They'll be there," Dave said as he walked off the floor. "Anyhow, right this way."

Russell draped his jacket over his arm and followed Dave through another entryway and down a short hallway before arriving outside a set of double doors leading into the team's locker room. Dave rubbed his ID badge against the security scanner and the two men walked in.

Russell strode to the middle of the circular room. This was more like what he expected. The soft, black carpeting was so plush that each step he took left an impression. His hands traced the large cherry-wood cubicles that lined the locker room walls under enormous pictures of some of the team's greatest players. Reading the nameplates that rested on the top of each locker, Russell found Lords's space. He laid his jacket down, sat on the black leather-cushioned bench in the locker stall, stretched out his legs, and leaned back.

"I must admit, this is pretty impressive," he said as he scanned the room.

Dave walked over and stood next to Steven's cubicle. "So are you a fan, Detective? Are you one of Lords's believers?"

"Nah, I haven't followed sports since I was in college."

Russell stood, then walked past Dave to have a closer look at a giant plasma television mounted at the head of the room. "And frankly, all this seems a little excessive when you consider all these guys do is play a game," Russell said. "It's a heck of a lot of money to house some basketball players, when right across the street you have homeless people sleeping on cardboard boxes and begging for a little something to eat. What a waste."

"We aren't oblivious to our community. We take our

charitable contributions very seriously. You'll be happy to know the organization donates money to all sorts of charities throughout Miami and South Florida," Dave said. "Some of the players themselves have their own charitable foundations. In fact, Karen, Steve's wife, is head of the Steven Lords Foundation. With Steven's help they've done a lot of good things, here and around the world."

A set of rear doors swung open and a paunchy, middle-aged man wheeled in a white bin. Russell watched the man stop at each locker and carefully hang the players' uniforms in their stalls. After he left, Russell walked over to one of the stalls and fiddled with the sleeve of the warm-up jacket. "How long have you known Lords?" Russell asked Dave.

"Since he's been in the league, I guess. We're talking seven years," Dave replied.

"So what's your take on him?"

"My take? I think he's a great player and a good guy."

Russell laughed. "Come on! A few minutes ago you were asking me to fix a misdemeanor for your nephew, so don't give me the company man routine," he said. "Give it to me straight. Just like you did with that bet. What's the deal with Lords? We both know some of these superstars can be real head cases in one way or another."

"Not even close, "Dave said. "Steven's different from a lot of the other guys you see on TV. Not that they're bad people . . . but what you see with them isn't always what you get. Even though the shoe commercials try to deify him, he's the most down-to-earth guy you could ever meet."

Russell sneered as he walked over to Dave. He was trying to convey the standard company line, but this guy wasn't telling the whole truth. "How do you explain his pregnant girlfriend, then?"

Dave shrugged his shoulders. "Hey, that's his business, all right? It's not my place to judge. I don't hang out with him and I don't get involved in his personal affairs. So if you're looking for somebody to dish dirt or whatever, I'm not the guy. Sorry."

Russell snickered as he walked back to Steven's locker. He reached down to grab his jacket, but instead decided to take Steven's warm-up jacket off its hanger. He draped the jacket over his shoulders, allowing the sleeves to exceed Russell's arm length by about six inches. Russell looked down to see the jacket hem dangle slightly below his knees.

"This is some jacket. Feels a lot lighter than it looks."

"If you like it, you can buy a replica in the store," Dave said.

"What's the difference between these and the replicas?" Russell asked. "Cheaper material?"

"Not too much. The biggest difference is these have the players' names and numbers stitched over the heart. The replicas don't. They just have the team logo there and also on the back."

Russell took off the jacket and draped it across its hanger. He heard Dave's cell phone ringing from his hip pocket.

"Excuse me for a minute, would you?" Dave said. He walked away for a moment and then returned, putting his phone back in his pocket.

"That was our GM. He said practice is over and Steven should be heading down here any minute."

"It's about time," Russell said.

"Let's head upstairs to my office and give Steven a chance to get cleaned up before you talk to him."

"I've already wasted enough time. How long is this gonna take?"

"Ten, maybe fifteen minutes. While we wait, I can get you that parking pass for the game."

CHAPTER 16

Locker room, 11:30 a.m.

Steven sat on his locker bench with a Gatorade towel draped over his shoulder and his head hung low. The sweat ran down his head and dripped onto the black carpet between his feet as he breathed long and slow, trying to cool down. It had been a tough practice. The guys had got after it that morning, maybe too hard. But it was good to focus on something else for a while, besides the sadness festering inside him.

He still couldn't believe Michelle was gone. He had barely gotten any sleep the previous night. He couldn't bear to watch any television or listen to any of the reports about the murder. Instead he relegated himself to his workout room and the basketball court to help him cope.

He knew he should call her folks but didn't have it in him. Not yet anyway.

He stood and bent to touch his toes, hoping to stretch out a mild burning sensation in his lower back. With game one only three days out, maybe it wasn't a good idea to have practiced so hard. He wiped the sweat from his forehead and tossed the towel in the pile with the rest of the practice gear. Another teammate threw a cold glare at Steven as he tossed his own towel in the pile.

"That was a good run up there, Ricky. Way to work," Steven said.

"Psssh. Whatever, man," Ricky said as he turned and walked off.

Steven bobbed his head. Things had gotten out of hand on the court. In the heat of competition, some harsh words had been exchanged, which had led to a few shoving matches. He looked down a few stalls and saw that Nate was still scowling. A hard foul on a breakaway lay-up had almost resulted in them coming to blows.

Steven sat back down to take off his shoes. He had definitely let his emotions get the better of him. The last twenty-four hours had been tough. Having an affair go public and grieving over Michelle's death was a lot to deal with. But it was no excuse for taking it out on everyone else.

Steven took a deep breath and stood in front of his stall. "Hey, fellas, I just want to say I'm sorry if you thought I was trippin' earlier today at practice," he said. "I've got a lot going on and I guess the shit is starting to get to me. But I didn't mean to take it out on y'all."

Rev, the starting center and oldest member of the team, walked over to Steven. "Don't worry about it, all right?" he said. "I'm sure I speak for everyone when I say no harm done. We know what you're up against and we're behind you all the way."

Nate walked up to Steve and hugged him. "You know it's all love, baby."

"Rev's right," Kyle said. "You don't have nothin' to apologize for."

Steven smiled. "I appreciate the hell out of y'all for real," he said. "It means a lot to hear you say that."

Coach Hollis had joined them in the locker room with a stranger in tow. "I hate to break up this love fest, but before you guys get gone Warren Crane from legal would like to have a few words with you," he said. "I've got to go upstairs and get ready for this press conference. None of you are required to stay, and if you want to leave after you get treatments or whatever no one has a problem with that. But remember practice is the same time tomorrow. Steven, when you're dressed they want you in Jeff's office. So if there's nothing else, here's Mr. Crane."

His mind preoccupied, Coach Norman Hollis headed for the GM's office, where Kevin Daniels and Vice

President of Basketball Operations Jeff Lane waited for him. It was no secret to anyone he was worried about Steven, who had been doing his best to keep himself together, but whose slip was starting to show. The outbursts at practice may have only been the tip of the iceberg.

Norman glanced at a newspaper on Kevin's desk as he sat next to Jeff. The headline read "Lord Only Knows." It looked like the sharks smelled blood and were already starting to circle. It'd be a full-on feeding frenzy by tip-off and if Steven wasn't careful, the press was gonna eat him alive. That was something the team could ill afford.

"Hey, Coach. I hear the team looked good in practice today. Are we gonna take it to them in game one or what?" Jeff asked.

"That's the plan," Norman said. "We got some good work in on some situational stuff—before things got a little heated."

"A little heated?" Kevin asked. "What happened out there?"

"Steven got into it with a few of his teammates, is all. A couple of guys had to get in there and separate them."

"Well that can't be good for team chemistry," Kevin said. "It's way too late in the season for this kind of behavior. We don't need any more distractions."

"It's really not a big deal. Practices can sometimes get a little testy," Jeff said, patting Hollis on the back. "Norm and I have both been in this league long enough to know that. Steven's a competitor, and he's four wins away from his first championship. He's entitled to kick a little ass in practice to make sure everyone's on the same page. If anything it'll help team chemistry and get them focused."

"I know what you're getting at," Norman said. "But you didn't see him in practice today. He was all up in guy's faces and yelling at coaches about foul calls during scrimmages. I almost tossed him out of practice, but I understand what he's going through."

"I'm telling you, Steven's a warrior," Jeff said. "He blew off some steam today—no big deal."

"I've been around Steven since he was a rookie and what I saw at practice today wasn't just about him blowing off some steam. That girl's death is taking a toll on him."

Jeff threw up his hands and shrugged. "Of course it's going to bother him. But I think you're making too much of it. There's nothing more important to Steven than winning his first championship. He'll deal with it and it'll all blow over and that will be that."

"I don't think you're making enough out of it, Jeff," Norman said. "His girlfriend was murdered. He was seen leaving that hotel. I don't know if you've noticed, but Karen and his little girl haven't been at the games lately. Steve's carrying some major baggage and I'm very concerned."

"How are things with the team now?" Kevin asked.

"Before I left, Steven was apologizing to the guys. But

look, you know they'll rally around him. That's what this team does. I'm more concerned about Steven's mental state. This thing with his murdered girlfriend and him leaving the hotel is only getting started. You know it's gonna snowball from now until the finals."

"I was just on the phone with the league office. Stan called. He told me Doug is concerned about the league's marquee name being connected to this murder and having this scandal overshadow the finals," Kevin said.

"That's exactly why we're holding this press conference today," Jeff said. "There are a bunch of reporters here, and hopefully we can redirect some of this attention off Steven and back on the finals."

"That's all well and good, but what else are we going to do for Steven?" Norman said as he picked up the front page of the paper. "I'm looking at those newspaper headlines— 'Oh, Lord . . . You Devil!'—and it looks like we've got quite a storm brewing."

"At this stage of the game, what else can we do?" Kevin said. "If this thing takes a turn for the worse, you know we'll do everything we can to help him. But right now, my responsibilities are to the team. I'm trying to squelch some of the distractions so they can focus and prepare. At this point there's a whole lot of speculation out there, especially after the statement the chief of police made."

Hollis sat up in his seat. "Which was?"

"Oh that's right—you were at practice and missed the

police press conference. The chief said Steven was a person of interest in that murder. They sent a detective over to talk to him. He's in Dave's office waiting right now."

Norman sat back in his chair with his hand over his mouth. "Does Steven know?"

"He will in a minute. I just saw him walk into your office, Jeff," Dave said as he walked in. "His agent is there with him, and I'm sure he's telling him."

STEVEN SAT ON A BROWN LEATHER COUCH WITH HIS HEAD back and his hands over his eyes. This couldn't be happening. It wasn't enough to try and cope with the death of a close friend—there also needed to be a Q & A from some cop about it? No way this was for real.

After all, Steven Lords was the biggest name in sports. How in the hell could someone even think "The Lord" could have or would have anything to do with someone getting killed?

"We've talked about this, Steven," Allen was saying. "You knew it was a very good possibility you'd be questioned in Michelle's murder."

Steven lifted his head and looked at Allen. "Yeah, I guess. But why here and why now?" he asked.

"Would you rather it be at the police station with news cameras all over the place? I wouldn't," Allen replied. "This was my call. In here you're comfortable and relaxed. There are no reporters and no cameras around. It's just like being at home."

"I understand that, but do they honestly think I had something to do with what happen to Chelle?"

"Right now you're a person of interest. You haven't been formally charged with anything and the odds of it going any further than that—"

"What the hell is a 'person of interest,' then? Am I a suspect or something? Because if I am, we can just go downstairs to that press conference and squash all that shit right now."

"Listen, you're not a suspect and you aren't going to make any statements to the media right now. What you are going to do is answers this guy's questions—"

"That's exactly what I plan on doing, man. I'm not gonna have him think I'm capable of killing somebody. I'm gonna tell him the truth—that he can forget any thoughts he had about Steven Lords murdering somebody."

"That's what I want you to do. But when he asks you a question, I want you to answer that question. Don't tell him anything other than what he asks. If he asks what color your car is, you tell him black. You don't tell him it's a black BMW X5. Only answer what he asks, all right?"

Steven nodded. Anything to get this whole ordeal over with.

"I think he's coming," Allen said. "I'll be right here with you, so don't worry. Just stay calm and relaxed."

CHAPTER 17

Russell heard the chirping of phones echoing through the offices as Dave guided him down a hallway of frosted glass walls. Watching all the commotion reminded him of the cops at the station. Everyone around here was scrambling like the chief had put them on a deadline.

They went through a doorway into the much quieter executive area and then into a nicely appointed office Dave said belonged to the team's vice president. "Detective Howard," Dave said after they entered the room. "Meet Steven Lords and Allen Warner."

Russell's heartbeat quickened as he took in the sight of Steven Lords in the flesh. The camera was supposed to add ten pounds, not ten inches. Lords seemed to be about twice as tall as a lot of the guys on the force, and he was sitting. Russell trained his eyes on Steven as he walked closer to him. With his model good looks, Easter Sunday haircut, and impeccably trimmed goatee, it was easy to see why the guy was so sought after for product endorsements. He seemed relaxed in his baggy blue sweatpants and a T-shirt with his crucifix logo on it: a cross with a net hanging from it, only the "hoop" looked like a halo. That Lords could use something as sacred as the cross as a marketing gimmick emphasized to Russell he was way more self-centered than people realized.

But how could he not be? Even if he were totally innocent, and that was a big "if," the events of the past couple of days had to be wearing on him. His effort to look so relaxed, casually chewing gum the way he was, somehow struck Russell as contrived—maybe even cocky. The scene had a staged look to it, but there was no way to know whether the interview delay was actually due to Lords being at practice or simply a stall tactic.

Russell looked Steven in the eye as he sat and pulled a notebook from his inside pocket. All he had to do was stick with the plan and let Lords hang himself with his own rope.

"So, Allen is it? What business do you have here?" Russell asked as he took the cap off his pen. "Do you work for the team?"

"I'm Steven's agent, actually."

Russell should have figured. The guy looked like a lawyer. He wasn't slouching like Lords. His posture was more rigid and purposeful. His blond hair was trimmed in a trendy but professional style. Even his eyebrows looked waxed. Custom-tailored suit, six month's worth of a detective's salary on his wrist; if Lords was trying to look relaxed, this guy personified cool. Russell sat back in his chair as Allen crossed his legs and smirked at him.

Russell raised an eyebrow. "Well, this is a private matter, so it might be best if I talked to Mr. Lords alone."

"Sorry, but that's not going to happen," Allen said. "I can stay, or if you'd prefer, we can get Steven's lawyer in here. Your choice."

Smug bastard.

Russell nodded and turned to Steven. "Mr. Lords, just so you know, you're not being charged with anything. I'm here to clear up some things about your whereabouts on the night of Michelle Tibbs's murder and to try to get to the bottom of what might have happened to her. I'm assuming I can count on your cooperation?"

Steven nodded stonily, but said nothing for a moment. "Of course," he then said hoarsely. "I've got nothing to hide. I don't know who could have done this but if there's anything I can do—"

A glare from Allen stopped Steven cold.

"Mr. Warner, this is a police investigation, not a contract negotiation. So I'd really appreciate it if you'd give us some privacy."

"Sorry, Detective. Just go on as you would. You won't even know I'm here."

"All right then," Russell turned to Steven, whose brow was slightly furrowed. "Is it okay if I call you Steven?"

"Sure. Whatever."

"Great. So tell me, Steven—did you see Michelle Tibbs on the night of her death?"

Steven looked down at his lap. "Yeah, I saw her that night."

"About what time?"

"About two."

Russell nodded as he scratched on his notepad. "And what happened when you went to see her?"

Steven looked over at Allen and took a long breath. "We just talked, all right? She called me after the game and asked if I could come over and talk."

"I see. What did you two have to talk about?"

"Not too much. She just wanted to congratulate me on getting to the Finals."

Russell laid his pen on the polished teak table and raised an eyebrow. Steven's fingers were rapidly tapping his knee. "I'm going to give you another chance to answer that question. As a matter of fact, let me help you out. When I looked through Miss Tibbs's belongings I found a bottle of folic acid pills."

"So?" Steven said, after a moment of uncomfortable silence Russell wasn't about to break.

"So . . . I don't know if you know this, but folic acid pills are used to prevent birth defects in newborn babies. So are you sure she just congratulated you on your win?"

Russell picked up his pen as Allen whispered in Steven's ear.

Steven took another deep breath and then looked at Russell, almost relieved. "She called to talk to me about the baby she was carrying."

"Your baby, right?"

Steven nodded. "Yeah, the baby was mine," he said as he dropped his head. "That's what she said, anyway."

"And that night you two met in her room at the Murcielago? To talk about the child?"

Steven looked up and glanced over at Allen. "We talked about what to do about the baby," he said. "You have to understand, it wasn't an easy decision to make. We both agreed it would be in our best interests if she had an . . . if she terminated the pregnancy."

"She decided or you decided?"

"We both decided."

"So did the money you offered her entice her to go along with it, or did she just agree to it for the greater good?"

"There was no money offered to Michelle for an abortion," Allen said. "Whatever you may have heard is purely rumor."

Russell looked at Allen skeptically. Steven was too easy to read. His wandering eyes and twitchy fingers gave him away. There was something going on. Russell had heard the voicemails and talked to Michelle's sister, and Steven's answer wasn't consistent with what he already knew. Maybe it was time to raise the stakes.

"How's your marriage?" Russell asked after a moment.

Steven resumed his gum chewing. "My marriage is fine."

"Karen? Your wife's name is Karen and she runs your charitable foundation and everything, yes?"

"Yeah, that's right."

"Did she know about you and Michelle? Did she know Miss Tibbs was your main squeeze back in the day and you were still seeing her behind her back?"

Steven sat motionless. He hung his head as Allen placed a hand on his shoulder.

"She did know, right?" Russell continued. "And I'm guessing Michelle wasn't the only other woman, was she? Is that why Karen left you?"

The gum chewing stopped. Steven's jaw started quivering.

Russell continued. "When one of your girlfriends gets pregnant, I can't imagine that going over well at home. I can't imagine that going over well to the public, for that matter. People have to believe in the idea and the family-man, holier-than-thou image you and your agent put out there. That's why companies like Nike pay you all those millions of dollars. So let me ask you: What happens to those lucrative endorsements if word gets out that—"

"Now hold on just one minute, Detective!" Allen said. "I see where you're going and nothing could be further from the truth. What happened to Michelle was a tragedy, but Steven had nothing to do with it."

Russell grinned. "Did I say he did?"

Without waiting for an answer, he turned back to Lords. "Steven, let me tell you what I do know. I know Michelle was pregnant with your baby and I know you didn't want her to have it. I also know you paid her to have an abortion and she refused. She wanted the baby. I also know your having a child out of wedlock could easily cost you millions in endorsements, not to mention who knows how much in alimony and child support."

"You have quite an imagination," Allen said. "But if I were you I'd stick to facts and not wild accusations."

Russell leaned closer to Steven. "So why don't you give me the facts then? Because so far I'm not fully understanding what happened that night."

Steven took a deep breath. "Michelle called and wanted me to come over to her hotel—"

"And what time was this?"

"About two. I told you before—I went to see her around two."

"Just making sure," Russell said. "Please continue."

"Anyway, I went to her room and we talked about plans for the baby."

"The baby you went over there thinking you'd both agreed to terminate, correct?"

"Hold on, man! That isn't true. I actually went to talk to her about maybe keeping the baby!"

Russell leaned forward and smirked. "Oh, so now you wanted to keep the baby? A few minutes ago you wanted her to get an abortion and now you offered to let her keep it? I'm confused. Which was it?"

"At first I thought an abortion was the right thing to do but then I changed my mind. I mean, there was no reason why she couldn't have the baby and be taken care of. We just had to do it the right way."

Russell tapped his pen against his notepad. "Did she go along with your change of heart?"

Steven looked at Allen, who didn't look too pleased with his client's candor. "Not at that time. All she said was she'd think about it."

Russell sat back in his chair. Steven's jaw had stopped quivering and his hands were perfectly still in his lap.

If Steven had been anticipating an answer from Tibbs, then the message he left on her phone made sense.

But when Russell heard more whispering he looked up, noticed a slight grin on Allen's face, and cocked an eyebrow. There was no doubt about it: Steven had been coached. It was time to get him out of his newfound comfort zone and back on the hook.

"I did some digging and found out Michelle was pregnant by you before and that pregnancy ended in a miscarriage. Is that right?"

Steven nodded.

"I'm guessing at some point after that you met and married Karen. But maybe out of some kind of sympathy or guilt about the child you lost, you continued a relationship with Michelle?"

Steven scowled. "Look, man, you don't know anything about what happened between me, Michelle, and that baby, so don't talk about stuff you don't know nothing about."

"Well educate me, then," Russell said. "You still continued a relationship with Miss Tibbs after you were married, right?"

"That's right."

"That's a pretty expensive suite Tibbs stayed in. You probably got her the Amex Black Card she used to reserve that room, didn't you?"

"Yes. Yes I did."

"See, here's where I'm having a problem. Tibbs was working temp jobs and staying in a five-star suite. She had the latest designer bags, upscale makeup, and all sorts of expensive accessories that you were obviously bankrolling." Russell closed his notebook and leaned toward Steven. "What does Karen think about all of that? You say your marriage is fine, but that's not what I've been hearing. And if this is the kind of crap she's having to put up with I don't blame her for—"

He stopped when he heard Allen chuckle. "Again, this is just idle gossip that's—"

"Just sit there and be quiet!" Russell pointed a finger at Allen then turned to Steven. "I think you offered Tibbs money for that abortion. You have too much at stake to allow her to have that baby. But my guess is Tibbs didn't want the money. Why would she? A child puts her in your pockets for at least twenty years, and that's worth a whole lot more than whatever you were offering. Plus, she probably saw the handwriting on the wall and knew her time with you was about up."

Steven's hands had started twitching again. All Russell had to do was give him a little push.

He was about to go in for the kill when he thought about his superiors' admonition and the bigger picture. Lords wasn't going anywhere and he was clearly rattled. So Russell just smiled and stood up, closed his notebook, and tucked it back into his jacket pocket. "This interview was just a formality. Next time we meet, I suggest you get your boy a good lawyer."

Russell started toward the door. Before he left he stopped and looked back at Steven and Allen. "Thank you for your cooperation," he said. "We'll be in touch."

CHAPTER 18

As soon as the door closed Steven slumped back in the couch let out a long sigh. "I don't know who that detective thinks he is, Al, but he had one thing right. I'm getting a lawyer and I'm gonna fight this shit," Steven said. "But first we need to make a statement or something because I can't have people thinking the same thing that cop was thinking. I didn't do a damn thing!"

"I know, Steven, I know. I'm sorry you had to go through that, but we aren't about to hire a lawyer because of some rookie cop's fishing expedition," Allen said, fumbling for his cell phone. "Just let me take care of it."

"Fishing? He's doing a lot more than fishing. He knew we were paying her to have an abortion. He knew about Michelle losing our first baby and Karen leaving. How the hell did he know all that?"

"He's a detective, Steven—it's his job to know. He

probably has Michelle's cell phone. I bet she never bothered to password-protect her phone, much less put a password on her voicemail. She was always so damn careless."

"This is all so fucked up. You told me to be honest. You said answer the questions. Why the hell is he trying to pin Michelle's murder on me?"

"He was trying to railroad you, Steven. You're probably the only suspect he has, so he's grasping at straws, trying to make his case. But you can't go to pieces."

Steven took a long breath and rested his head in his palms. He looked out over his hands. "Okay then. How about we put our own press conference together. Let me tell my side of the story and let people know I didn't kill anybody."

"It's not that simple."

"The hell it ain't! Come on, Al—you work for me. I'm telling you to put a press conference together. Let's go at these suspicions head on and crush all these rumors before people start treating them like facts."

"The problem is Michelle's the tip of the iceberg, Steven. Denying guilt in her murder is all fine and good, but that's what everybody expects. Your saying you didn't do it isn't going to surprise anyone or convince anyone. But what it will do is give a bunch of nosy reporters the opportunity to dig deeper and start dishing dirt. They'll start asking about Michelle, then the baby she was carrying—and if there was anyone else."

"But—"

"Just hear me out, would you? Problem is, there *were* lots of other women you've slept with since you've been married to Karen. None of whom are above going to TMZ and telling their story if this shit starts trending. We open this can of worms and there's no telling who's going to come out of the woodwork, trying to get a payday."

Steven thought for a moment. "Maybe, but that could happen anyway. And if it does, we handle it. But I'm not about to let people roast me or try me in the news over a murder I didn't commit. I've worked too hard for everything I have to let it get taken away like this."

"You've worked too hard? *We've* worked too hard," Allen said. "You listen to me. Nobody is going to take anything away from you, Steven, not a single goddamn thing. When wolves are at the door, what do you do?"

"Get a gun and start shooting!"

"No. Let me put this another way. When a hurricane is coming, you hunker down and ride it out. When the storm blows over, then you get up and enjoy the brand new day."

"What fortune cookie did you get that out of?" Steve said, rolling his eyes. "What the hell? I don't need a weather report. I need to clear my name, man."

"You're missing the point. Lay low. Let me handle this. Like you said, I work for you, so let me work."

"What are you going to do?"

"What you pay me to do. Protect your best interests,"

Allen replied. "Now listen, I don't want you to make any statements to the media. I don't want you to say anything. I don't want you to go anywhere."

"Where could I go? Everyone knows my face."

"You can thank me for that later. I know it doesn't look like it now, but this is good for us."

"I don't understand."

"A scandal days before the Finals? Do you know what this is going to do to the ratings? Hell, this has just increased your marketability."

"You can't be serious."

"I'm trying to put a good spin on it. I don't need you nervous and tense right now. I need you to focus on your game. Trust me, when this is all over, you're gonna be hotter than ever."

CHAPTER 19

Although Allen meant every word he'd said about the potential upside of this scandal hitting right before the playoffs, he couldn't shake the unnerving sense that the whole thing could end badly. There were too many variables to know what the outcome would be, so the best thing Allen could do for damage control was to pull whatever strings he could and try to keep Steven from getting too uptight.

The temptation to turn Eddie over to the police and let him take a well-deserved fall was difficult to deny, but nothing was more likely to send Steven sailing over the cliff than thinking his best friend killed his girlfriend. There was no telling what that would lead to, and as much as he wanted Eddie out of Steven's life forever, Allen couldn't take the risk.

He had stepped outside Jeff's office and shut the door

behind him, to collect his thoughts and figure out his next move. He was standing in the hallway contemplating an idea when he felt a tap on the shoulder accompanied by a whiff of Cool Water cologne.

Speak of the devil himself.

"So what's the deal, Al?" Eddie asked. "I got your text and came right over. Is everything okay?"

"No, everything is not okay," Allen said, half-whispering through gritted teeth. "You've really screwed the pooch on this one, you know that? A detective was just here grilling Steven about Michelle. They're calling him a 'person of interest,' but he made it pretty damn clear he's their lead suspect."

"But Steven didn't do anything!" Eddie blurted." I'm sorry, Al. I really am. But you know I wouldn't have gone up there if I didn't think I could help."

When Allen didn't say anything, Eddie nodded toward the office door. "Is he still there?"

"You need to get him out of here right away," Allen said. "But don't just drop him off. I need you to stay with him and try to keep him distracted. Word of what's happening is going to spread like wildfire so keep him away from his smartphone and his TV, all right?"

"No problem," Eddie said. Then, after an awkward pause, "Allen, man, listen . . . before you dip up out of here, do you think you can help me out with something?"

"Help you out how?"

"Well . . . if the cops are on to Stevie, then it may only be a matter of time before they're onto me. You know I was only trying to help my dawg out, so is there anything you can do for me?"

Allen put a hand on Eddie's shoulder and looked him in the eye. "You fucked up big time, Eddie. But I think everything will work out fine. Plus, I know how much you mean to Steven. He probably wouldn't be here if it wasn't for you, so no . . . don't worry about a thing. I'll do everything in my power to keep you out of trouble. But you need to clean up your act and try and get some of this nonsense in your life under control, you hear me? It's not good for you and it's not good for Steven."

Eddie smiled. "Thank you, bro. I know we've had our beefs and all that, but I'm glad you're on our side, you feel me?"

Allen nodded. "That warms my heart. Now get in there and do what you need to do, all right?"

EDDIE'S STOMACH CHURNED WHEN HE SAW HIS FRIEND slouched forward on the couch, head in his hands, looking as depressed as he'd ever seen him. He didn't even look up at the sound of the door closing.

Maybe Steven had been right all along. For all her attitude and self-centeredness, Michelle did care about him, and maybe she would have come around if she'd had more time. But there were all sorts of reasons Eddie hadn't trusted her, and he knew in his heart she'd been bad news for Steven. He wanted to feel good about what he'd done— stepping up for his boy, dealing with a major problem— but standing there, looking at his friend, all he felt was shame and regret. He'd made a huge mistake and had no idea how to make it right.

"Hey, are you okay?" Eddie asked after a moment.

Steve turned and looked up with surprise. "Eddie . . . hey . . . I guess I'm all right."

"I just ran into Al in the hallway and he told me about that cop that came through here," Eddie said. "That's crazy, man. Anybody who knows you would know you wouldn't do anything like that. But I wouldn't worry about it. Ain't no way that shit's gonna stick."

"Yeah, but still—"

"Yeah, nothing! Don't let this shit mess with your head, man," Eddie said. "Just try and relax, and this will all be over before you know it."

Eddie reached out to help Steven off the couch. Before they got to the door of the office, Steven stopped short and let a heavy gaze fall on Eddie.

"I've been meaning to talk to you about something . . . remember that night we were going to the hotel to see Michelle and you asked me if I wanted you to take care of things?"

Eddie froze, throat tight. He turned toward Steven but couldn't quite meet his eyes. "Yeah?"

"Well . . . you didn't go up there and do anything stupid, did you?"

Eddie's stomach churned harder as he shook his head and said, "No, bro. I ain't have nothin' to do with that. I told you I had to go to the bathroom that night. Man, I drank so damn much I threw up all over the place."

"Yeah, well I want to find out who did this, Eddie. I need to do something and I'm thinking maybe you can help."

"You name it. What's on your mind?"

"You know some people in the streets," Steven said. "Maybe we could offer a reward or something. Fifty thousand for any information, man. Get at your man Jimmy, too. Get him to ask around the hotel and see if anyone he works with knows anything. Make sure you let him know about the reward."

"I got you, bro. I'll put it out there. Don't worry about a thing."

STEVEN WATCHED AS EDDIE PUT ON SHADES OVER HIS bloodshot eyes and headed into the hallway. His friend seemed anxious, so much so his hands shook a little bit. He was definitely on edge about something, and more and more these days Steven had the feeling the booze and coke was taking its toll on Eddie's nerves. And the past few days had been especially bad.

They didn't talk about Eddie's habits much and whenever Steven brought it up, Eddie's line was always the same: "If there's ever a problem, I'll tell you."

Steven was about to say something when his phone buzzed. It was his mother calling, and no doubt she was upset. By then she had to know about Michelle, and she was probably looking for an explanation. Steven gathered his thoughts before answering. He had to make her believe everything was okay, somehow, and the whole situation was overblown.

"Hey, Mama," he said, catching the call just before it went to voicemail.

"Stevie, tell me what's going on. I turned on the television to watch Judge Mathis you know, and I see news reports saying you're a suspect in some kind of murder."

"Mama, don't believe anything you hear. None of it's true—I promise."

"None of it? What about that girl, Michelle? What on earth happened?"

"I wish I knew. All I can tell you is something bad went down, and not too long after I saw her after the game. But I don't know who did it or why. All I can tell you for sure is it wasn't me."

"Of course it wasn't. I didn't think that for a minute. But you can't believe what's happening. I've got newspeople all outside my door and all in Willie's yard and down the street blocking Gwen's driveway. I don't like this, Stevie. I don't like it at all. Do I need to come out there?"

"No, Mama. I'm okay. Just stay in the house and don't say anything to the newspeople. And promise me you won't believe a word of what you hear on TV, okay?"

"I'm about to throw some bleach at them out there if they knock on my door again!"

"Well, it's all just a misunderstanding. I'll explain later," Steven said. "I got to go now, Mama. I'll call you later. I love you."

Steven hung his head as he put the phone back in his pocket. He hated to rush his mom off like that, but once she got started with her questioning there was no stopping her. And he couldn't deal with that at the moment. They could talk more tomorrow, but for the time being all he wanted was to keep her from worrying.

"How's your moms doing?" Eddie asked.

"There are a bunch reporters at her house. They're all down the street, in the neighbors' yards and everything."

"I hope they ain't in Mr. Willie's yard. He don't play about that grass," Eddie said, smiling thinly. "I still don't know why she didn't just let you buy her a new house somewhere closer. The news was bound to find her."

"Well, we need to get her out of there. I don't like people messing with my moms, man."

"Me neither. But first things first—I need to get you out

of here," Eddie said. "I promised Allen I'd get you home right away."

"I can drive myself, man," Steven said. "I don't need no chauffeur."

"You sure? You're okay to drive?"

"I ain't crippled, am I?"

"Okay, good. Tell you what, though. It's going to be crazy over by your house if the media's gotten wind of this. Why don't you crash at my place?"

Steven paused to consider Eddie's idea. He didn't want to go home. That interview was still heavy on his mind and he could use the company.

"You know what? That sounds like a good plan. Maybe it will help me clear my head."

"Cool! It'll be just like old times. Hey, remember when we used to lay sleeping bags on your mom's living room floor when we were kids? Y'all ain't have no couches, so we laid out on the floor."

"Yeah, but this time we don't have to sneak and watch the dirty movies on late-night TV. C'mon, man—let's get outta here."

CHAPTER 20

Miami-Dade Police Station, 2:20 p.m.

The more Russell thought about it, the more plausible it seemed Steven Lords was his man. He had a long way to go make his case stick, but the pieces were starting to come together.

"So you still think he really could have done this?" Morales said after Russell had finished his rundown of the interview.

"All I know for sure is that Lords was lying through his teeth," Russell said. "But yeah, I think he may have done it. And that's why I sort of went after him when he started lying to me."

Morales stiffened in his chair and leaned forward, lips tight. "What do you mean you 'went after him'?"

"I tried to break him, you know? Told him I knew he was lying and he'd better get a lawyer."

Morales leaned in closer, his brown eyes blazing. "Are you telling me you interrogated him in a way that might have been seen as aggressive or hostile, with his agent present?"

"You're damn right I did. I've only got forty-eight hours, Art. Not a lot of time for bullshit. He got nervous and I thought I could sweat him."

Art looked away and let out a sharp, angry breath. "You may have really screwed up on this one, my friend."

"How? How did I screw up? The guy was on the edge and I tried to nudge him over the edge. What's wrong with that? I've seen you do it hundreds of times."

"Not when I don't have any real leverage."

"But I *did* have something. I knew he was hiding something when he told me that lie about Michelle calling to congratulate him and some bullshit story about them together deciding on an abortion. It was all lies, Art."

"Doesn't matter. Certain people carry a certain cache in this town and as much as you or I don't like it, you have to handle them with kid gloves," Morales said. "Plus, nothing I've heard here justifies what sounds to me like a very bad decision to get into it with someone who isn't even officially a suspect."

Russell thought about that for a moment. Had Steven Lords been someone else—anyone else—there was no way Russell would catch flak for applying a little heat. But whatever. If he had to play the game, so be it.

"That's bullshit, Art. I saw an opportunity and I went for it. Not hard, but enough to let him know I knew he was bullshitting. If that was the wrong move, I'll try to be more considerate next time."

"That's the right idea," Morales said. "But you gotta have leverage. Hell, I'm not sure that's going to change anything. The captain wanted to see you as soon as you got back. After hearing this I'm guessing it probably has something to do with the way you conducted that interview."

"The captain?" Russell's eyes widened. "Where's Lieutenant Herrera?"

"Frank put in for a one-week vacation this morning. He saw this shitstorm coming after he read your report. Figured it was a great time to take the kids to Disney World."

Russell stared at Morales, who stared back at him, smirking. "That's why I tell you to take time to build your case. You'd better hurry up, Junior. Cap's waiting for you in his office."

Russell scoffed as he straightened his tie. It was good to know Morales could find some humor in all this. The one thing that he loved more than listening to himself school young detectives on the right way to conduct an investigation was watching the consequences when they didn't adhere to his rules. Usually it was a come-to-Jesus meeting with Lieutenant Herrera. But today would be like swimming with the sharks, with Captain Stewart playing Jaws. As he left the detective pool, Russell looked back at Morales, who still sat at his desk smirking. *You win, Art. Make sure there's leverage before sweating a suspect. Lesson learned—jerk.*

Three years on patrol, eight months as a detective, and never so much as a peep out of Captain Stewart. It came as a shock that the captain spoke so highly of him to the chief. It wasn't like Russell had worked many cases during his brief career, so it was a surprise the captain even knew his name. Still, a ringing endorsement from a superior did a lot for one's confidence, and maybe some of that had gone to his head.

With his head hanging low, Russell walked down the hall to the captain's office.

"You wanted to see me, sir?"

"I just got a call from the mayor's office and it wasn't pleasant," Captain Stewart said before Russell even had a chance to sit. "I don't know what you said in that interview with Steven Lords, but you sure pissed some people off."

"Sir, if I can explain—"

"I don't want to hear your explanation, Detective. I left you on the case because Frank assured me you could handle it. But now it's become obvious he was wrong."

"But, sir, I—"

Stewart waved a hand at Russell. "That's enough, Detective. From what I understand you were blatantly unprofessional, and I can't have a detective taking cases personally. You blew it. You're off the case."

"With all due respect, Captain, if I can just explain—"

"Save it, Detective. Just go home. You're done."

CHAPTER 21

Miami-Dade Police Headquarters, 8:00 a.m.
Two days until the Finals

The next morning Captain Stewart sat at his desk, taking sips from his lukewarm coffee. It was no secret Miami loved a winner. The town would bend over backward for you if you brought some star power to the table, and unfortunately that also applied to City Hall. Detective Russell hadn't been around long enough to know the protocol for interviewing someone like Steven Lords. Art said he told him to take it easy, but when you were trying to break a case this big, it was easy to get swept up.

Stewart felt badly about pulling him off the investigation. Rookie detectives were prone to let their emotions run high and make mistakes. But the heat had come down from City Hall and he had no choice. Word had come down that the mayor had the gall to send someone in—a "consultant"—to babysit the police as they worked on the case. The gloves had come off and Captain Stewart was pissed.

The loud buzz of the intercom echoed through the office. "Sydney Farrell is here to see you."

"Thanks, Judy. Tell him I'll be right out."

Stewart took a deep breath as he got up from his desk. Time to play host to whatever pencil-pushing desk jockey the mayor's office sent over. All he could hope for was that the guy would have some kind of clue as to how an investigation was supposed to be handled.

He stepped out of his office and stopped short when he saw a woman in her early thirties with a coffee-colored complexion, dressed in designer jeans, couture T-shirt, and wool blazer. Her long hair was pulled back into a tight ponytail, revealing elegant diamond-stud earrings.

As he approached he tucked in his shirt a bit tighter and straightened his tie.

"Sydney Farrell?" he asked, hand extended. "I'm Captain Philip Stewart. "Pleased to meet you."

"Likewise, Captain," Sydney said as they shook hands. "I'm looking forward to working with your department on the Tibbs case."

"We're happy to have you aboard. If you'll follow me, I can fill you in on what's been happening."

He offered her coffee, which she declined, and then led her into his office. "So is it Miss or Mrs. Farrell . . .?"

"Why don't you call me Syd?"

He sat across from her and handed her a manila folder. "Okay, great. Here are the reports from Detective Howard's investigation. That seems like the best way to start."

He watched as she flipped through the pages. "I'm curious, Syd—have you ever worked a homicide case before?"

Sydney looked up from the folder. "I was actually a special agent with the FBI for six years in their violent crimes division. So yeah, I've worked a few homicides."

"I'm glad to hear that. I've been asked to extend you every courtesy afforded to a visiting detective. The department is at your disposal. If there's anything you need, feel free to ask."

AFTER BEING SENT HOME THE PREVIOUS DAY, THE LAST thing Russell expected was a call from the chief requesting a meeting first thing the next morning. The chief's tone was stern and direct, so it was difficult to discern what kind of mood he was in or what he wanted. But when the chief asked to see you, you showed up. Russell dressed quickly in his best gray suit, fearing the worst but hoping for the best.

"Good morning, sir. I hope you haven't been waiting long."

"I don't have a lot of time so let's make this fast,"

Cavanaugh said after Russell sat. "I heard your interview with Lords didn't go very well."

"No, sir. It didn't go well at all. Captain Stewart pulled me off the case, but I'm not sure whose decision that was."

Chief Cavanaugh leaned forward and folded his arms on the table. "I remember when I was a young detective just starting out," he said. "I was investigating this murder and one of the suspects had political ties in Tallahassee. To make a long story short I got reassigned to another case because somebody made a phone call to my captain."

"Sir, I'm sorry about what happened yesterday. But sir, I think there's more to what Lords told me and it's worth staying with my theory of the crime. I may have lost my head and I didn't use very good judgment. I want to get back on this case and—"

"I know you do. Problem is Lords's agent is golfing buddies with the mayor, which is why you got tossed off in the first place. I've always hated when politics get involved with police work. There's no place for it."

"So what can I do, sir?"

Chief Cavanaugh sat back in his chair and sipped his coffee. "You know, I liked your work on the Maldonado case a lot. A whole lot of people were convinced Alex Maldonado committed suicide. But you believed otherwise. I know what you did went unnoticed by a lot of people, but sometimes it's the smallest detail that makes or breaks a case."

"It really wasn't much of anything, sir. I simply looked at

the evidence," Russell said. "Alex suffered a gunshot wound to his right temple. All I did was study the crime scene photos and noticed the mouse on his computer was on the left-hand side. Made it highly unlikely he would've shot himself on the right side when he was left-handed. Any detective would've eventually picked up on that."

"But any detective didn't do it, son. If it weren't for you, who knows if Councilman Maldonado would've ever confessed or the truth about his drug smuggling operation would've ever surfaced."

"Damn shame. Innocent college kid with nothing to do with it had to lose his life," Russell said. "But I didn't do anything special. I just had a hunch Cesar's story about his son's suicide didn't seem right."

"Sometimes that's what police work is. Hunches and details. You could have a bright future, young man, and that's why I don't want to let the nonsense from city hall get in the way. I'm not saying I agree Lords did this—but if he did, I damn sure want to see him held accountable."

"Sir?" Russell asked, now completely confused as to where the conversation was going.

The chief pushed his chair away from the table and stood. "The mayor used his power to help his friends. So I'm going to use mine to put you back on the case. This is police business, not an opportunity to help campaign contributors or whatever the hell he thinks he's doing."

Russell nodded in agreement. "That's great—"

Cavanaugh held up a hand. "That's the good news. The bad news is, the only way I could get away with putting you back in the saddle here is by agreeing to let City Hall arrange for a consultant who'll be in on the case. From what I understand she's a former FBI agent and comes highly recommended. Although I'm not too sure by whom."

Russell leaned forward and paused before speaking. "With all due respect, sir, that doesn't make any sense. This is a *police* investigation. How can any outsider even be considered on a case like this?"

"That's Miami politics for you," Cavanaugh gathered his car keys and cup of coffee and started toward the door. "All I can say is good luck, Detective. The clock is still ticking on your investigation, so I suggest you don't dally."

TEN MINUTES LATER, RUSSELL WAS IN HIS CAPTAIN'S office doing his best to feign nonchalance after the introduction to Sydney Farrell. It was a total joke to even have her involved in this case. But if she was even half as good a detective as she was good-looking, maybe this situation wouldn't be so bad after all.

"My friends call me Syd," she said after shaking Russell's hand and offering a warm smile that seemed genuine. "I know the situation here is a bit unusual, and I'm just here to help in any way I can."

"It is unusual," Stewart said. "And that's why we now

officially have a gag order on this thing. I don't want either of you saying a word to the media about this, you got it?"

Russell and Sydney both nodded. Russell was relieved Stewart hadn't said anything about his being taken off the case and was happy to leave it that way.

"Good. Then I'll let Detective Howard here show you around," Stewart said. "He'll get you up to speed on what he's learned so far. If you need anything else, let me know."

IRATE AS HE WAS ABOUT HAVING A BABYSITTER ON THE case, Russell couldn't deny Sydney made a great first impression. He hadn't known her more than five minutes, but he already felt confident she was smart and competent and not there to bust anyone's balls. The mayor may have sent her for all the wrong reasons, but that wasn't her fault. Best thing he could do was give her the benefit of the doubt—and enjoy the scenery—while they worked together.

"I understand we don't have a lot of time to consider the possibility that Lords may have done this," Sydney said while Russell, walking a step behind her, followed the rhythmic swaying of her hips.

"That's right," Russell said, pleased that she seemed open to the possibility of Lords's culpability. "Chief gave me forty-eight hours and they started yesterday."

"That could be a problem, based on what I've seen. I've

been looking at the information you've gathered so far and I have to say your case looks pretty weak so far."

So much for not busting balls. "Weak?" Russell said. "Is that years of FBI training talking or some directive from the mayor's office?"

Sydney smiled knowingly and waved her arm dismissively. "I'm trying to come at this as objectively as possible. I'm not saying you're wrong about Lords lying in your little grilling session yesterday, but if you're going to make this case against him stick, you're gonna need something more than a handful of circumstantial evidence."

"Have you read the reports?" Russell said, struggling to keep the irritation from his voice. "We've got connection, we've got motive, we've got opportunity. It's as simple as connecting the dots."

"No, detective. It's not that simple. You have a plausible theory of the crime and good reason to look carefully at Lords. But I don't see a shred of proof here that he killed this girl, and without it I'm not even sure *I'm* confident he's our man. And I'm on your side here."

"Are you?"

She thought for a moment and answered calmly without a hint of aggravation. "Let's come at this another way then. What makes you so sure Lords did it? I mean besides what you've already told me."

"Well for one thing, I talked to the night staff," Russell said as he walked over to his desk. "They all remembered seeing Lords at the hotel, and they all noticed he looked upset about something. A bellhop at the hotel also confirmed he left around 2:45—"

"So did a lot of people. That's still circumstantial," Sydney said. "And as far I can tell, none of these witnesses saw Lords anywhere near the victim or could even confirm that's who he was there to see."

Russell shook his head. "Do you think it's circumstantial that a woman he's been messing with was found murdered hours after he left her room? A woman, by the way, who was also pregnant with his child? Is that what you call circumstantial? Is that what they taught you in the FBI?"

"They taught me to look at the big picture and all the evidence before I rush to judgment. So let's do just that, okay? So far you have him at the scene—he admitted as much to you but no one saw him there. You've also established a relationship between Lords and the victim—"

"That's right. She was his pregnant girlfriend and he has a marriage in trouble because of it. That goes to motive."

"Okay, so what about the murder weapon?"

"What weapon? If you read the reports, it looks like she may have been strangled. There was bruising on her neck and severe damage to her throat. Strangulation usually indicates a crime of passion. Given their past history and current circumstances, that seems pretty fitting, don't you think?"

"Maybe, but we're still talking about a guy with no criminal history, who's at the apex of his sports career, strangling a pregnant woman to death, and with her his unborn child." She paused and shook her heard pensively.

Russell wasn't so quick to believe the "no criminal history." Lords simply hadn't ever been caught.

"I'm still not sold," she said. "I think we should talk to Peter Owens again. Something about his statement doesn't sit right, and I have some questions of my own I'd like to ask him."

"But I've already talked to him," Russell said. "Deputy Chief Garcia got on my ass about the security tech on duty that night. I need to go talk to him. He was supposed to be on duty last night, but he never showed. He may hold the key to this whole thing."

"That sounds good. But let's talk to Owens first. There are a few things that need to get straightened out."

"Like what?"

"Like don't you find it a little strange he showed up in the hotel parking lot on the same night he supposedly had words with Lords during the postgame interviews?"

"So I've heard." Russell said. "What of it?"

"I saw the postgame press conference and it wasn't pretty. I checked out some sports blogs this morning and word is Owens and Lords had a heated exchange in the hall after the press conference. So Owens supposedly got some anonymous call telling him Lords was at the Murcielago Hotel? I'm not buying that and from what I've heard, you're too good a detective to buy that either."

Russell hated to admit it, but she might have a point. Owen's source may have been suspicious, but there was no way his story was suspect. The video that Owens showed of Lords leaving the hotel didn't lie—not to mention that Lords himself admitted going to see Michelle. Plus, whatever happened between Owens and Lords was immaterial to what happened at the hotel. It was a waste of time talking to Owens, but it wouldn't take long and he didn't want to seem uncooperative.

"Okay. We'll do it your way. We'll go and talk to Owens. Then we'll go and find out what happened to that missing video," Russell said. "But I'll bet you anything Owens will be a dead end."

CHAPTER 22

"A representative of Steven Lords made this statement on his behalf: I am grief-stricken over the loss of a very dear friend. While there are allegations that I had something to do with Michelle Tibbs's death, nothing could be further from the truth. I am confident the police will uncover evidence that will clear my name of this heinous crime and bring the true perpetrators to justice. In the meantime, my thoughts and prayers go out to her family during this difficult time . . ."

Steven sighed as he sat in Eddie's living room, flipping through channels and seeing himself as the main discussion topic. He'd gotten calls and text from several neighbors telling him about the vans that had been canvassing the neighborhood and news helicopters circling overhead. So much for Star Island's reputation for seclusion and privacy.

The idea of staying at Eddie's had made sense at the time, but Steven's jaw dropped when he saw the condition the place was in. The smell of stale beer, rotting food in takeout cartons, and a sink full of unwashed dishes—it was enough to make him gag. The floors and walls were filthy and the dust on the glass coffee table was so thick Coach Hollis could have drawn up plays in it.

Eddie's once-pristine white leather couch was sagging and marred by several burns and stains that hadn't been there a few months ago. A three-foot Grapphix bong stood on the end table, opaque with resin, emitting an acrid odor that Steven suspected wasn't weed.

That the place smelled like a frat house had Steven worried, but even worse was that Eddie didn't seem the slightest bit embarrassed or even conscious about the mess.

Steven rubbed his eyes as he continued flipping through the channels. It seemed like every station was condemning the man who a few days ago had been the epicenter of the sports world for all the right reasons. Seven years of carefully crafting an image, shot to hell in a matter of moments. No one was talking about the amazing shot that won the game a few nights prior. All anyone cared about were allegations of cheating and murder.

Eddie was moving slowly that morning and seemed pretty zoned out. But after a few moments of watching the TV, he turned to Steven and said, "Hey, did you really make that statement?"

"No," Steven replied. "Allen must've come up with that. I had nothing to do with it. He scowled at Eddie. "Man, what's wrong with you? All that sniffling is getting on my damn nerves. You know, I asked around and I have a number for a guy I think you should call. Maybe he could help you get your act together."

"Naw, bro, ain't no thing. Just coming down with a summer cold is all," Eddie said. "Either that or my allergies are acting up."

Summer cold my ass! Who was Eddie trying to kid? He'd barely slept all night and his swollen, bloodshot eyes told the whole story. "Well get some tissue or take something, would you?"

Eddie sipped his beer and the two watched in silence as reporters and legal analysts attempted to predict what lay ahead for Steven and his career.

"Man, can't we watch something else?" Eddie said. "No sense sitting here watching this bullshit."

"It's not bullshit, Eddie. This is my life these people are talking about."

"No it ain't. It's a bunch of people who don't know shit, tearing you down piece by piece. Hell, half of them were begging to have you on their shows two days ago."

Steven changed channels until he noticed his picture on CNBC. What in the hell did they have to talk about? Did somebody suddenly rob Wall Street in a Steven Lords mask and jersey?

"The potential trouble Steven Lords is in has caused a slight ripple on Wall Street. Since the story broke about Lords's illicit affair and his alleged involvement in the murder of Michelle Tibbs, some of the companies Lords endorses have announced intent to drop him as a spokesman. One company went so far as to say he no longer embodies their ideals and ethics.

"There has been no word from Nike as to whether or not they've terminated his contract, but they are delaying the shipping of his new shoe that was due to hit stores next week. They have also suspended any ad campaigns indefinitely. Their CEO issued a statement saying they are fully supporting Steven Lords during this difficult time and are hoping for a speedy and favorable outcome to the investigation."

Steven changed the channel and his jaw dropped when he spotted a familiar face on E!

"Women are beginning to come forward with details about their affairs with basketball superstar Steven Lords. Actress and model Veronique Esperanza claims she's been having an affair with the basketball superstar for the past year."

Steven looked at Eddie, whose sunken eyes went wide with surprise. The idea of Karen having to hear this, along with everything already going on, fueled the growing sense of shame and despair that had been eating at him all morning.

Eddie snatched the remote from Steven. "I'm tired of this mess," he said as he began whizzing through the channels. "I know there's something better on than this."

He stopped at a news report of some sort showing a crowd of people with one person holding up a Steven Lords jersey. He tossed the remote back to Steven.

"I'm standing outside of a Foot Locker shoe store where a crowd of fans has gathered in support of Steven Lords," a reporter said. "Steven Lords's number-fourteen jersey is already the top-selling jersey, according to retailers. But since his game-winning shot the other night and reports of his involvement in his alleged girlfriend's murder, it's the hottest thing out there."

"Sir, if I may have a word?" the reporter asked one of the men in the crowd. "What do you think about all the allegations surrounding Steven Lords?"

"I don't think nothing about them! I'm still gonna show the love for the best basketball player in the world! He's the man."

Another man yanked the microphone over. "Lords is innocent. This ain't nothing but some mess the media cooked up to bring a good man down. But 'The Lord' is too strong. He's righteous. Blessings to him and his fam!"

The reporter looked through the crowd and found a female to interview. "What about you, ma'am? How do you feel about what's going on with Steven Lords?"

"Well . . . if you ask me, he's wrong for cheating on his

wife, but you know that's how these athletes are these days. But I don't think he killed nobody."

Eddie looked at Steven and smiled. "You see that, man? You still have some people down for you. Focus on that. I know you ain't kill Michelle and there are a million people out there that know that too. When it's all said and done everybody's gonna come running back to kiss your ass, and after you bring Miami a trophy, you'll be bigger than ever!"

"But at what cost? My reputation is ruined. Ronnie and all those other chicks coming out—that's gonna mess things up with Karen for sure."

"Look at it like this. You win that championship and all this shit goes away. That's the beauty of the game, man! People forget your fuckups when you win. Who's a better winner than you?" Eddie said. "And give Karen some time, man. You may have stepped on your dick in a serious way, but give it a little time and I bet that'll work out too."

Steven didn't say a word. Some of what Eddie said might be true, but a championship wouldn't bring Michelle back. And it damn sure wasn't enough to make Karen forget about his extracurricular activities.

He'd give anything if he could turn back the clock and make some better choices back when he'd had the chance. But that wasn't the way things worked.

He muted the TV and sat with Eddie in contemplative silence as he flipped through the block of sports channels.

He stopped and turned up the volume when he saw Peter Owens live via satellite split screen on CNN.

"Peter, you first broke the story on your sports show in Miami, Florida," the anchor was saying. "How'd you get the story?"

"A good reporter never reveals his sources."

"So we'll say you got a tip?"

"Let's just chalk this up to good investigative journalism," Peter replied.

"Fair enough," the anchor said. "Are the police currently looking at any other leads right now?"

"Miami Police would have you think they're looking at other possible suspects, but my sources tell me you can forget about what you heard at their press conference yesterday—Steven Lords is their prime suspect."

"You've been covering Miami sports for over ten years and you've interviewed Lords quite a bit during that time. Do you honestly believe he's guilty?"

"It's not my job to presume guilt or innocence. We'll leave that up to the courts. But I do know he had an affair with Michelle Tibbs and I also know he was at the hotel the night she was murdered. And no matter what Lords did or didn't do, this is a terrible tragedy for everyone."

"You live in Miami. How have the fans and community reacted to the allegations that Steven Lords is involved in a murder?"

"I'd say they're in shock. Up until now he was a perfect

role model. A family man who exemplified good values and strong moral fiber. But now we've seen an ugly side to Steven Lords, who's clearly anything but a saint. "

"Enough of this shit," Steven said as he grabbed his cell phone. "I need to do something about this right now."

"Whatcha doing, man?"

Perched in his chair with his thumb on the keypad, Steven waited for the phone number to flash across the screen.

"It's a call-in show, right? So I'm gonna call in and set the record straight."

Eddie shook his head. "That ain't a good idea, man."

"I don't think you have a say in this!"

Eddie held out his hand. "Give me the phone, Steven. Remember what Al said. Stay off the damn phone!"

"Since when have you given a damn about what Al said?"

"I don't. I've been saying for the longest time you don't need his ass. But I think he may be right, you know? Calling into this show is a bad move."

Steven rolled his eyes. "How is standing up for myself a bad move, Ed? Please tell me."

"First of all, you're all emotional right now. You ain't thinking straight. If you call into this show you're playing on their court, and right now you ain't prepared. You don't know what they'll ask or what they'll say. Plus whatever you say will be played over and over. You can't take that shit back."

"So what am I supposed to do? Just sit here and watch my life go up in flames?"

"I know you're upset. But you need to chill—"

"Chill? How can you even say some shit like that? It ain't your life playing out on television. Honestly, I don't think you understand the situation because if you did you would've handled shit a whole hell of a lot better."

Eddie scowled at Steven. "What are you trying to say? You saying this is my fault?"

Steven stared back, eyes blazing. "I don't see anything about the reward I'm offering. What's up with that, Ed? I thought I told you to put it out there. I'm watching people talk about me like I'm some damn monster. Why don't I see anything about that?"

"Come on, man, that was just yesterday! I know you're tripping, but don't go taking this shit out on me! I'm just trying to help—that's all I've ever done is try and fucking help. No matter what happens don't ever forget that, all right?"

Something in the way he said it bothered Steven. But before he could respond, his phone buzzed.

CHAPTER 23

Steven headed for the kitchen to take the call. There, he noticed a chalky mirror wedged between the dirty dishes in the sink. His mother had called three times since their brief chat, but Steven had hesitated to answer. How did you explain to your mother that you'd been living a lie for the past seven years and everything she taught you about honesty and good character was thrown away? How did you tell her your actions caused a lot of pain to the people who loved you and may have even brought about the death of a dear friend?

There was only one solution he could think of. He needed to get it over with.

"Hey, Mama! Did Allen get you all settled in?"

"Boy, don't you 'Hey, Mama' me! I've been calling you since yesterday! You couldn't pick up a phone and call me back like you promised?"

"I know you've been calling," he said. "But I stayed at Eddie's last night and I didn't feel like talking to anyone."

"I don't give a damn where you were last night! I'm your mother! I've been worried sick about you. Is it too much to call me and let me know you're okay?"

"No, you're right," Steven said. "I should've called. I'm sorry. Is everything all right?"

"I'm fine. I'm over here at Sandra's house. All those damn newspeople were all over the neighborhood."

Steven chuckled. "You should've let me buy you a house in a nice, secluded neighborhood so you wouldn't have to worry about any reporters."

"Remind me where you live and where you slept last night," his mom said. "It don't matter where I am or where you are—these people will find you. I should've had that driver take me to the airport!"

"I told you I'm okay, Mama. Everything's fine. There's no need to worry."

"Fine? I'm sitting here watching these people on television talk about how you could go to prison for a long time for killing that girl and her baby, and you're telling me everything is fine?" I know you didn't do it, but I'm so damn mad at you for putting yourself in that kind of situation. I've always taught you better than that. I never understood what you saw in that girl in the first place."

"Michelle was all right, Mama," Steven said. "You never gave her a chance."

"I don't mean to speak ill of the dead, but she was a hot-ass fast little girl then, who turned into a tramp and a homewrecker later."

"Come on now, she wasn't that bad."

"Maybe not to you, but that's because you've been defending her since you were in school. She sure had her hooks deep into you."

Steven rolled his eyes. "Eddie said the same thing."

"He did? Well, maybe he ain't as dumb as he acts. Hell, I don't understand why you keep his sorry ass around."

"He's one of the good guys, Mama. I got tons of people around me and most of 'em want something. But not Eddie. He's one of the only ones I can trust."

He heard her clicking her tongue. "I wish I could believe that. But how are you holding up, Stevie? For real now."

Steven paused and stared out over the front lawn. He could feel the wetness in his eyes as his lips started to quiver. "Not so good, Mama."

"I'm sorry, baby. I know this has been hard on you. Have you talked to Karen?"

"I've been trying to call her, but she won't answer."

"She's probably mad at you and embarrassed by all those women saying they've been with you. I can't say I blame her either. She has every right to be. You got another woman pregnant! What were you thinking, boy?"

"I don't know, Mama. I wasn't thinking. That's the problem."

"Well I guess you don't know do you? Look at what you did, walk around like God Almighty and now you stepped in some mess you can't easily get off of your shoe," she said. "But I've fussed at you enough. Why don't you tell me what's on your mind?"

Steven paused. A hundred thoughts swarmed around in his head, but none seemed to be coming to his lips.

"Come on, Steven, out with it. What's going on in that head of yours?"

He let out a long sigh. "I'm just hearing all these people say all this stuff about me, you know? These are some of the same people who were praising me and saying how great I am and all that, a few days ago."

"Stevie, you've been in the public eye long enough to know how this works. They love you one minute and they hate you the next. But this will pass, I promise you that."

"I know, Mama. I know I messed up big time and I'm just disgusted with myself when I think about how I've been acting. I offered to do the right thing and take care of the baby—"

"The right thing isn't taking care of Michelle's baby. The right thing is taking care of your own house and leaving all that other trash on the curb."

"You're right, Ma. But now I got people calling me a murderer and willing to believe I'm capable of killing somebody. It just . . ."

"Just what, baby? Tell me how you're feeling. You don't need to put on any kind of show for me."

"It hurts, Mama. I'm watching TV and putting myself in the shoes of someone who doesn't know me and thinking 'who is this guy,' you know? To be honest, I'm not sure I like the answer."

And that was it. He'd been exposed as a liar and cheat, and that's what he was.

He'd always known it was wrong to sleep around but that's where the thought had stopped. He'd never given much thought to what it said about his character. Christ, what kind of fantasy world had he been living in? How had he managed to convince himself it was okay to cheat on Karen and sleep around like some kind of playboy?

"You can't let yourself get all worked up because some people are calling you something you know you're not. And as for the women, well, Son, you brought that on yourself. You aren't the first man to do that, and you damn sure won't be the last. But it sounds to me like as hard as this is, it's also a good opportunity to take a good, hard look at yourself and maybe think about making some changes."

His mom was right. And there he'd been, worrying about his best friend because he liked to party too much.

"I know this will come out all right in the end," his mother said. "It's funny how things work. You've let this image of you that really isn't you take over, and now that image and all those lies you've been telling have been exposed. Nothing tells on a person quicker than being something you aren't."

Steven nodded. His mother's words were truer today than they were all those years ago. Maybe this was a punishment for all the lies and deceptions. Losing Michelle was a terrible price to have to pay and worse, the debt still might not have been settled.

"I'm scared, Mama. I feel like I might lose everything."

"What do you mean everything?"

"Everything, Mama! The house, the cars, all my endorsements could be in serious trouble. Hell, I've already lost some of them."

"Stevie, I'm surprised at you," his mother said. "That house and those cars and all the money in the world don't mean a thing! We never had all that stuff when you were growing up and we did just fine. You have plenty to be concerned about, but all that material stuff isn't it."

"I know, Mama. But sometimes I feel like it's all I have. I know this stuff isn't important, but I also remember coming home from games and you'd be passed out on the couch from working two jobs. I promised myself I'd take care of you and make sure you had everything you wanted."

"Baby, I've always had everything I wanted," she said softly. "I never cared about you playing pro ball. I remember when you wanted to be an architect. I remember you used to draw so well and your teachers said you had good math skills. But you loved that ball so much."

"Because I knew it could help me take care of you. Look at everything the game gave us."

"But look at what it took from you, boy. It made you into something you're not—you're cheating on your wife with all these no-count skanks. It's been taking little bits from you since you were a kid. I guess some of it is my fault."

"None of it's your fault, Mama. How can you even think that?"

"I knew there were people like Eddie, Michelle, and that Dub character around you, taking advantage of you, and I should've stepped in and said something. But they were doing things to help you I wasn't able to do. If I would've said something or did something, things would have probably been different."

"Mama, Eddie looked out for me when we were in school. He's had my back for a long time. I'm not gonna argue about Michelle with you and we're so far from Dub now it's not even worth talking about."

"I still should've done something. I let that man take advantage of you."

"Mama, don't do that, okay? Dub's no longer an issue. Besides, he did a lot of good things that helped me get here. If it wasn't for him, we might not have some of the things—and some of the opportunities—we have now."

"Stevie, I just told you I don't care about all that. I just wanted you to be happy."

"Well, I was happy," Steven said. "At least I thought I

was. But now it seems like everyone in the world is against me."

"That's only temporary, baby."

"With the fans, maybe. But with Karen, I just don't know."

"There's nothing you can do about that. You're pretty much at the mercy of whatever she chooses to do. You're the one who messed up. All you can do is try to convince her you'll change and things will be better from here on out. Have you talked to Michelle's family?"

"I wouldn't know what to say to them."

"Well, it may not be what you can say so much as what you can do. I don't like the situation anymore than you do, but you and that girl were friends at some point. Maybe you could offer to pay for the funeral arrangements."

"I don't know about that, Mama. The press would have a field day with that. I can see the headlines now: 'Lords pays for girlfriend's funeral.' That would be an even bigger nightmare."

"Stevie, you can't live your life according to public opinion. If anything, this trouble you're in should tell you that. Sometimes you have to put aside what people might think and do what's decent. Find a way to do it quietly."

"I hear you, Mama, and maybe you're right. I'll try to make some arrangements."

"You know it isn't too late for me to hop a flight. I could be there by dinnertime."

"Naw, it's okay. I got a lot going on with practice and trying to get ready for the game. I feel better just talking to you though. Thanks for listening."

"Are you sure?"

"Yeah, Mama, I'm sure. I can handle this."

"Okay, baby. If you need to talk to me you know you can call, right?"

"I know, Ma. I love you."

"I love you, too."

CHAPTER 24

Allen watched from the back seat of a black Lincoln MKZ as his driver turned from Detroit's Livernois Avenue onto an ordinary neighborhood street lined by rows of two-story brick houses with small lawns separated by driveways.

He wasn't at all surprised to see news vans parked and several camera crews set up outside the Lester residence, nor that the curtains were drawn and the front door was closed. Allen was about to ring the bell when a large black man with a thick moustache opened the door holding a baseball bat, shaking it menacingly. "I told you fuckin' people we ain't talking to no damn reporters! So get the hell off my porch before I make you wish you had!"

Allen had forgotten Mr. Lester was so big. "I'm sorry to bother you, Mr. Lester. We've met before. My name is Allen Warner and—"

"I don't give a frog's fat ass who you are! Get off my porch before I knock you off!"

Allen looked back at the reporters across the street, then back up at Mr. Lester. He didn't need this turning into a sound bite on the evening news.

"Mr. Lester, I think there's a mix-up. I'm not a reporter, I'm—"

"Uncle Allen!" Cassidy Lords beamed as she ran toward the screen door. She was bigger than Allen remembered but cute as a button in her yellow dress and pigtails.

"Hi, Cassidy," he said, smiling warmly.

"*Uncle* Allen?" Mr. Lester said, looking bewildered as the child tugged on his pants.

"Grampa, that's Uncle Allen. He works for Daddy."

Mr. Lester looked down at his granddaughter, who was jumping up and down around him. "Back up, baby girl," he said as he tried to nudge Cassidy behind him.

"Is Daddy here too?"

"Judy, come get this girl!" Mr. Lester yelled. She's out here acting the damn fool."

"Allen?" Mrs. Lester asked, squinting as she got closer. "Allen, is that you?"

"Yeah, Gramma, it's Uncle Allen," Cassidy said.

Allen sighed with relief. He didn't come all this way to

end up as a stain on Mr. Lester's Louisville Slugger. "Yes, Mrs. Lester, it's me. I'm really sorry to bother you. I tried calling Karen several times, but I didn't get any answer. Is she here?"

Mrs. Lester backed Cassidy away from the door and pushed her husband aside. "She's upstairs. Come on in and I'll let her know you're here."

"Wait a minute, now!" Mr. Lester said. He held his bat against the screen door to prevent his wife from opening it. "You're sure we know this fool?"

"Put that bat down!" his wife said. "This is Steven's agent." She lowered the bat and opened the door. "I'm so sorry about this. Please come in. You can have a seat in the living room and make yourself at home."

As Allen sat, Mr. Lester, bat still in hand, took a seat in a chair directly across from him. "So what's all this I see on TV about Steven and this other woman?" Mr. Lester asked. "I keep hearing people saying he killed that girl. What's really going on?"

Allen cleared his throat. "I wouldn't believe any of that stuff, sir. We all know Steven and he isn't capable of anything like that. This is just sensationalistic journalism and gossip."

"Like hell! You saw all those cameras and reporters outside my house! They've been knocking on my door, knocking on my neighbors' doors, asking all kinds of mess about my daughter. This ain't no damn gossip, man."

"Mr. Lester, I know this has been a very trying time for everyone but I assure you everything is being done to make sure the truth comes to light and Steven will be proven innocent."

"Oh yeah? So what exactly is being done? This whole thing is embarrassing to my daughter and my grandchild. So how is this gonna get handled?"

"Let's just say Miami police is working this case around the clock, and I have every assurance Steven will not be charged."

"And what are you going to do about all these other women?"

Allen was about to answer when he heard footsteps coming down the stairs. He smiled when he saw Karen rounding the banister. Dressed in baggy, black sweats and a light blue camisole that looked good against her peanut-butter-colored complexion, Karen stopped at the bottom of the stairs. Her black hair was twisted up around two dark-brown hair sticks that stuck out from the back of her head.. Her eyes were puffy like she'd been crying all morning. She'd probably been glued to the news.

"What are you doing here?" Karen asked.

Allen stood and walked over to greet her with a kiss on the cheek. "You look good, Karen," he said. "Are you holding up okay though all this?"

"Oh, please! I look like hell, and I know you didn't come all this way for small talk, so don't waste my time. What do you want?"

"Is there someplace we can talk?"

"Y'all can sit down and talk right here," Mr. Lester said. "I'd like to hear whatever you came to say."

"Whatever he has to say is none of your business," Mrs. Lester said as she came down the stairs with Cassidy following. "Why don't you two talk in the kitchen. Can I get you something, Allen?"

"No thank you, Mrs. Lester. I won't be here long."

"Well, you two go ahead. I'll take the baby upstairs with me," Mrs. Lester said. "Charlie you go on and finish watching *Bonanza* and leave them alone. If you feel you need to do something, how about fixing that running toilet upstairs like I been asking?"

"That's okay." Mr. Lester said. "I'll go see what Ben Cartwright is up to."

KAREN LED ALLEN TO THE KITCHEN TABLE. SHE WASN'T happy about him showing up at her parents' house, but with everything that had been going on the she was actually surprised to see him.

"Wow, Cassie's really grown a lot since the last time I saw her," Allen said, sitting at the table. "She's sprouting like a weed."

"Stop with the small talk and tell me why you're here."

She watched the fake smile leave his face, which seemed to darken and become more serious.

"I'm here because I need you to come back to Miami with me. I'm setting up an important interview at your house tomorrow to address some of the allegations levied against Steven, and we need you there."

"Then you just wasted a lot of time," Karen said. "Because I'm not going anywhere."

"But Karen, he needs you. You see what he's up against. They're persecuting him in the press."

"I'm sure he'll be okay. But he got himself into this mess, and I'm not about to—"

"It's not the murder case I'm worried about. It's the public relations hit he's been taking through all of this. He's lost three sponsorships with two more sponsors considering terminating his endorsement contracts. This whole ordeal has already cost him millions, and that may only be the beginning."

"Is that what this is all about? Did you come here to tell me about some endorsements? To hell with the endorsements, Allen! Are you watching television? The man is being investigated for murder. Every hour some new girl comes out of who-knows-where with a story about how she's been sleeping with my husband. I came here to get a little sanctuary, but now I've got reporters circling my parents' house like vultures and talking to neighbors, prying into our personal lives. So now it's like we're prisoners in our own home. I can only imagine what this is doing to Steve's mom!"

"She's already been taken care of," Allen said. "She's fine.

I could move your parents until this thing blows over, you know? Put them up someplace nice with a lot of privacy, away from all this attention."

"That's not the point. It's not about my parents or his mom. It's about my husband being a cheating bastard and getting caught up in his own mess. That's what this is about. Now here you go asking me to come back to Miami for some interview to help his PR? Are you out of your mind?"

"Karen, you know no one cares more about you and Steven than me. I love you guys. But I'm his agent and his best interests are my main concern. Right now those concerns are his image and his family, and those two things happen to coincide at the moment."

While Karen listened her dad lumbered into the kitchen to get a snack from the fridge. "If you ask me, you should stay right here. No need getting yourself in the middle of Steven's crap," he said. "Let his agent get him out of this mess. You and Cassidy should stay put."

Karen rolled her eyes. "Daddy, stay out of this please."

"I'm just saying that boy done lost his damn mind. You don't need that kind of mess."

"Take a look outside, Mr. Lester." Allen said. "Those reporters aren't going anywhere anytime soon. You should probably expect them out there until this whole ordeal is resolved."

Her father shook his head as he left the kitchen with a bowl of grapes.

"The spotlight will stay on Steven through this, and don't think you won't catch some of the glare as well. You can't hide here forever. What we need to do is take back some control over the situation. We need to make a statement and send a message that we're stronger than this. Like I was saying earlier, I'm setting up this interview to do just that. But in order for this thing to work, I need you there."

Karen folded her arms on the table. Those reporters and cameras wouldn't stop until they got the story they sought. They would hound them all no matter where they went and strip every bit of privacy away from her family. But was she ready to look Steven in his face after everything that had happened?

"I don't know, Allen. I just don't think I'm ready to go home."

"Come on, Karen. All this nonsense outside isn't fair to your neighbors or your parents. Come on back to Florida and let these people have their lives back. Those reporters are only here to see you. Come on home—we'll do the interview and a lot of this attention will go away."

She stared out the kitchen window.

"Karen, you know coming home is the right thing to do," Allen said as he took Karen's hand.

She snatched it back and glared at him. "I'm not the one who's been doing the wrong thing, Allen, so don't go lecturing me all right? I've stood by Steven while he went out and cheated on me. I didn't fail him. He failed me and worse than that, he failed Cassidy. So don't try to make it seem like it's my duty to do some damn interview you put together."

She stood and pointed a finger in Allen's face. "Do you know how embarrassing this is for me? Do you know how foolish I feel? Of course you don't, Allen! So if you're done telling me what's 'right,' don't let the door hit you!"

She pushed her chair away from the table. "Me and Cassidy have some errands to run, and I know you don't want to miss your flight back to Miami, so—"

"Hey, y'all may wanna come and take a look at this," her father shouted from the living room. "It looks like Steven might have another problem!"

CHAPTER 25

Karen and Allen rushed into the living room and stood in front of the television as Mr. Lester turned up the volume.

"What happened, Daddy?"

"The commissioner was just on, and he said he was thinking about suspending Steven for the Finals," Mr. Lester said. "Serves him right if you ask me."

Karen shook her head. "That's really gonna hurt. He's been waiting his whole career to play for a title, and if he misses those games—"

"You don't have to worry about that," Allen said, taking out his cell phone. "That's not going to happen, Karen. No way he's getting suspended."

He found the league commissioner on his contact list and headed back into the kitchen, pacing the floor as the phone rang. Deep down, Doug was a businessman. The reason why the league had been so profitable was because he realized his athletes' marketability only enhanced fans' interest. So it was hard to see why he'd suspend his marquee talent and try to shy away from all the interest Steven's situation was generating.

"I was expecting this call. Christ, Allen, your boy really screwed up!" Doug said without any kind of hello. "What the hell was he thinking?"

"What do you mean? You don't actually think Steven had anything to do with that woman's death, do you?" Allen said. "And since we're getting right to the point here, what makes you think you can up and suspend Steven like this anyway? He hasn't been convicted. Hell, he hasn't even been *charged* with anything."

"But he's a person of interest," Doug said. "And that's enough to violate the player personal-conduct policy in the last collective bargaining agreement. It's at the league's discretion to suspend a player whose off-court conduct is detrimental to the overall image and integrity of the league."

"The players' association won't allow it. They'll fight—"

"The players' association can appeal, but Steven's actions have clearly breached that policy and I'm being forced to act."

Allen paused to consider that for a moment. "Forced?"

"Title sponsors have been flooding this office with phone

calls wondering what I intend to do about this mess Steven made for himself."

"Sponsors? Since when did you start caving to pressure from sponsorship?"

"Since the image of this league has been tarnished by a murder investigation right before the championship series," Doug said. "And these aren't just any sponsors. We're talking about major corporations like McDonald's, ConAgra, and Coca-Cola. Companies that already dropped Steven as an endorser."

"It's just formalities and damage control, Doug. You know how it is. They're all just trying to distance themselves so it looks good to the shareholders. But after the truth comes out, this won't be an issue."

"That's where you're wrong, Al. The issue isn't just this murder case. It's Steven's viability as an ambassador of the game and a role model for the kids," Doug said. "The people over at McDonald's watch the news, and they know about Nicole Aniston and Abella Anderson. So they're damn sure not going to put Steven's face on Happy Meal boxes."

"So you're willing to send Steven up the river to save face?" Allen said. "Look at what he's done for this league! Thanks to him this sport is more profitable than ever. Popularity is at an all-time high and that's opening up new markets overseas. You're willing to overlook all of that on a whim from some sponsors? Come on, Doug. I thought you were smarter than that!"

"I don't need you to tell me what Lords's impact has meant. I don't want to see him suspended any more than you do, but I have an obligation to—"

"Your obligation is to do what's in the best interests of the league. And we both know that isn't suspending Steven, especially with the television rights up for renewal at the end of the season."

"TV rights have nothing to do with what we're talking about right now."

"Doug. Television rights have everything to do with it. All this controversy surrounding Steven is doing nothing but heightening interest in the Finals," Allen said. "Think about it: Everyone following this investigation will want to tune in to see how all this affects Steven on the game's biggest stage. That's a ratings boost you can't ignore. If you suspend Lords, I guarantee you won't have the numbers you want, and it'll hurt those network negotiations."

"I already know the numbers and I'll deal with the negotiations this offseason. Meanwhile, I have an immediate situation that needs immediate attention and, like I started to say before you interrupted me, I have an obligation to preserve the image of this league."

"You also have an obligation to the other owners, and suspending Steven isn't honoring that obligation," Allen said. "You said it yourself—you didn't want to suspend him, so you already know the impact that would have on the Finals. Why don't you present those numbers to the sponsors? Explain to them that they stand to lose a lot of exposure if our boy doesn't play, not only this year but also possibly in the years that follow."

"He's not my boy, Allen. And frankly I'm disgusted with the bigger picture that's emerging. But even if this did satisfy our sponsors, we still have our superstar in the middle of a murder investigation. What do you plan to do about that?"

"I'm going to let the investigation play itself out," Allen said. "And you should do the same. Why don't you wait a couple days to give the justice system a chance to work before you think about a suspension?"

"That's just it. We only have a couple days before tip-off! I need to act on this immediately."

"No you don't, Doug!" Allen said, pacing the kitchen and running his fingers through his hair. "You make a statement saying you'll wait until the investigation is done before you decide on a suspension. By then you'll see nothing will come of those murder allegations and all you're left with is a guy with some family issues. No big deal . . . hey, could you hold for a second? I've got Steven calling in on the other line."

WHILE ALLEN WAS ON THE PHONE, KAREN HAD GONE back upstairs to her room. The last place she wanted to be was lying on her old full-sized bed, staring at her old pink walls still decorated with Ginuwine, Tupac, and Aaliyah posters. A Fox News report played in the background as the tears trickled down her cheeks. Karen laid her head on her flower-print pillows. Michelle's murder was a tragedy, but it was hard to suppress a deep feeling of satisfaction. For years that girl had victimized her family. At the very least Michelle should've gotten a Motown beatdown a long time ago.

The backlash would be catastrophic to Steven's image. Karen wiped the tears from her face. The steady stream of tears had started to stain her pillowcases. It always came down to "The Lord's" image. Everything was handled according to how it would affect Steven's brand, so that had made kicking Michelle's ass out of the question. It was a real shame because it would've solved a whole lot of problems she created *and* served as a warning to the rest of those bitches. It probably would've saved Michelle's life, too.

But the murder and the investigation weren't the issue. In spite of the trouble Michelle caused, it was almost laughable to think Steve could've killed her. As image-conscious as he was, he loved himself too much to subject himself to the possibility of prison.

Karen's mom cracked open the bedroom door. "Baby, are you okay?" she asked as she peeked in.

"Yeah, Momma, I'm fine, "Karen said, wiping her face with her hands.

Her mother slowly opened the bedroom door and walked in. "You don't look fine to me."

She sat on the edge of the bed and began stroking Karen's hair. Years ago, it had seemed like that was all Karen needed to make the pain go away. Mom would hum some old Sam Cooke song, Dad would go and get a pound of fried shrimp from Miley & Miley, and her problems would seem to disappear. Too bad times had to change and those problems had gotten a whole lot more complicated.

Karen's mother took the remote and turned off the television. "Look, baby, I don't want to get in your business—"

"So don't, okay? Just let me handle this."

"All right, but let me tell you something. I remember when me and your daddy were dating, he had this dark-blue 1967 Pontiac. It was such a beautiful car. He used to pick me up and we'd go for rides around town in it. I felt like Diana Ross. Your daddy was no slouch, either."

Karen shook her head as she rolled to one side. "Mama, I'm not in the mood to hear stories about you and Daddy," she said. "I have too much on my mind right now and—"

"This won't take a minute. Your dad also told me he had this great apartment with all kinds of fancy leather furniture and a big color TV. Acted like he was heaven-sent. Well, come to find out the apartment he said he had turned out to be a little room over a nightclub, and the car belonged to his best friend Earl. He had this raggedy old motorcycle that smoked like a broke stove. The man could tell a lie.

He didn't tell them to be mean or anything, but he always wanted to make himself seem more than he was."

"Mom, your point?"

"The point is, I knew what your daddy was before I married him and I married him anyway. You knew what Steven was before you married him and you married him anyway. There are no surprises, baby. He's the same man you fell in love with."

"I know, Momma, and I'm so mad at myself for being in this situation. He made so many promises and said so many things, and he went back on all of it. I knew what was going on and I just sat there. I didn't say a word—I just let it all happen."

"Yes, you did, and you see where that got you. But crying and feeling bad isn't gonna fix any of it."

Karen's eyes welled with tears as she sat up in her bed. "Mom, you've seen the news. Do you know how embarrassing this is?"

"Well, if it's that embarrassing, don't tell me about it. Tell Steven. It's time you stopped hiding from the world and being mad at yourself. We've raised you to be strong and independent. I heard what you were telling Allen downstairs, and you need to tell that to your husband. You owe it to yourself. You need that peace of mind."

"So you think I should go home?"

"I think you need to talk to him, that's for sure. Whether you choose to stay with him is your choice. But you can't just sit here with your head in the sand. Think about that. I'm getting ready to take Cassidy to the store." With that, her mom got up and walked over to the door.

"You're going out there with all those cameras outside?" Karen asked.

"Cameras or no cameras, we still got to live."

Karen stood and closed the door behind her mother. She dried the tears from her eyes as she rested her head against the door. In her own down-home sort of way, her mother had hit the nail on the head. She'd spent too much time shouldering the blame and not holding Steven responsible. Staying in her bedroom and crying wasn't going to help. The situation needed to be confronted head on. That meant going home to Miami.

She took a couple of suitcases out of her closet before heading downstairs. Her heart wasn't into going back home, but she couldn't spend the rest of her life hiding at her parents' house. She could hear Allen's voice coming from the kitchen and by the sound of it, he was getting what he wanted. No big surprise there; he usually did.

"Good news," he said after he hung up. "Steven won't be suspended unless the police get something more definitive. So I guess I'll be on my way."

Karen took a deep breath. "I'm going with you. What time is our flight?"

CHAPTER 26

Downtown Miami, 10:21 a.m.

Peter Owens stood in line at Starbucks, waiting for his daily macchiato. God only knew why the lines were always so long in the morning. Didn't these people have jobs or somewhere to be?

He had just gotten his coffee and was reaching for a few extra napkins when he saw Detective Russell Howard heading his way.

Howard got right down to business. "Sorry to bother you, Mr. Owens, but this is Sydney Farrell. She's a consultant on the Lords investigation, and she wants to talk to you about what you saw at the hotel the other night."

Russell sounded anything but enthusiastic.

Sydney smiled as Peter shook her outstretched hand. "I

was going over some reports, and I just wanted to talk to you about a few things in your account of that night."

Peter's eyes shifted between Russell and Sydney. "Sure thing," he said after a moment. "Let's make an appointment to sit down and talk tomorrow. I have a very busy schedule today. As a matter of fact I have to do an interview soon, so—"

"This will only take a minute," Sydney said. "We're sorry to trouble you. We went by your office and the secretary told us you usually stop here before you head in. So I promise this will be quick."

Once they were seated Sydney took out her notebook and started flipping through the pages. "Would you mind going back over what you saw at the Murcielago?"

"No problem," Peter said. "I was in the parking lot when I saw Lords coming out of the hotel. I remember he was standing at the top of the stairs of the hotel, looking sort of lost. He walked down the stairs and looked around a bit and headed back into the hotel. He looked confused about something. Actually, I'd say he looked anxious."

"How'd you know to go to the hotel in the first place?" Sydney said.

Peter took a bite out of his scone and a long sip of his coffee, enjoying making her wait for an answer. "It's just like I told the detective, I was finishing my story on the game when I got a call from a number I didn't recognize. The person on the other end told me if I wanted to get a good story on Steven Lords I should get to the Murcielago hotel right away."

"You didn't know who made the call. Is that correct?" Sydney asked.

"Yeah, that's right."

Sydney leaned forward. "So do you usually get anonymous phone calls for stories? Do you blindly follow the suggestions of strangers on the other end of anonymous phone calls?"

"No, not normally. But I do like to leave my card with a lot of people because you just never know." Pete shrugged his shoulders. "Look, I went over all this with the detective."

"I know. I read your account in Detective Howard's report." Sydney said. "But humor me. So what made this time so special?"

"Well, the caller said Steven Lords was at the hotel, and I know he likes the ladies and his marriage was in trouble. So I figured it was worth taking a look."

"How'd you know he wasn't there visiting his wife?"

"I didn't. All she said was that Lords was going to be at the Murcielago and if I wanted a good story I should get right over there."

"She?" Russell said. "You never mentioned that the caller was female."

Peter bit his lip as he glanced at Russell, who had become more attentive to his replies. "Christ, don't I have the right to protect my sources?" Peter asked.

"So it was a woman who called you?" Sydney asked.

"Yeah, it was a woman's voice. But that's all you need to know."

"Okay, we'll play your game." Sydney said, sitting back in her chair with a coy smile. "It just seems odd to me that you get a call that late and head over to the hotel without any idea who it was you were talking to."

"That's how it is sometimes when you're a journalist. When a story's out there you can't wait. You gotta act on it—otherwise someone else will," Peter said. "Now if you good people will excuse me, I have to get going."

"I don't think we're finished yet," Russell said.

"Well, that's too bad, isn't it?" Peter pushed his chair away from the table. "I'm done talking. I only agreed to sit down out of courtesy, but I'm not obligated to answer your questions."

"Before you go, Mr. Owens, maybe you can answer this: Do you remember Justin 'Popeye' Willis?" Sydney said.

Peter's brow wrinkled. He hadn't heard that name in years. What in the hell could Popeye have to do anything? Peter scooted his chair back to the table.

"Yeah, I remember Popeye. He was a pitcher in the bigs," Peter said. "He had a nasty hundred-mile-an-hour fastball, but he blew out his shoulder and was never the same again. So what?"

"Anything else you remember about him?"

"It was a sad case, really. He had a botched surgery and

spent the rest of his career in the minors. He was never able to recapture his stuff."

"That's right," Sydney said. "Rumor had it he got seriously hooked on painkillers to boot. Vicodin, Oxycontin, Demerol . . . do you remember hearing anything about that?"

Pete attempted to look bored with the conversation. "It's a sad story, sure, but why bring it up? Seems like ancient history to me."

"You wrote an article on him. It was a real insightful piece about how he lost his career to addiction."

"Yeah. I wrote that. I still don't see what that has to do with anything."

"Popeye died of a drug overdose shortly after your story came out."

"I remember. Can't say I was surprised either, as he was in really bad shape. It was only a matter of time. But I fail to see—"

"Then let me explain. When I worked for the FBI we investigated a guy named Dr. Rene Mettier from Toronto. He was involved in illegal trafficking of steroids and other opiates into this country," she said, smiling thinly.

Peter hunched his shoulders. "So what? I don't see what you're getting at."

"I think you do, Mr. Owens. Considering you were one of his so-called patients."

"Where on earth did you—"

"Dr. Mettier was a meticulous recordkeeper, as it turns out. Quite a habit you had going there, apparently."

Peter laughed nervously. "Okay, you got me. I bought some painkillers. I had knee surgery years ago and I couldn't get a prescription after mine ran out. But that was a long time ago."

Sydney nodded sympathetically, but there was a hard look in her eyes.

"Well, you might also be interested to know my father was a cop for the Buffalo Police Department and he actually knew Popeye pretty well. Arrested him on several occasions for petty drug-related crimes. Dad loved baseball, you see, and was a big fan of Popeye's. He helped him get clean. When he died of that overdose, Dad always wondered what caused him to relapse. That's about the time your article came out."

"So what? I wrote an article on the guy. Big deal."

"You did more than that. When my dad helped Popeye's family clean out his place, he found a bottle of pills. It turned out that bottle came from Dr. Mettier. A look at the doctor's records showed he never sold to Popeye, but he did sell to you. Funny how Popeye's overdose coincided with a story you wrote on him?"

"So what are you getting at?" Peter said. "Popeye was a junkie. He could've gotten those pills anywhere."

"But he didn't." Sydney said. "Look, I can make a phone call and have copies of Popeye's toxicology report and the good doctor's records sent to your editor at the *Post*. With your reputation, do you think—"

Peter's eyes grew wider. "What the hell is this? Some kind of shakedown?"

"It's a simple quid pro quo," Sydney replied. "You tell me who was on the other end of that call, and I won't tell your editor about how you fixed that story."

Peter sat silently, biting his lower lip and drumming his fingers on the tabletop. *I should've left when I had a chance.*

"All I need is the name," Sydney said. "If you tell me, I'll forget Popeye ever existed."

Peter cut his eyes over to Russell. "I also don't want you coming after me with charges of obstruction or anything like that. Is that a deal?"

"Look, Owens, if you know something that will help this case, just say it," Russell said. "I won't come after you unless you did it."

Peter looked back at Sydney and said. "It was Michelle."

Russell leaned forward and placed his elbows on the table. "Are you saying Michelle Tibbs called you right before she was murdered and you're just telling me now?" He shook his head. "I checked her hotel phone records and her cell phone calls. No record of a call made to you that night."

"Actually, Detective, we were instant messaging on Facebook that night, and she let me know Steven was on his way over to the hotel."

"You'd better start from the beginning," Russell said. "How did you know Tibbs?"

Peter looked at his watch before answering. "I met her about a year ago while I was covering the team. I knew she was having a thing with Lords and I thought maybe at some point she might want to dish a little dirt on him. A few months later that's exactly what she did. Apparently Lords broke it off with her abruptly, and you know what they say about a woman scorned."

"So what'd she say?" Russell said.

"She called me a few months ago and asked if I knew of any publishers who might be interested in a book about the real Steven Lords."

Russell's jaw dropped. "You mean something *she* was writing?"

"That's right," Pete said. "A tell-all exposé—and let me tell you, it was steamy!"

Russell sat back in his chair. "So what exactly did she have on Lords?"

Peter grinned. "Well for starters, she had intricate details about their own little affair and a few other flings he's had with some of Hollywood's A-listers."

"Revealing some affairs isn't enough to kill her over," Sydney said. "Even if Tibbs was pregnant with Lords's child, I doubt—"

"That wasn't all," Peter said. "She told me she'd recruited

an old friend of Lords who gave a damning account that points—"

"Speculations and hearsay," Sydney interrupted. "The woman has an ax to grind with a man who most of country believes can do no wrong." She chuckled as she shook her head. "No one would believe it, let alone spend money to read about it."

"That's exactly why she came to me," Peter said. "She was looking for a way to pitch her story. I told her I thought it might not be a good time for a tell-all about Lords. His image was a little too clean for people to take that seriously, so we came up with a way to dirty him up a bit."

Sydney nodded. "So the questioning after the game was . . ."

"It was all a part of the plan," Peter said. "I was gonna ask him questions about his wife and kid, cast some shade on his reputation, and then expose him. Michelle told me she was pregnant with his baby and he'd been pressuring her for an abortion. I told her to get him to the hotel that night and let me know when he got there. That way we'd have him on video leaving the hotel. I just didn't expect him to kill her."

"So it was all a setup?" Sydney said.

"'Setup' is a bit harsh. All we were trying to do was bring the truth to light," Peter said. "Lords has been coddled his whole career. It's high time he finally gets exposed."

"You mean to tell me all of this started because Tibbs wanted to get back at Lords for breaking things off?" Russell asked.

"Pretty much," Peter said. "The plan was she'd go public with the affair and the love child she was carrying. The book would come out and I'd get the exclusive interviews. That's one thing about the media, see—we love to build them up and we really love to tear them down."

"Why didn't you mention all this before?" Russell demanded.

"That girl got killed because of my idea. I felt a bit responsible for it. I know you think I'm heartless, but I do care."

"I think you're a bottom-feeding lowlife," Sydney said. "You didn't feel responsible. What you felt was the possibility of an even bigger story that you had the inside scoop on."

Pete gathered his coffee and what was left of his scone, then stood with a grin. "Think whatever you want, honey. But you know what? This really doesn't change anything. All this does is make Lords look even more guilty, which makes the story I write all the better. You people enjoy the rest of your morning."

RUSSELL IMMEDIATELY MOVED TO A SEAT OPPOSITE SYDNEY and leaned in close so no one could hear them talk. It was hard to look her in the eye, knowing she had made the right call by insisting they talk to Owens. But that the sleazy reporter had strengthened the case made his job a lot easier.

"Sounds to me like we have a new motive," Russell said. "If Lords knew anything about this little tell-all Tibbs was planning, that'd give him even more reason to want her silenced."

"Slow down, Detective. I'm still not sure Lords is our man," Sydney said.

Russell rubbed his face. "He had motive and opportunity, so what don't you get? This may be as open-and-shut as we can ask for. Time to throw in your cards and fold."

"I don't know," Sydney said as she shook her head. "There's something else that bothers me."

Russell threw up his hands. "Are you kidding me? There is nothing else! What are you, president of the Steven Lords Fan Club or something? The facts are the facts and it's time you take a look and see them for what they are."

"The only problem is that there isn't a shred of proof that he did this, nor that Peter Owens is telling the truth. And what's your deal anyway, Detective?" she said, for the first time showing a hint of lack of composure. "Why are you in such a rush to wrap up this case and arrest this guy?"

"Because he's scum, that's why!" Russell shouted. He dropped his voice when he caught glances from others in the coffee shop. "Sorry, but it seems like everyone's ignoring the obvious because this guy's a celebrity. Sometimes if it walks like a duck . . ."

"I'm telling you this case isn't as open-and-shut as you think," Sydney said. "Owens said he was Facebooking Michelle the night she was murdered. But you saw her phone—it's not Internet-enabled. That means she may have had a laptop with her. I don't remember seeing a laptop with her personal effects. Did you find one at the scene?"

"No. We didn't find anything like that. Maybe she had her book manuscript on it and Lords took it with him after he killed her," Russell said.

Sydney rolled her eyes. "What is your problem? Why are you pushing so hard to pin this on him? Are you resentful of Lords's wealth or fame? Or is this just good, old-fashioned Southern racism?"

"Now you hold on right there!" Russell said, finger pointed at Sydney. "I may not like what Lords represents, but that doesn't make me a racist. I'm trying to do my job by solving this case and—"

"And put someone away for this horrible crime," Sydney said. "That's all I'm trying to do as well, but in order to do that I need you to stop being so close-minded to the possibility that Steven Lords may not have killed that woman."

"Why, because you say so? I mean, you're the hotshot consultant."

"That has nothing to do with it. But after talking to Owens again, something has to have changed in your mind."

"Oh, something definitely changed in my mind," Russell said. "I think Owens just provided me with a better motive. What did it change for you?"

"It created the possibility that whoever took that laptop also could have killed Tibbs."

"Which again goes back right back to Lords," Russell said, standing.

"Where are you going?"

"While this little visit has been educational, I still have some real police work to do," Russell said as he checked his pocket for his car keys. "I'm going to go ahead and humor you about that computer because it helps my case."

"Fine, but we still don't know for sure what happened in the hotel room and with the lack of forensic evidence, it'll be hard for you to even get an indictment, much less a conviction."

"Which is exactly why I have to go and talk to the security manager on duty that night," Russell said. "The last time I talked to the hotel staff they hadn't seen him since that night. The deputy commish has a feeling he could be the key to all of this."

"You haven't interviewed him yet?" Sydney asked. "I know you like Lords for the murder, but you could've at least done your homework and checked all leads."

"For your information the address the hotel had on file for him was for his baby's mother's place. She said he hadn't lived there in almost a year," Russell replied.

"So do you have the correct address now?"

"Neither the DMV nor the post office had a current address for him, but I was able to find a co-worker who's been taking him home recently. Feel free to tag along if you like, but please stay out of my way. Let me do this my way."

"No problem, Detective. You've done a great job so far."

CHAPTER 27

Liberty City, 12:19 p.m.

Russell drove slowly down the street of a Liberty City neighborhood with his attention divided between the bleak, ghetto cityscape outside the window and his passenger's stony demeanor. Sydney hadn't spoken since getting in the car, and that suited him fine, given the magnitude of what Owens had told them and how much stronger the case against Lords looked. She might be bitter about having to eat crow, but at least she'd have to stay the hell out of Russell's way and let him do what he needed to without distraction.

Next up was to talk to James Cooper, who had either himself tampered with the security footage at the Murcielago or could lead them to the person who did. They'd already wasted a lot of time, so the best Russell could hope for was to sweat a confession and hope Steven Lords had put Cooper up to it. But he had a nagging feeling it wasn't going to be that easy.

Cooper lived in a neighborhood worn ragged by years of neglect. The stucco houses were old and covered in graffiti. The yards were strewn with trash and choked by weeds. It was a residential neighborhood, but there were no young kids or old folks or anyone who didn't look like some kind of thug. A couple of dreads sitting on turned-up milk crates looked up in alarm when someone screamed, "Aye yo, po-po, y'all!" right after Russell turned onto their street. But other than that, no one seemed to notice or care.

"Here we are," Russell said, breaking the tense silence. "There's a car out front, so maybe we'll get a break and actually catch him at home."

They stepped out of the car and headed up the cracked walkway to the front door. A rusty chain-link fence surrounded a yard overgrown with burnt-out crabgrass and raggedy hedges that didn't look inviting—but then again, this wasn't exactly Mr. Rogers' neighborhood.

Russell knocked on the door, then took a step back and waited.

He knocked again and put an ear to the door. "Mr. Cooper. This is the Miami-Dade Police Department. Would you please open up?"

"Maybe that's not his car after all," Sydney said.

"I hear the TV on," Russell resumed knocking, harder now. "We didn't come all this way to come up empty. I don't care if I have to camp out on this guy's porch. I'm not leaving until I get some answers."

Russell pounded even harder on the door and stepped back in surprise when it slowly swung open.

"This can't be good," he said after inspecting the shattered doorjamb on the inside. He quickly reached for his shoulder holster and drew his gun. "Are you packing or what?"

"What do you think?" Sydney replied. "Former FBI here in a consultant capacity?"

Russell rolled his eyes. *Great.* "Okay then. I'm going to have a peek inside. Keep a lookout for anything suspicious."

"Have you forgotten where wc are? Everything looks suspicious," Sydney said. "Why don't you just—"

"Take a step back, would you?"

With gun in hand, he eased through the door and into the house. The storm shutters over the windows darkened the living room but the TV emitted enough light to show Russell the room was empty and the place was a pigsty.

He kept his gun in front of him as he cautiously moved through the living room. His breath caught in his throat when he entered the dining room. That smell wasn't a good sign.

He stopped in his tracks when he got to the kitchen. The refrigerator door was wide open. Broken bottles were scattered all over the kitchen floor underneath a dead James Cooper, who must have been leaning into the fridge when he'd been shot.

Sydney walked in and stood over Russell while he inspected the two holes in the back of Cooper's head.

"Looks like Excedrin headache number nine-millimeter," he said. "I guess we can call this lead a dead end."

"Has anyone ever told you you aren't funny?"

"I'll tell you what isn't funny. Now we may never know what was actually on that video."

"So what now?"

"I don't know yet. Without this guy, we may as well be back to square one," Russell said as he stood. "I'm gonna call this in. Why don't you go talk to the neighbors and see if they noticed anything we might want to know about?"

"You really think that will do any good? People in areas like this don't make a habit out of talking to police."

"Well, that's good because you aren't exactly a cop, are you?"

Russell smirked when he heard the door slam shut. She might have been miffed, but she was out of his hair, so he could work without someone looking over his shoulder. At least until Morales showed up.

A young man named Darrell and his friend Rodney sat on a couple of patio chairs in the driveway of the house next to James Cooper's. They had spent the morning trying to make a few dollars selling nickel bags of weed—that was, until they saw an unmarked white Crown Victoria pull up to Coopers' house. An old paint can made a convenient hiding place for their stash, and they sat and watched whatever was going down.

Darrell nudged Rodney when he saw Cooper's door open. Two cops had gone in but only one walked out. That wasn't good for Jimmy, and that damn sure wasn't good for the block. If something had happened to Jimmy, and he guessed something had, then the law was gonna have everything around there roped off.

Darrell shook his head as he watched a pretty lady cop approach with a smile on her face. Police or not, she was wasting her time coming over because ain't nobody got nothing to say.

"Shouldn't you boys be in school?" Sydney asked as she walked up the driveway.

"Naw. I'm home sick and my boy stopped by to bring me some soup," Darrell said.

Sydney smiled. "Well, you don't look sick to me," she said as she put the back of her hand to the side of Darrell's face.

Darrell jerked his head to one side. "What you supposed to be? You some kind of a doctor or some shit?"

"My name's Sydney Farrell and I'm working with the Miami-Dade Police Department. I was hoping to ask you a few questions about your neighbor."

"I don't know nothin' 'bout him," Darrell said.

"Whatever you want to know about Jimmy, ask Jimmy," Rodney added.

"Well, I'd like to ask Jimmy, but we just found him dead on his kitchen floor," Sydney said. "I'm hoping maybe you boys might have seen something that could help us find out who did it."

"Naw, lady, I ain't seen nothing over there. Sorry," Darrell turned to stare off into the distance past her. "But don't worry . . . if I hear something, I'll be sure to report it to the local authorities."

Darrell laughed and shot a knowing glance at Rodney. This lady had to be nuts, thinking she could come into the hood like this, flash a pretty smile, and get some answers. She'd better take that shit to Coral Gables or something because snitches got stitches around this neighborhood.

Sudden activity from next door drew his attention to the other cop, who had exited the house and was approaching quickly.

"CSI is on their way and I need you to see something," the man said.

"In a minute, Russell," Sydney said. "I wasn't quite done here yet."

Rodney laughed. "Oh but we done with you! Why don't you just go on back over there with your partner? We just told you we'd call if we had some info for you."

The guy named Russell raised an eyebrow. "Are these gentlemen being uncooperative?"

"A little, but I was about to see if I could persuade them to be good citizens and help us out a little," she replied.

"I think I may have an idea," he said, stroking his chin.

Darrell's heartbeat quickened. He looked over at Rodney, who looked like he was trying to swallow a lump in his throat. A cop had that same look on his face when he jacked up Lamar in the Pork 'n' Beans Projects a few months prior, and he was still sporting a limp from it.

"Hey, man, go 'head on with that shit," Darrell said as looked around nervously to see if anyone was in the area to witness any act of police aggression. "Me and my boy ain't doing nothin' but sitting on my grandmomma's porch chillin'. We ain't have nothin' to do with what happened next door."

"What are you talking about?" Russell asked. "All I was going to do was ask if you guys liked basketball."

"Why? What's it to you?"

"Well it just so happens I have two lower bowl tickets to game one of the Finals. I don't care much for the game. I was gonna give them to one of the detectives in my precinct, but if you guys are interested—"

Darrell's eyes widened. "Hell yeah, we interested! Where they at?"

"Check it. I have to be there in person to pick up the

tickets from will-call on game night, but I'll give you my card so we can meet up right before the game. All you have to do is give me and my partner here a little information about Cooper."

"I don't know, D," Rodney said. "A cop with seats like that to game one? Sounds like some bullshit to me."

Darrell nodded. "How I know you ain't tryin' to run some game on me or somethin'?"

"You don't. You can either trust he has those tickets or you can stay home and watch it on television," the lady cop said. "But it's gonna be the biggest game of the year, and you know how Steven Lords plays during big games. It may be a career night for him."

"Aye, yo, you know, 'The Lord' gon' clown in that game," Rodney said. "All you see on TV is people talking 'bout the girl that got killed at that hotel Jimmy worked at. Skip, Wilbon, Stephen A., and all of them been talking 'bout how that's gonna be a distraction and mess The Lord all up."

"That's exactly why we're here, actually. Now, do you guys want these tickets or not?"

Darrell sat back in his chair as he watched the cop reach into his jacket pocket. Cops usually couldn't be trusted, but what kind of cop bribed people with basketball tickets anyway?

Darrell took the card Russell handed him and scanned it before handing it over to Rodney. "Okay, Detective Russell

Howard, I want the tickets," Darrell said. "This better not be no hustle or nothing. What you want to know?"

"Did either of you guys see anything suspicious over there the past few nights?" Sydney asked. "Cooper's door-jamb was busted, so I'm wondering if maybe you heard someone kicking in the door."

"Man, that door's been kicked for about a week," Rodney replied. "People just used the backdoor."

Darrell shook his head. "Jimmy always had people running in and out of that house all times of night. It's been the same deal up until about two nights ago, when people stopped coming around."

"What do you think was he doing over there? With all that traffic, I mean?"

"I know he was selling the shit he stole from people at that hotel," Darrell said.

"Hell yeah. While he was selling dope up out of that place, dude was robbing them people, man," Rodney added. "He took watches, necklaces, all types of shit, and then he'd sell it to the niggas in the neighborhood."

"Well that solves that mystery. When I talked to hotel security they said they'd had some thefts. Now we know who was doing it," Russell said. "Is there anything else you can tell me? Did he have any enemies? Do you know if he'd pissed anyone off lately?"

"I heard he got into it with some thugs from Carol City," Rodney said. "They might have popped his ass."

"Did you guys hear any gunshots or anything?" the lady asked.

"Nope," Darrell replied. "All I know is I was outside trying to holla at this girl and some dude pulled up and went up in there."

"You think you could identify the person? Or maybe the car?"

"It was dark and I was just minding my own business with my attentions elsewhere," Darrell said.

Rodney chuckled as he and Darrell exchanged a fist bump. "All I can tell you was the car I saw was a dark blue Caddy with gold rims."

"Well that's something," Russell said. "I appreciate the help. I'm going to be next door for a while. If you think of anything else, come on over and talk to me."

"Oh we gon' be talking to you!" Rodney said. "Right . . . at will-call tomorrow night."

Russell sighed as he and Sydney headed back to Cooper's place. A careful inspection of the house turned up few clues as to what had happened, other than the obvious. To make matters worse, as she had at Starbucks, Sydney had provided another credible lead. At least she had helped with this one. But there was no way those kids would've told her anything if it wasn't for those basketball tickets.

"So what did you have to show me?" Sydney asked.

"I found where Cooper was hiding some of the drugs and the stuff he stole from the hotel," Russell said. "In a hollowed-out dictionary in his bedroom, if you can believe that."

"So that corroborates the boy's story and blows a breaking and entering theory out of the water. Who's going to kill him and rob him but leave the valuable stuff behind?"

"Somebody who wasn't looking for drugs or watches," Russell said.

Sydney scoffed. "The boys did say he was beefing with some guys. Maybe that's what this is. We don't know if it's related to that laptop or anything else having to do with Lords."

Russell shook his head. "This doesn't sound like some Carol City beef. There were two bottles of Budweiser on the coffee table. I'm guessing Cooper was entertaining whoever came to see him," Russell said. "Probably the arranged pick-up for Tibbs's computer and then the tie-up of a loose end."

Russell looked up to see the CSI van and a couple of marked patrol cars approaching. He was glad to see they'd sent Davis again.

"You'll find the victim in the fridge," Russell said, after introducing Sydney. "I'll need your boys to tape off this block and two more blocks behind it."

"You know my team is nothing if not thorough. If there's something there, we'll find it," Davis said. "By the way, I got that message you left on my desk this morning. Thanks for those tickets. Consider our bet squared. My kid's gonna be pumped when I tell him the news."

"Oh yeah about that . . . I'm afraid I had to use those tickets to bribe some information out of some kids next door. But you know you didn't win that bet anyway."

"So what's the plan now, Detective?" Sydney said, with an exaggerated look of disinterest at their banter.

"With those uniforms' help, we're going to talk to everybody within a three-block radius," Russell replied. "Somebody around here had to have seen something."

CHAPTER 28

Coach Hollis patted his full belly and smiled at Steven as the two men sat on patio chairs around the swimming pool looking out at the inlet. Inviting Steven over for dinner—just the two of them, away from all the pressures of the game and news media—had been a good idea. And the weather couldn't have been more cooperative.

Hollis didn't get to entertain much, and when he did it was rarely one-on-one with his players. But he and Steven had always gotten along and after that incident in practice the previous day, Hollis figured it was as good a time as any to invite him over and see where his head was.

With dinner finished, Hollis grabbed a couple of Coronas from the patio fridge. "So, are you ready to tip it up?" He popped the caps off the beers and handed one to Steven. "You all set to go?"

Steven smiled. "Hell yeah I'm ready, Coach. After everything that's gone down the last few days I really can't wait to get back on the court and get people talking about something besides my personal life, you know?"

"Good. I think that's a great way to look at it."

"How about you, Coach? You feeling all right about our chances?"

Hollis smiled. It was always good to see the players confident, but as a coach there were too many other variables to consider. But he did feel like it was their time, as long as Steven could stay focused and be on his A-game. But there was no need to pressure Steven. He knew all too well what was at stake.

Both men took long drinks of their beers as they listened to the faint sounds of calypso music playing nearby. Steven closed his eyes and bobbed his head gently to the rhythm.

Coach Hollis took another swallow of beer as he watched Steven's head sway back and forth. "Can I ask you something?" he asked.

"Sure, Coach, anything. You know that."

Coach hesitated. He took a long swig of beer and asked, "I know this week's been crazy for you. But how are Karen and Cassidy holding up through all this?"

Steven stopped swaying. He looked down at his bottle and said, "I'll know more when I see them tomorrow, but I think they're doing okay. At least as good as can be expected, under the circumstances."

Hollis nodded.

"I'm doing this interview tomorrow to finally let the people hear from me directly that I didn't have anything to do with Michelle's murder. I wouldn't blame Karen one bit for not joining me for it, but as of right now it looks like she's going to."

"Was that your idea? To do it the day before the Finals?"

"Nah, Allen's idea," Steven said. "I guess he's hoping it can turn public opinion back my way before we get back on the court. I don't know."

"Well it sounds like a decent plan to me. Plus, you've got Karen on board so that should help."

"Allen got Karen involved, not me," Steven said. "She won't even talk to me, if you want to know the truth. And maybe that's a good thing because I wouldn't know what to say to her if she did."

Hollis thought for a minute before answering. "Well, don't kid yourself. She isn't coming back because your agent asked her to, that's for sure. You'd better believe she has her own reasons for coming back."

"That's what scares me," Steven said. "What if she's had it? What if she's coming home to tell me it's over?"

Hollis couldn't tell what to make of Steven's tone. He sounded worried by the prospect of divorce but not exactly heartbroken. Maybe he was already trying to separate himself emotionally and mask the pain. It wasn't Hollis's place to ask, but he privately wondered how good a fit Karen was as a life partner for Steven.

"That's a possibility," Hollis said, relieved that Steven seemed comfortable with the conversation. "But there's no sense in worrying about that unless it happens. In the meantime, it sounds like a good time to reevaluate your whole situation."

"That's all I've been doing the past few days, Coach!" Steven put his beer on the ground and sat up in his chair. "It's really hard to believe just how bad I messed up."

"You made some mistakes, sure, but you're human just like the rest of us," Hollis said. "You're what, twenty-six years old? You're still a young man. Don't let this define who you are. Besides, over time people will forget all this. That's the great thing about playing professional sports. Championships have absolved more sins than the Pope."

"That's what people have been saying. I need to put all this behind me, play my game, and everything will be okay," Steven said. "But it's been hard sitting on the sidelines and letting other people take care of all this. It's been hell, man . . . I can't go anywhere or do anything or even make a single statement about my own guilt or innocence without having to consult with someone first. It's like I'm trapped by all my fame and celebrity."

"Fame is a prison of your own design, son," Hollis said.

"Well, then I guess I've been doing time since high

school," Steven gazed out at the water. "It wasn't always that way, though. This one time back in high school I remember being at this party standing against the wall by myself not knowing a soul.

"Not even Eddie?" Hollis said. "Seems like he's always been around."

Steven smiled. "Oh yeah, Eddie was there, but he was hopped up on something and busy trying to get up on some of the girls. He and his boys weren't paying any attention to me, and I was standing there like an idiot, feeling very self-conscious, you know?"

"Sure do," Hollis said. "No one likes to feel like the odd man out at a party."

"Well, there I was just wanting to get the hell out of there when I noticed these girls looking at me and giggling. There was nobody standing next to me, so I figured they had to be looking at me, right? So part of me is psyched because I'm getting these looks and part of me is scared shitless because I don't have a clue what to say or how to act even."

"So what'd you do?"

"Man, I think I almost pissed myself I was so nervous," Steven said. "The only girl who had ever paid attention to me was Michelle, and honestly, I had no idea how we even got together. But there I was, this awkward kid holding up the wall and I had these really cute girls pointing and staring at me."

"So what happened?"

"It turned out I didn't have to do a thing. They knew my name, where I played ball, my jersey number—they even knew I was dating Michelle. Once word got around the party who I was, I didn't have to lift a finger to get a rap. All that night I had all these girls coming up to me and asking me to dance and giving me their phone numbers." Steven smiled wistfully and shook his head. "From that moment on things kinda changed for me."

Hollis nodded. "Not bad. From a shy kid to a ladies' man overnight."

"Kinda. Now that I think about it, I'm guessing Eddie might've said something about who I was to kind of get the ball rolling. But that was just the beginning. My high school team kicked some serious ass that year, and after word got around that scouts had been watching the games and talking about this new kid from Suncoast High, people really started to take notice.

"It wasn't long before I felt like something of a celebrity. I had people coming at me left and right asking for pictures, autographs—even my shoes—and it's been that way ever since. One minute I'm reading comic books and watching *Star Wars* movies; the next minute everyone wants a piece of me."

"No doubt about it—this game changes you if you don't have a strong sense of who you are," Hollis said. "Once you get caught up in the madness it's easy to lose yourself. You have to stay grounded."

"That's the one reason why I've always liked having Eddie around. He's one guy who can help me keep it real."

"Yeah, I guess," Hollis said, trying to keep disapproval out of his voice. Eddie was probably an okay guy at heart, but his gangsta routine worried Hollis sometimes.

"It's good to stay in touch with your roots," Hollis said. "But remember money and celebrity can spill over to those around you and warp their sense of reality, too. You have to keep it together for you and your family."

"Coach, you played the game. You were in the league. How did you handle it all?"

Coach Hollis rolled his eyes. "When I played it was a different time, but that doesn't mean I didn't make some of the same mistakes you did."

"Really?" Steve cocked his head. "You mean like . . ."

Hollis put his beer down and looked at Steven. "This doesn't leave this patio, all right? I didn't have half the talent you have, but whatever I had was enough to get me noticed. I was a happily married man and probably too young and naive to know any better, just like you. But when I signed with Chicago, it didn't take more than a few weeks for me to mess up and do something really stupid once people started recognizing me and the opportunities started coming."

"Opportunities," Steve said. "That's just it, isn't it? I get so tired of people moralizing about cheating on your wife. They're right of course, but it's a bit different when you have beautiful women coming up to you all the time."

268 | PERSONAL FOUL

"It is," Hollis said. "It was fine for a while, but then one night me and my wife had a big fight before a game. I went out afterward to celebrate with some of my teammates, and sure enough this woman started looking at me from across the bar like she knew exactly what she wanted."

"I know those looks, Coach."

The thing is, after you give into it once—and I did that night—it gets hard to stop. Next thing you know I was out there screwing around regularly, and it was only a matter of time before I got someone. You know as well as I do that's a hard pill for a woman to swallow. Sometimes they can overlook the cheating. But when you bring a child into it, it can get messy."

"That's another thing that's got me twisted," Steven said. "When Michelle first told me she was pregnant, I was completely thrown. I didn't know what to do. An abortion seemed like . . ."

Hollis saw an expression in Steven's face like he'd never seen before.

"I'm sure you made the best decision for you and your family," Hollis said softly.

"That's what I kept telling myself," Steven said. "But the truth is I made a decision based on what I thought would be convenient. I told Allen about it and he thought Michelle's baby could be bad for my future marketability. So he told me she had to get an abortion."

Steven shook his head reflectively and let out a long sigh.

"I never gave any thought to the child she lost when I was away at school. That child probably meant the world to her, and I treated the whole situation like an inconvenience."

"You live and you learn," Hollis said. "I was lucky the girl I got pregnant didn't wanna make any waves. She just wanted me to support Natalie and I did. It cost me my first wife, but I did what I had to do."

"That's what I was trying to do before, you know?" Steven said. "I mean lately I've been thinking about that child. The cards will fall where they may with Karen, and I can't blame her if she does leave. But I just love Cassidy to death, and I can't imagine life without her. And here I was trying to deny Michelle that same pleasure—of being a mother—and I realized that wasn't right . . ."

Hollis waited, but Steven said nothing further.

"Well you know Karen a lot better than I do, but I'm guessing if Michelle would've had that child you'd certainly be headed for divorce court."

"Can't argue with you there, Coach."

"So you may not have made the right choices, but at least you were trying to protect something valuable with the wrong one. Does that make any sense?"

Steven looked at him, then thought for a moment and grinned. "You know, it does!"

Hollis smiled back at him and then got up and headed over to his stereo. He picked out a favorite Coltrane CD, grabbed two more cold beers, and sat next to Steven.

They sat for a while longer, not talking much, sipping their beers and enjoying the salty night air.

CHAPTER 29

Murcielago Hotel, 9:30 p.m.

Russell returned to the Murcielago with waning hopes that his case could be salvaged. "Sorry to bother you again," he asked the night manager, "but have you or any of your staff recalled any new details about the night Michelle Tibbs was killed?"

"Not to my knowledge, Detective. No one has mentioned anything to me. And everyone here has been instructed to inform either the police or Miss Sydney Farrell if they do think of something."

Russell's tilted his head and squinted. "Sydney? Who told you to contact Sydney Farrell?"

"We got a phone call from the Deputy Chief of Police the day she checked in—"

"Wait—she's a guest of this hotel?"

"That's right. When she arrived, we were told she'd be assisting with the investigation and we should treat her the same as we would any other detective in regard to the case. Would you like me to call her room for you?"

Russell nodded. "Yeah, that'd be great."

He walked to a sitting area where he noticed a *Sports Illustrated* with Steven Lords on the cover and the caption "The Lord Be Praised." He picked up the magazine, thumbed through the pages, then tossed the magazine face down on the table. *What a joke!*

He was about to sit when he saw Sydney get off the elevator. Her tan pants hugged her slender contours and her waist-length white camisole revealed a glimpse of her midriff. She really wasn't hard on the eyes.

"Hey, Russell, what are you doing here?"

"I should be asking you the same question. I didn't realize you were staying at the Murcielago," Russell said. "Are the taxpayers of Miami footing the bill for your visit?"

"My travel arrangements are well taken care of, thank you very much. But you didn't answer my question."

"I stopped by to talk to the night crew again."

"Dead end, I'm guessing?"

"Pretty much."

"Same here, I'm afraid. I did some asking around after our little adventure this afternoon. Talked to a few bellhops and clerks when I got back and their stories were pretty much the same."

"That's too bad," Russell said, racking his brain to figure out if there was anyone else to talk to. The manager needed to know about what happened to Cooper, but not right away.

"Listen, I know what it feels like to have a case get away from you," Sydney said, eyeing him sympathetically. "Why don't you let me buy you drink."

The couple walked into a nearby tavern and took a seat at the bar. After the bartender took their orders, Russell sat back and massaged his temples, hoping to soothe his throbbing head. That day had produced more questions than answers. The biggest question was: Where did the investigation need to go, now that it was back at square one? The bartender placed their drinks and a couple of glasses of water in front of them. Russell grabbed his drink. Nothing like a little Jack Daniels to help you to relax. He looked at Sydney as he held up the glass and downed its contents.

"You're drinking like a cop with a lot on his mind," Sydney said. "Dad used to drink a few Miller High Lifes when he had a bad day on the job."

He motioned the bartender for another before answering. "Getting dealt a 3–7 to start a hand of Texas hold 'em is a bad day. I'm on the verge of blowing the biggest case of my short career."

"So you *are* a bit of a gambler?" Sydney said, as if affirming something she'd heard.

"Not really," he said. "I just like to play the odds sometimes. Compete against chance and see what happens."

"You ever bet on sports?"

"Used to. Not in years though."

"Let me guess—too many losses?"

"More like one big loss, but I don't care to talk about it." Russell said as the bartender brought him his second drink. He took a big swallow and savored the burn.

"I was thinking about it last night and how I'll probably take a transfer if this thing blows up in my face." Another drink materialized, and he snatched it up and swallowed it down. "It'll beat getting an OTH."

Sydney looked puzzled. "OTH? Other than honorable discharge? You were in the military?"

"Army . . . Fort Benning, Georgia."

She leaned toward him with a look of surprise but said nothing.

"That's right," Russell said, nodding. "Extenuating circumstances led me to enlist, but it really wasn't a good fit."

"How long did you serve?"

"Eighteen months. I won't bore you with the details, but I got discharged."

"Fair enough," Sydney said. She held up her drink and put a hand on his arm. "Here's to being all you can be, right?"

"Whatever." Russell said, opting for a sip from the glass of water.

"So what made you choose police work, anyhow?"

"I don't know. After I left the Army, I needed to find a job and the police department was hiring, so I figured why not? Thought my service record would keep me out, but it didn't and here I am."

Russell reached for the bowl of peanuts and grabbed a handful. He threw his head back, poured a few into his mouth, and looked at Sydney, who was still nursing her first drink. "So what about you?" Russell asked. "What's your story?"

"Not much to tell really. My dad was a cop in Buffalo, so I guess I followed in his footsteps."

"Did he push you into law enforcement?" Russell said. "I can't see somebody like you just wanting to join the FBI out of the blue."

"What's that supposed to mean, 'somebody like me'?"

"No offense, but you aren't too hard to look at. You could've been a model or something. Why the hell'd you want to be a cop?"

She smiled, eyes almost twinkling, but then her face became serious.

"Just watching my dad. He could size people up and know off the bat whether or not they were lying to him. He was always aware of everything and everyone, anyplace he went. I thought that was so cool."

Sydney took another dainty sip of her drink and then glared at him. "Beside, who says a good-looking woman can't kick a little ass sometimes?"

"You're right. You're absolutely right," Russell said. "I bet your dad's very proud."

Sydney nodded and took another sip. "What about your folks?" she asked. "Were they military as well?"

Russell rolled his eyes. "Hardly. My dad's idea of work was beating against the spread. Sometimes Mom had to get a second job to make ends meet because Dad was known to put his money on long shots that usually didn't pan out."

"I'm guessing you two must be a lot alike," Sydney said. "I mean, going after Lords for this murder is really a long shot. I must admit, not a lot of cops would even want to do that."

"Dad always said, 'scared money don't make money.' Besides, everything points to Lords and I still like him for it. If only I could make this case stick."

"Well time's winding up, Russell, and you don't have many options left," she said. "I know it's the hardest thing to do, but maybe it's time to cut bait and work a new angle."

Russell nodded as he stared down at the bar. She was right. Sometimes you had to take your lumps and move on. It had been a long day of disappointments and disagreements, but in the end maybe Sydney wasn't so bad.

"Russell, I think we may have gotten off on the wrong foot today," Sydney said.

"Yeah, I think so too. But how would you feel if someone was sent in to babysit you and tell you how to handle your investigation?"

"Good point. I guess I may have come on a little strong, and I'm sorry about that. So how about we start fresh? I'll apologize for whatever I said that may have offended you, and you'll forget everything you were thinking about me?"

Russell nodded. "I think a fresh start is exactly what's needed," he said as he got off his stool.

"Where are you going?"

"I think I'll head over to the station and take another look at my reports and some of the crime scene photos. There has to more to this murder than what's already come out. There just has to be. Maybe I overlooked something."

"So you still like Lords for it?"

"There's too much on the line and too much at stake for him not to be involved. My gut tells me there's something there. Call it a long shot."

"You really are your father's son, Russell."

Russell smiled. "Scared money don't make money."

CHAPTER 30

Miami-Dade Police Headquarters, 8:24 a.m.

"Hey, Russell, wake up!" Art Morales said as he pounded his fist on Russell's desk. "What'd you do, pull some kind of all-nighter?"

Russell slowly opened his eyes, lifted his head from his desk, and wiped off the drool that had leaked out of the corner of his mouth. "As a matter of fact I did. Just going over everything, hoping to find something I might've missed."

"Any luck?"

"Hardly. That security guy Cooper getting killed messed me up big time."

Morales nudged a stack of folders to the side and sat on the corner of Russell's desk. "So that lead fizzled?" he asked. "Without a name or another lead, what's your next move?"

Russell yawned and stretched his arms. That's what he'd been asking himself all night.

"All I'm saying, Junior, is maybe it's time to look at other possible suspects," Morales said. "Maybe you need to accept that someone else could've killed this woman."

"You sound like Sydney, you know that?" Russell said. "Tibbs was killed to shut her up and protect Lords. Yesterday, Owens told us she was writing some sort of book that could take him down pretty hard. Owens also said he'd been chatting online with Tibbs before she was killed, and in all her personal things I didn't find a computer. So whoever killed her probably took it with them. If that's the case, then that missing surveillance footage may be my only link finding out who did it!"

"Okay, Junior, calm down. I'm just trying to open you up to some other possibilities."

"I don't understand why it's so hard to believe Lords could've killed Tibbs. He has a motive; he had the opportunity. What is it you guys aren't seeing?"

Morales leaned closer to Russell. "I understand where you're coming from, Junior, but you need to realize something."

"Oh yeah, what's that?"

"How this looks to your superiors. For whatever reason, you've been gunning for Steven Lords since the get-go. You've been grasping at straws long enough now, and it's high time you start looking someplace else. Stick with this purely circumstantial line of thinking and you'll look like someone with an ax to grind. Not a detective."

Russell nodded as Morales stood from the desk. It was just after 8:30, and there wasn't much time left on that forty-eight-hour deadline the chief had given. He was going to want an account of how the investigation was going. Russell held his face in his palms. It was gonna be tough to tell Chief Cavanaugh that as far as proving Lords to be the killer, the last two days had been a total waste of time.

"Why don't you go to the break room and get yourself a cup of coffee? Maybe it'll take some of the edge off," Morales said. "You look like hell, by the way."

The galley area was quiet as Russell poured himself a cup of coffee. He added a few spoonfuls of sugar and stirred it before taking a sip and then dumping it right down the sink, his stomach recoiling from the acidity. When he heard a breaking news alert, he looked up at TV mounted on the wall.

"With game one scheduled to begin tomorrow in Miami, Steven Lords will finally break his silence by conducting an interview scheduled to air this evening," the reporter said. "I'm standing outside of Steven Lords's Miami Beach home, where he'll be doing the interview and is expected to answer questions about the allegations levied against him as well as the controversy that's been surrounding him."

Russell scoffed at the report. It was no coincidence he was

holding a press conference today. His people were probably expecting him to walk unscathed away from this situation. They'd probably spin the story some way to make him look sympathetic, like some hapless victim.

After returning to his desk, Russell grabbed the deck of cards out of his drawer and started shuffling them. Maybe it was finally time to work on a new theory of the crime.

"What's with the cards, Russell?" Sydney asked as she approached his desk, holding two manila envelopes, smiling broadly, and looking fresh as a spring daisy.

Russell put the cards down on his desk. "Helps me think sometimes," he replied. "I've been going over reports all night, and frankly, I'm absolutely nowhere."

Sydney pulled up a chair next to him. "I'm sorry to hear that. I guess it won't help to tell you I saw Chief Cavanaugh on my way up here. My guess is he's gonna be looking to get an update on your case."

"I wish I could say I wasn't expecting him," Russell sighed and looked at the envelopes Sydney put on his desk. "What are those?"

"A couple of envelopes a girl at the front desk asked me to give you," Sydney picked up the envelopes and handed them to Russell. "One looks like the coroner's report on Tibbs. Not sure about the other, but it feels padded to me."

Russell tossed the coroner's envelope aside and ripped open the padded one. "It's the copy of Owens's show I asked for," he said as he opened the DVD case.

"Why did you want that? What do you think you'll be able to get from it?"

"Since the hotel's security cameras have blind spots in the front entrance, Owens had the only unobstructed view of that area. I wanted a closer look at the video he shot to see if there's anything significant."

"Sounds like a long shot."

"Welcome to my world," he said with a grin.

He opened the CD tray on the desktop computer and loaded the disk. He sat back and watched Owens on the show's set with a coffee table in front of him and a monitor behind him.

"Hey, Pete, how much of this video do you want us to air?"

"Gimme at least the first minute or so and then get me as tight on Lords as you can before you freeze frame."

"Okay. I'm gonna load it up and let it roll on the monitor behind you. I have it on the AVID, so when you want to stop it, give a holler and I'll mark it."

Owens walked over to the large monitor and watched as the Murcielago Hotel doors opened and Steven Lords rushed out. Lords looked around and paced on the walkway while fans approached. He stopped to sign a few autographs, still desperately looking around.

"Okay, let's stop it right there and get me as tight on Lords's face as you can get it. I want people to be able to see it's him," Owens said as he walked away from the screen.

"Got it. I'll cue it up for the final segment."

"Sounds good," Owens said. When he heard the argument he'd had with a parking lot attendant, Owens turned around to see the video still playing.

"Are you sure you've got it? The video's still running. There's nothing else we need on here."

"Yeah, I got it marked up here. Don't worry you're dealing with the best production staff in television. We don't make mistakes. This broadcast will have everyone talking. I can guarantee that."

Russell leaned closer to the computer monitor. By that point, Owens had laid down his camera as he got out of his car, so the footage was slanted. He looked at Sydney with a smile. "This must be some footage that didn't get aired on the show. And we may still be in the game after all."

Russell drummed his fingers on the desktop as he stared at the screen.

"Hey, Russell, brass wants to see you two in the conference room," Morales shouted.

Sydney looked up and nodded. "Come on, Russell, it's time."

Russell didn't budge. He watched Steven pace the sidewalk as people kept trying to approach him. Russell's eyes stayed trained on every detail and every face he saw in the video.

"Russell, they're waiting," Sydney said.

He tapped his fingers faster as he watched members of hotel security come out to usher guests into the hotel and away from Lords. *There must be something here. Why did Lords keep looking around like that?* Russell watched as Lords stood still and checked his watch. *He's waiting for something. What is he waiting for?*

"Give it up. Your case is done. It's time to move on," Sydney said. "You need to face the facts. Steven Lords—"

"Had *help* to kill Michelle Tibbs," Russell said. He clicked his mouse to rewind the video. "Lords didn't do it alone."

"What are you talking about? What do you mean he had help?"

Russell smiled as he replayed the video. "See for yourself."

They both watched Lords pace the sidewalk. "You see how he keeps looking around?" Russell said. "He's looking for something, or better yet, someone."

"Yeah, but how—"

"Wait for it."

Lords checked his watch again and continued pacing. Onlookers gawked and snapped pictures of him as he waited until a silver Aston Martin pulled up alongside the curb. Steven opened the door and got in, and the car sped off into the night.

"Did you see that?" Russell asked. "Did you see what he just did? He got into the *passenger* seat of his own car. That means Lords wasn't alone in the hotel that night. I bet you anything that whoever drove him there also accompanied him to Tibbs's suite."

Sydney sat slack jawed. Her eyes rolled as she rubbed

the back of her neck. "Maybe, but you can't know that for sure. And this gives us no idea who was driving the car. With those tinted windows rolled up, we never get a look at the guy."

Russell sat back and ran his fingers through his hair. He had a guess, but there had to be a way to positively ID Lords's driver. Maybe there had been other eyes in the sky outside in the parking lot that could help reveal Lords's accomplice. With a little luck, maybe the accomplice had been holding a laptop when he got into the car.

"What are you doing, Russell?" Sydney said. "We've got the chief waiting and we're already late!"

"Chief can wait a little longer," Russell said as he pecked away at the keyboard. "I'm looking up the number to the hotel. I know somebody who works there who may be able to help us identify the wheelman."

Russell tucked the phone between his ear and his shoulder while he pressed numbers on the keypad to bypass all the hotel's automated messages. "I need to speak to Chris in security, please."

"I'm sorry, but Chris isn't in at the moment. Would you like his voicemail?"

Russell slammed his fist onto the desk.

"We really need to go," Sydney pleaded. "They're waiting."

Russell wrinkled his brow and he held up his index finger. Her nagging wasn't helping anything move any faster.

"Listen, I really need to speak to someone in security," Russell said. "Is anyone available?"

Chris picked a hell of a day to be M.I.A. Russell looked at Sydney, who had already gotten out of her seat and was leaning against his desk, pointing at her watch. He shrugged as he waited on hold.

"This is Luis—how can I help you?"

"Listen, do you have security cameras out in the parking lot?

"Yeah, a few. Why? Who is this?"

"My name's Detective Howard, and I need you to do me a favor," Russell said. "I'm investigating the Tibbs murder, and I need you to check the surveillance videos from three nights ago between one and three in the morning. You're looking for a silver Aston Martin. I'm looking for footage of whoever was driving that car."

"I'm about to walk out the door, so what I'll do is leave a note for the guy on next shift to look that up for you. Do you have a number where he can reach you?"

Russell shook his head. Apparently Luis did not understand the gravity of the situation.

"Hey, Junior, what's wrong with you?" Morales asked as he approached Russell's desk. "They're waiting for you in the conference room. What the hell are you doing?"

Russell waved him off. "I don't have time to wait, Luis. I need you to do this for me right now."

"I'd like to help you, but they're hell on overtime around here. I'm a minute late from punching out, I get my ass chewed out," Luis said. "The next shift starts in just a few minutes. I'll have someone call you."

"Luis, are you a basketball fan?" Russell asked as he ran his fingers through his hair. "Are you a Steven Lords fan?"

"Yeah, man! Who isn't?"

"Well then you know what he's up against, and right now you're the only guy who can help him," Russell said. "If you can't do what I'm asking you to do, then Lords may be in some serious trouble—he could face serious prison time. So do you think you can take a few minutes to help him out?"

"Okay, I'll see what I can do. It may take me a little while, though," Luis said. "Do you have a number or something where I can reach you?"

Russell gave Luis the number. "I'm running late for a meeting, but Sydney Farrell will be waiting for your call," Russell said as he nodded at Sydney. "I really need you to get back to me within the next ten minutes,"

"I'll do my best," Luis said. "Because there ain't no way 'The Lord' killed that girl!"

Russell rushed through the hallway toward the conference room. Chief Cavanaugh had been waiting for almost fifteen minutes and was sure to be as hot as fish grease, but at least now Russell had something to go on.

An Aston Martin was too expensive to let anyone drive around, so Lords had to have been with someone he trusted and someone who could stand to lose a lot if Tibbs went public with her pregnancy. Plus, if that book she was writing would've found the light of day, then Lords's earning power would've taken a hit. But at the end of the day, how many people would've been affected enough to be an accessory to murder?

It had to be Warner, the agent. The answer had been there the whole time. Nobody other than Lords had as much on the line as that guy did. It explained why he wanted to sit in on the interview, why he'd helped Lords cover it up. It all made sense. Only nobody had counted on Owens being in the parking lot recording them. All that was left was convincing the chief, and without an ID of Lords's driver, that wouldn't be easy.

Russell slowly opened the conference room door. He was relieved to not see the panel of high-ranking officials he'd originally thought would be there, but he shook his head when he saw the man seated at the head of the table.

"You're late, Detective Howard. I don't like to be kept waiting," Deputy Chief Garcia said.

"Sorry for the delay," Russell said. "I thought Chief Cavanaugh was meeting me."

"The chief had a last-minute meeting with the mayor. But I decided to stay and meet with you and Miss Farrell. Where is she, by the way?"

"Actually, that's part of the reason why I'm late. There's been a last-minute break."

As Russell sat and explained this latest discovery, he noticed Garcia tapping his index finger on the table with no other reaction to anything he said. The guy could clean up at a poker table.

"So let me see if I got this right. You believe Mr. Lords's agent may have been involved with the murder?"

"I believe Lords had an accomplice and—"

"And you don't have corroborating evidence as to who this accomplice is?"

"Not at the moment, but I'm expecting hotel security to call any minute with whatever footage they have that will help ID the guy."

"And if that doesn't pan out, then what?"

"I was thinking of going to talk to his agent," Russell said. "I want to ask him—"

"Out of the question," Deputy Chief Garcia said. "Stay away from Lords and his agent."

Russell's shook his head. "With all due respect, I think speaking with his agent has to be our next move. He may have been involved with the murder and the cover-up. We can't just let this go!"

"*May have been* are the key words. You don't know anything at this point, and I'm not going to let you test your theory by harassing those people. Unless you get something concrete, stay away from Lords and his agent. That's an order, Detective."

Russell was biting his lip as he stared across the room.

If Chief Cavanaugh were there he wouldn't see a problem with talking to Lords or his people a second time, so what was the deal with this guy?

"If there's nothing else, we'll conclude this meeting," Deputy Chief Garcia said. "But a word to the wise? Start looking for a new suspect. The Steven Lords lead is dead in the water and you've wasted too much time chasing it. If I were you, I'd—"

"I'm sorry I'm late," Sydney said as she walked into the conference room. Her timing couldn't have been better, and judging by the smile on her face she had something that might just save the day.

"Miss Farrell, I'm happy you could join us," Garcia said. He looked down at the folder she carried. "I take it you have something relevant to share."

Sydney laid the folder on the table. "Luis from the hotel came through with a picture of the guy who was driving Lords's car," she said as she took out the picture. "I scanned the image but it's likely to be awhile before we'll know if we can get a positive ID."

Russell looked at Deputy Chief Garcia. "I think I found my new suspect," he said. "Is this concrete enough to warrant another questioning?"

"Against my better judgment, I'm going to give you another twenty-four hours to make this stick. By this time tomorrow, if you haven't built your case, then it's over," Deputy Chief Garcia said. "One other thing. If the mayor's

office gets another call about your conduct during questioning, I promise you I'll have your badge."

CHAPTER 31

"Everything look okay, Mr. Warner?"

Allen shook his head at the image on one of the monitors sitting on a table in the Lordses' living room. The lighting wasn't right at all, and he was stunned anyone involved could have thought otherwise. *Fucking dolts!*

"Let's open up the blinds a bit, okay?" Allen said, keeping his voice light.

He watched the scene carefully as a production assistant adjusted the blinds until the room brightened and Steven's and Karen's faces got completely out of shadow. He checked the monitor again and after suggesting a few more tweaks to the lighting, finally gave the director a thumbs-up. The devil was in the details, and this interview was way too important to let any detail slide.

Next up was a checkup on Heather Shaw, who was looking at her compact and applying some extra lip gloss. Allen smiled as he watched her pucker and dab at her full, pouty lips like she was performing surgery. Her light pink suit projected a nice blend of femininity and professionalism, and her blouse was open at the neck, revealing a hint of cleavage but not enough to be inappropriate.

When she looked up from her compact, he smiled at her encouragingly. She really was the perfect choice to do this interview—a pretty face without any kind of agenda.

Word from his people was she'd gotten tired of a fluff lifestyle show she'd been doing and was looking for a taste of something more substantial. When he approached her with the idea of doing the interview, he immediately sensed she was desperate enough to play it exactly like he told her.

After she finished preening, Allen put a hand on her back and gave it a friendly pat. "So are you all set?"

"Yes, Mr. Warner, I'm ready to go. But I've got to say, I read over your questions this morning and this interview seems a little soft. More soft than I expected, I mean."

He looked at her but said nothing. He was in no mood for games.

"I don't mean any offense, but this seems more like the puff pieces I told you I'm trying to get away from."

"Listen," Allen said after pausing. "I'm giving you the

opportunity to advance your career here, but this is my interview and that means you need to play by my rules. And what that really means is putting your journalistic ego on hold and letting this be a chance for Steve to make a public statement."

"But I think these questions . . . they're so—"

Allen held up his index finger and wagged it as he sucked his teeth. "Don't think. Just do what I tell you," he said. "I've gotten dozens of other requests from everyone from Bob Costas to Oprah, begging me to do this interview. So if this isn't hardball enough to suit you, let me know and I'll get someone else."

"Good," he said, once she assured him that wouldn't be necessary. "Now fix your hair and then go ahead and take your mark," Allen replied as he winked. "We're almost ready to start."

KAREN SAT ON THE SOFA NEXT TO STEVEN, GETTING HER makeup touched up while the production staff hurried around tending to last-minute details. She tried not to scowl while the makeup brush fanned against her face, but her powder-blue-and-white striped sweater didn't seem to fit correctly. It seemed a lot looser than it used to be. But it matched Steve's light blue shirt, so Allen insisted she keep it on.

The makeup was stupid, the pinned-up hair was clichéd,

and whatever sentiment generated would be manufactured at best. The whole spectacle was almost as pathetic as the matching powder-blue outfits, she thought.

Steven put his arm around her and pulled her closer. He looked over at her with a big smile and kissed her cheek. As hard as she tried to flex the muscles necessary to return something that resembled a smile, the best she could do was raise the upper left corner of her mouth. This was all so pointless. And what the hell was he smiling about? Why was he sitting over there grinning like everything was okay? Was he really that stupid? Did he think this television interview would fix everything?

"Karen, I can't thank you enough for making the trip back with me," Allen said after the director got his crew in place. He stiffened when he saw her frown and put a hand on her shoulder. "Are you sure you're okay? Do you need anything? Can I get you a bottled water?"

"I'm fine," Karen replied. "I just want to get this over with."

"And it will be, soon," Allen said. "There's actually a question in there for you as well. When Heather asks you where you've been through this whole ordeal, just tell her—"

"I know my role, Allen. Let's just get through this, okay?"

ALLEN WAS FINISHING HIS INSPECTIONS WHEN HE SAW Eddie in the far corner of the room, talking to the director.

"Hey, wassup, Al? I was telling the director here that Stevie's left side is his—"

"What the hell do you think you're doing here?"

"I thought it'd be good to stop by and help out, you know what I'm sayin'? This here is pretty important for Stevie."

Allen shook his head. "We don't need your help," he said. "You've done enough. In fact, you've already done way more than you should have."

"But I think I can do more. You feel me?" Eddie said, smirking.

Allen shrugged. "What on earth are you talking about?"

"The other day me and Stevie was talking about that cop that had came and talked to y'all and I had a thought—"

"First time for everything," Allen said.

Eddie stiffened and stepped out from around the camera, motioning for Allen to follow him out of earshot of everyone else in the room. "You need to stop frontin' and think about how you feel about obstruction of justice and conspiracy-to-commit-murder charges?"

"I'm not following you," Allen whispered through gritted teeth. "I never lied about anything and I certainly never conspired with you to kill anyone. So why don't you just run along and—"

"Not this time," Eddie said, barely under his breath. "You're in this shit just as much as me, you know that? Your covering all this up makes you as guilty as an accessory. How do you think a conspiracy-to-commit-murder charge would look to those future draft prospects in the prison yard?"

Allen took a few deep breaths before responding. The situation was clearly escalating, and Eddie's angry demeanor was starting to attract attention. God only knew what the idiot was on.

Eddie nodded. "So how you like me now?" he said, smiling. "You know, you always talking to me like I'm stupid is gonna stop. I'm gonna have just as much pull around here as you do, and you better start respecting that!"

Allen nodded at the director apologetically and motioned to Eddie to keep his voice down. *Had he totally lost his fucking mind?* Eddie was standing there with his chest puffed out and a dumb look on his face.

"Do you really want to make that play?" Allen asked in a harsh whisper. "So you think you're ready to have a seat at the adult table?"

"Man, quit talking to me like I'm some damn kid," Eddie said. "You think you better than everyone else but you ain't. You ain't no different than the rest of them hustlers me and Stevie left back in the Wood."

His red, sunken eyes got wild as he looked at Allen. "And you know what? You can be gone just like them."

Allen glared back at him and smiled when Eddie broke eye contact. "Listen here, Eddie. I don't know what the hell you're on, but you need to calm down and get your ass out of here, okay? There are too many people and too many cameras around for this kind of nonsense."

"Nonsense?" Eddie said "You think I'm playin'? You keep disrespecting me like this and I swear—"

Allen leaned close, saw Eddie's defiant expression, and realized he needed to change tactics. "Did you hear what I just said? Now if you want to do this, whatever this is, then we'll have to do it later. But right now, just trust me and take my word for it that it'd be better if you left. You look like hell, for one thing. Why don't you go home and get some sleep?"

Eddie glanced at a mirror over the fireplace then looked back at Allen. He couldn't have liked what he saw.

"It's almost lunchtime over at Johnny Ray's. I think I'll head over there for some pork chops, but I'll be back later to settle this."

"Fine with me," Allen said. "But you may want to go to the bathroom and take care of that nosebleed first."

RUSSELL AND SYDNEY ARRIVED AT THE LORDSES' HOUSE amid the chaos of the production crew's final preparations. Russell's eyes shifted around the foyer as he tried to look at the faces of each person that walked in and out of the house. If this interview was as big a deal as the news reported, then Lords's driver was bound to be here somewhere.

"Excuse me," Russell said as he approached a harried girl who looked like some sort of production assistant. "I'm Detective Russell Howard and this is my partner Sydney Farrell. We're investigating the Murcielago murder and we need to talk to Steven Lords."

"I think they started doing the interview," she said. "I'm afraid you may have to wait a little bit."

"Is his agent available?" Sydney asked.

"I think so. If you wait here I can go and get him for you."

They both watched as the girl went into the living room. Sydney turned to Russell with an eyebrow raised. "So I'm your partner now?"

"Don't let it go to your head," Russell said. "Right now I need you to stay sharp."

CHAPTER 32

"Hello, I'm Heather Shaw and I'm at the home of basketball superstar Steven Lords. Unless you've been living under a rock the last seven years, you know Lords has been one of the hottest names in sports. His likeness graces the covers of magazines, billboards, and newspapers, but lately he's been drawing attention for a different reason. Three days ago a heinous murder took place at one of Miami's finest hotels. It's been alleged Steven Lords was having an affair with the victim, and we have unconfirmed reports that the Miami Police consider him a person of interest in her murder . . ."

Allen smiled at Heather from his perch outside the view of the camera and gave Steven and Karen an encouraging nod. As long as everybody stuck to the script, this would go fine.

Heather quickly finished her introductions and gave Steven the floor.

"Let me start by saying this has been a very trying situation," he said, "and it's high time I cleared the air on some of the allegations and rumors surrounding me and my family."

"Let's get right to the heart of the matter, then, and the question that's been on the minds of a lot of people," Heather said, eyes locked on Steven's the way Allen had coached her. "Did you kill Michelle Tibbs?"

Steven looked directly into the camera and shook his head emphatically. "Absolutely not. Michelle has been a close friend since high school. I'd never do anything to hurt her."

"Then why do the police think you did?"

Steven shrugged. "I'm not sure they do. I haven't been charged with anything, just interviewed because I was seen on camera at the Murcielago that night after the game. They asked me some questions. The rest is just overblown speculation."

"Okay, then. So why were you at the Murcielago?"

The interview was live, so there wasn't a thing Allen could do except shoot Heather a warning glance and hope Steven could handle the unscripted question.

Steven thought before answering. "That's exactly what the police wanted to know. I told them why I was there, and that was that.

"Listen," Steve said, after a quick glance at Allen. "The police have an important job to do, and I think it's very reasonable they came and talked to me after realizing I was at the hotel and I knew Michelle. But I had nothing to hide, and while they may not have any other suspects yet, I'm sure it's just a matter of time before they do."

Steve was ad-libbing but doing great. Now if Heather would just get back to the script.

"Let's hope so," she said. "So . . . how have you been coping with the storm of controversy that's surrounded you these past few days?"

Steven leaned forward while Karen sat stiffly.

"It's been really upsetting to be accused of something I didn't do, but I'm confident the truth will come to light. The real tragedy here is that a young woman and her unborn child lost their lives. Our thoughts and prayers go out to Michelle's family."

"So what was your relationship to Michelle Tibbs?"

"We've known each other since high school and stayed good friends through the years."

"Did that friendship ever lapse into something more intimate? Maybe an affair?"

Steven looked over at Karen as he clutched her hand tightly. He took a deep breath and said, "I've made some mistakes, Heather—I'm not going to lie to you. Mistakes that have hurt me and hurt my family. There's been a lot of conjecture and lies circulating, but I'm afraid this is one rumor that has some truth to it."

Heather looked at Karen sympathetically and then nodded encouragingly at Steven.

"So you did have an affair with Ms. Tibbs?"

Steven nodded. "I'm not proud of it, but yes." With another deep breath, he looked into Karen's eyes. "Baby, I'm so sorry for everything I put you through. Knowing I've hurt you has made me do some soul searching. But I promise you I'll spend the rest of my life making it up to you."

Karen's flat response kept the on-air apology from having the impact Allen would've liked, but at least Steven came off as sincere.

Heather smiled and waited a polite moment before turning her attention to Karen. "Karen, you've been noticeably absent from Steven's entourage the past few months. Is there any truth to the rumors that you and Steven are in the midst of a separation?"

"At this time there's no truth to that rumor," Karen said, voice tight with hostility. "I'm not sure it's anyone's business, but my father was just diagnosed with diabetes, and I've been spending a lot of time back home so I can help take care of him."

"How has all of this attention affected you?"

"It's been very stressful. Steven's right that he's made some mistakes that have hurt our family," Karen said. "But God is all about love and forgiveness, and I pray that over time I can forgive Steven."

***

ALLEN FELT A GENTLE TAP ON HIS SHOULDER AND TURNED to face a pretty young production assistant. "Sorry to bother you, Mr. Warner," she whispered. "But there are a couple of detectives waiting in the foyer to see you."

Allen rolled his eyes, anxious but not surprised. He'd prepared himself for this.

Russell paced the floor while waiting for Allen. Things might have not have gone so well last time, but this time would be different. There was no more speculation. He had to stay cool and not push too hard.

Russell turned when he heard Allen approach. "Good to see you again, Detective," Allen said, smiling as if this was some kind of social visit. "Is this lovely young lady your new partner?"

"This is Sydney Farrell. She's assisting me with the investigation," Russell said. Allen looked genuinely at ease this time. Either he was putting on one hell of a poker face or something had changed.

"It's nice to meet you, Syd. I'm Allen Warner, Steven Lords's agent."

"I know," Sydney said flatly. "We're actually here to follow up with Steven after reviewing some video shot outside the Murcielago—"

"Are you referring to the video Peter Owens used on his show a couple days ago?" Allen said. "We saw that too, of course. I didn't see anything out of the ordinary aside from my client leaving at that late hour, just like he told you."

Russell stepped forward, eyes locked on Allen's. "What you saw was the broadcast footage of that video. The uncut version showed Lords wasn't alone at the hotel that night."

"As a matter of fact, we have a picture of the man your client was with that night," Sydney said as she opened her leather portfolio. She took out a copy of the picture and handed it to Allen, whose eyes widened when he saw it.

"Why don't we take a little walk?" Allen said.

Russell and Sydney followed Allen into an expansive detached garage. Allen flipped a few switches, bringing the lights up on a row of polished exotic cars parked in precise formation. The garage itself was decked out in an upscale fifties motif with a black-and-white checkerboard floor, two vintage gas pumps, and a collection of tin signs from companies like Gulf, Sinclair, and Sunoco.

The whole setup seemed over the top, especially the giant neon sign at the back of the garage reading "Lord's Garage" over a lounge area complete with a Wurlitzer jukebox and soda fountain.

But for all his condescension, Russell had to admit the collection was impressive. Russell recognized most of the cars—Bugatti, McLaren, Lamborghini—but he stopped at the fender of a make he'd never seen before.

"That's a Mosler MT900S," Allen said proudly, as if he were the owner. "It's made in Riviera Beach. Steven saw it on the Speed Channel and had to have one."

"Nice ride, but I don't see the Aston Martin he drove to the hotel," Russell said.

"That's in the other garage. This here is for his more exotic cars, which don't get driven nearly as much, for obvious reasons."

Sydney shot Russell an impatient glare and then turned her gaze on Allen. "So did you bring us in here to show off Steven's toys or do you have something to tell us?"

"It's a simple question," Russell added, "Can you tell us who that man in this picture is?"

Allen barely glanced at the image before releasing an exaggerated sigh and looking at Russell. "That's what I was afraid of."

"Why's that?"

"Because that's Eddie Brown, a very close friend of Steven's and a personal assistant of sorts."

"So Eddie was with Steven at the hotel that night?" Russell asked. "Why didn't he say that when we talked the first time?"

"He probably would have, had you asked him about it, Detective. But if memory serves, it never came up."

Russell scoffed as he shook his head, although he was sure Allen was correct. "Okay, Mr. Warner. You seem to know the scoop, so why don't you tell me what was Eddie doing at the hotel with your client?"

"It's simple. He went to see if he could make Michelle change her mind about getting the abortion."

"You mean Eddie or Steven?"

"Both actually, but Eddie had another thing to talk to her about. Steven didn't know about it, and that's why Eddie had to sneak up to Michelle's room and talk to her in private."

"And what did he need to talk to her about?" Russell asked.

Russell waited while Allen paused for dramatic effect. "It was a book she'd written. An exposé, really, casting Steven in a very unflattering light."

Russell looked at Sydney before responding. He could almost see the wheels turning as she contemplated the significance that Lords's agent and best friend both knew about the book.

"Steven had no idea about any of that," Allen continued, as if reading his mind. "It's my job to keep things like that from distracting him and affecting his play on the court. Eddie knew about it because he was, shall we say, 'involved'?"

Russell ran through the implications, trying to piece together the big picture in his mind. If Allen was telling the truth, then why would Eddie Brown betray a childhood friend and jeopardize a friendship that surely had its perks?

Sydney was wondering the same things and said as much.

"You know what they say, Detective—cocaine is a hell of a drug," Allen replied. "Eddie hasn't worked a real job a single day in his life, as far as I know. But he's got some expensive habits I'm quite certain have gotten him into some real trouble with some very bad people. My guess is he needed money."

"So he gets with his best friend's future baby mama and dishes some dirt on him?" Russell said, shaking his head. "I'm finding that very hard to believe."

"What can I say, Detective? It's the lifestyle these guys lead. Fast women, fast cars, and unlimited access to whatever you want when you want. Not everyone can handle it. Eddie was privy to a lot of things, and I'm guessing it all went to his head. Maybe even up his nose."

"Obviously, otherwise your client wouldn't be in this mess," Sydney said. "What I don't get is why he didn't go to Lords for the money."

"He couldn't. Steven got worried when Eddie started doing cocaine, enough to try and get him into rehab, but Eddie refused to go. He said he didn't need to go get help and he had everything under control. His habit is one reason Karen left home in the first place."

"What do you mean?" Russell said, jotting in his notepad as Allen talked.

"Lately, he's been having a problem handling things because he's coked up all the time. One of Eddie's jobs was to handle the travel arrangements for Michelle. About three months ago, Karen was supposed to go to New York on some business for the Steven Lords Foundation. While she was gone, Eddie was supposed to fly Michelle in. Problem was Eddie got the dates mixed up and Karen and Michelle wound up at the same game. There was Michelle sitting courtside wearing, of all things, Steven's warm-up jacket. Karen saw that, came home, and packed her stuff and left. Steven had been threatening to cut him off ever since."

"But how did *you* know about the book?" Sydney asked.

"It's my job to know these things," Allen said. "When Steven told me about the baby, I tried talking to Michelle in hopes of reasoning with her about getting an abortion. But Michelle was a bit of a hothead, and she ran her mouth off a little too much. We had some pretty heated words at one point, and she told me I'd better sell my Steven Lords stock sooner rather than later because she was working on a book that was going to bring him down and Eddie was helping her write it. I later confronted Eddie about it, and that's when he told me he got into all this trouble and needed money."

"That still doesn't make any sense. It would've eventually gotten back to Lords," Russell said.

"That's why they call it dope," Allen replied. "I made that same point to Eddie and told him he had to get that book back from her. Otherwise I had no choice but to let Steven know what he'd been doing. I knew Eddie was upset and was getting desperate. Considering he'd betrayed his best friend, why wouldn't he be? But I never thought for a minute Eddie would try to kill her."

"Still, how do you know Steven wasn't involved? I mean,

when you look at it, she was still threatening to have his baby and she was dishing the dirt on him," Russell said. "Fact is, he was in the hotel and his friend Eddie was with him. So it looks to me like they both may be guilty. Where was Lords when Eddie was choking the life out of his pregnant girlfriend?"

"When I heard about Michelle's murder, I confronted Eddie," Allen said. "He told me when he and Steven went to the hotel that night, Steven told him to stay by the car while he went up to talk to Michelle. Apparently, Eddie thought he could help matters if he went upstairs behind Steven's back and talked to her himself, and after he realized Steven was back in the lobby, that's exactly what he did. Unfortunately, things clearly got out of hand. Michelle was already angry after Steven's visit, and Eddie showing up right then only threw fuel on the fire. One thing led to another, and I guess he ended up strangling her."

"You guess?"

Allen nodded solemnly. "He was pretty hopped up on something that night. Doesn't have full recall."

Russell said, "This all sounds too fantastic to be believed. You could've saved your client a lot of grief if you would've been this up front from the start. Why didn't you mention this before?"

"I'm not here to do your job for you," Allen said. "My job is to protect my client's interests, and at the time those interests included Eddie."

"Are you kidding?" Russell got up in Allen's face, so close he could smell the agent's breath. "You deliberately withheld information about a confession. Why should I believe any of this now?"

"Quite frankly, I don't care what you believe," Allen said. "You came to me looking for answers, so obviously you couldn't come up with any on your own. Now if the evidence that you've gathered so far—and I'm willing to *bet* it isn't much—points you in a different direction, by all means pursue it. Then maybe you can come give *me* some answers instead of coming here looking for them."

Russell was so angry he could barely see straight. But if Warner's claim was true, then this meant a huge break in the case. It was more important than ever not to do anything that might bite him on the ass.

"With the Finals coming and all the deals I've got lined up, I can't have Steven focused on anything but basketball," Allen added. "Hopefully, we can put an end to these little meetings after today. The last thing he needs is to be thinking about how his best friend killed his mistress and unborn child."

"With all this bad publicity and sponsors dropping him left and right, how are those deals looking now?"

Allen smiled. "Believe it or not, pretty good. All the attention on the case means more people will watch the games. I've got a little sympathy interview going right now that will reel some wayward fans back. All Steven has to do is play his game tomorrow night and win this championship—and he'll be bigger than he ever was. That's the beauty of sports. You gotta love it."

"We still have a little matter of a dead hotel security technician," Sydney said. "You know anything about that?"

Allen looked puzzled. "Dead security tech? What's his name?"

"James Cooper," Russell said. "Did you know him?"

Warner shook his head and sighed. "I didn't, but Eddie did. They met at a team event at the Murcielago. I know Eddie used to bring him to games from time to time. I'm pretty sure he was one of Eddie's dealers. They were together a lot. How'd he die?"

"Gunshot wound to the head. Found dead in his own kitchen."

Allen let out a low whistle. "I don't know if this means Eddie did it, but I do know he has a nine-millimeter he keeps with him for security reasons. He also likes to think of himself as Steven's bodyguard."

"I have half a mind to slap you with an obstruction charge . . . anything else you want to tell me about this guy?"

"Just that he's probably carrying now and might be dangerous," Allen said. "But the gun's legal. It was like pulling teeth to get Eddie to register it and carry a permit, but he finally did."

Russell looked at Sydney and raised an eyebrow. "Florida requires registered gun owners to have their fingerprints on file with the state. Can you give Morales a call and ask him to pull up the prints for Eddie Brown?"

"His legal name is Edward," Allen said.

"Edward Brown? There must be thousands of Edward Browns in Florida," Sydney said.

"Well have him narrow the search to Miami," Russell said. "Come on, Syd, work with me here."

"He lives in the Trump Towers," Allen said, "if that's any help."

"There you go. That should limit the search," Russell said. "Have Morales check those prints with the ones Davis took off the victim."

"Wouldn't someone have done that already?" Sydney asked.

"Not necessarily," Russell said. "That may have slipped through a crack if the gun wasn't used in the crime."

While Sydney stepped away to make the call, Russell got back to business. "So, going back to Eddie Brown then . . . do you have any idea where we can find him?"

"We got into it a few minutes ago and I sent him on his way," Allen said. "I think he's headed over to a place called Johnny Ray's to get something to eat. It's not too far from here, on Northwest Eighth Street."

"Christ, you mean he was just here?" Russell said.

"He wanted to stay and help out, but I made him leave," Allen said. "I've been cautious about having him around Steven. He looked like complete hell and seemed really

antsy this morning. I figured he was coming off of something, and either seemed like
thing or just getting on something, and either seemed like
trouble. So I sent him packing and he said he was going to
Johnny Ray's."

"I know where that place is," Russell said to Sydney, who
had just ended her call with Morales. "Let's go. If we hurry
we can probably catch Eddie while he's having lunch."

"Wait, Russell," Sydney said. "You should do this by the
book. Don't you need an arrest warrant—"

Russell shook his head. "Not necessarily."

Allen smiled as he nodded. "That's right. If the arresting
officer believes the defendant has committed a felony—
and a murder would constitute a felony—then no warrant
needs to be issued," he said. "He's driving a silver Range
Rover with these giant chrome rims. If he is high and
armed, then he could be a real danger to himself, or maybe
to someone else."

CHAPTER 33

Johnny Ray's Cafe, 11:56 a.m.

Eddie sat heavily on a torn vinyl stool at Johnny Ray's lunch counter and put his Blackberry down with a sigh. Jimmy hadn't answered his phone in days, and a brother could damn sure use a fix. Listening to Steven bitch and moan the past few days would've been enough to make a priest want to get high, and Eddie's run-in with Allen that morning had his blood boiling.

He sat in silence, drumming his fingers on the Formica counter while Johnny Ray himself cooked up a pork chop and heaped a plate with mashed potatoes and greens.

"Looks good, Mr. Johnny!" Eddie said, when Johnny Ray put the plate down in front of him.

"You know it. Our cook's sick today, but I still know my way around the kitchen here."

He looked up from wiping down the counter when the door opened. "What can I do for you boys?"

Eddie was too engrossed with his lunch to pay them any mind.

"Hey, man, y'all making chitlins today?"

"Naw, son. Not today. We only have chitlins on Saturdays."

"All right then."

Eddie heard shuffling and then felt a bump on his shoulder. He looked up and saw two men walking toward the door, decked out in wife-beaters and baggy pants.

"Excuse you, man!" Eddie yelled out.

"Say what?"

Eddie sat up at the counter. "I said 'excuse you.' You bumped me while I was trying to eat."

"So what? What's up? You wanna do something?"

Eddie put his fork down on the plate. *If they think I'm with this shit they better think again.* Eddie turned on his stool and raised his shirt to reveal the gun tucked into his waistband. "I don't play games with kids."

"I see what it is," the taller of the two said, backing off. "It's cool. Our bad."

***

RUSSELL AND SYDNEY PULLED INTO THE CRUMBLING parking lot next to Johnny Ray's. Russell stepped out of the car and looked with disgust at the boarded-up windows and rusty, torn-down fences that gave the block such a ghetto feeling. The restaurant was cheerily decorated and looked decent enough, but the neighborhood surrounding it was an urban wasteland. It looked like the kind of place where you could get yourself hurt real easy if you weren't careful.

"At least the food smells good," Sydney said, nodding toward an open door off the kitchen.

Russell pointed to a silver Range Rover at the far end of the lot next to the restaurant. "Looks like we're in luck."

Sydney nodded. "Okay, so how do you want to do this?"

"Allen said he may be armed and possibly under the influence of something, so let's watch our step."

"I always do," she said. If she was nervous, she didn't show it.

Russell knelt down, raised his pant leg, and unsnapped his ankle holster. He took out a .22-caliber handgun and handed it to Sydney.

"I know you aren't armed, so go ahead and take this, all right? I may need you to have my back on this one."

Sydney grinned as she broke open the revolver. "With this little .22?"

"Sorry, it's my only spare. Anyway, when we go in, let me

do the talking. You stand back by the door and back me up. Keep the gun handy, but out of sight, so we don't spook him. You got it?"

"You're sure we shouldn't call for backup?"

Russell smiled at her and shook his head tersely. "For this? Not a chance. We may not know for sure if Eddie actually killed that woman, but if Allen turns out to be right about that, I don't want anyone stealing our thunder."

Sydney nodded and smiled knowingly. "Okay. Let's do this."

Russell felt his heart beating faster and his shoulders tensing as they approached the entrance of the building. The restaurant was almost empty except for a man behind the counter and Eddie Brown sitting at the lunch counter with his back to the door.

Even from that angle, Russell could tell Eddie was a lot bigger than he looked in the picture. But at least he was distracted and his hands were clearly visible. Sydney gave him a sharp nod to indicate she was ready, so Russell pushed the door open and stepped inside.

"Can I help you folks?"

"Yes, sir. It's awfully hot outside and I could really go for two cups of your sweet tea," Russell said. He walked over to the far side of Eddie, who was going at his lunch with gusto and didn't appear to be paying any attention to what was going on. No sign of gun on him, but a nine-millimeter would fit in his front waistband easily enough. Russell knew he'd have to be careful.

"You know that's a real nice Range Rover parked out there," Russell said. "I love those rims."

Eddie looked up and nodded approvingly. "Thanks, man. I appreciate that."

"Is that your car?" Russell asked.

"Yeah, that's all me."

"No kidding. So you must be Eddie Brown?"

Again, Eddie looked up, this time giving Russell his full attention. "That's right. What business is it of yours?"

The look in Eddie's eyes meant business. No telling what he was thinking or what he might try. So if this was going to happen, it had to happen now.

Russell reached for his gun and pointed it right at Eddie's chest. "You'll find out soon enough. Right now, just keep your hands where I can see them."

"What the—"

Russell was on him in an instant. He reached underneath Eddie's shirt, found the gun in his waistband and slipped it into his own jacket pocket.

"What is this, some muthafuckin' joke or something?"

With his still gun pointed at Eddie, Russell reached for his badge. "I'm Detective Russell Howard of the Miami-Dade Police Department. I'm putting you under arrest for the murder of Michelle Tibbs."

Eddie looked down the barrel of Russell's gun and then saw Sydney, who had her gun drawn as well. Russell folded up his badge and put it back into his pocket. "Now get up slowly and keep your hands where I can see them."

Eddie got slowly up off the stool. Russell's pulse eased as he patted Eddie down. This was going well—strictly by the book. No reason anyone had to get hurt.

"Officer, I think you got the wrong guy," Johnny said as he started walking over to them. "I've known this young man for—"

"For your own safety, sir, please back up. This man is very dangerous."

"You'd better listen to him," Eddie said. "I didn't kill nobody."

"Oh no. I got the right guy." Russell said as he wrenched Eddie's hands behind his back and clamped the cuffs on him. "You messed up big time, Eddie."

"This is some bullshit! You ain't got nothin' on me! You don't know what the hell you're doing."

Russell grabbed Eddie by the arm and jerked him toward the door while Johnny stood idly by with his mouth hanging open.

"You're making a mistake," Eddie said. "Seriously . . . I know some powerful people in this town and once they hear about this—"

"What, you mean Steven Lords and his agent?" Russell

stopped once they got to the door. "Christ, Eddie, who do you think gave you up, anyway?"

Eddie turned to look at the smile on Russell's face. "That's a goddamn lie. My people wouldn't do me like that! Stevie wouldn't let that happen."

"You'd better think twice about that. How do you think we found you? Why do you think we're here?"

Sydney held open the door and Russell steered Eddie out into the parking lot. She handed Russell his handgun as the two of them walked Eddie to the car.

"Wait a minute!" Eddie said. "You got this all wrong!"

"I don't think so," Sydney said. "Allen told us everything about your little confession, and after we match the shells from your gun to the casings we found at James Cooper's place, you're going to need a very good lawyer."

"Jimmy? What happened to Jimmy?"

"Can the stupid act, would you? You know damn well what happened to James Cooper," Russell said, pushing Eddie around to the driver's side of the car. "You killed him to shut him up because he knew what you did to Michelle Tibbs."

"Jimmy's dead?" I ain't even have anything to do with that or none of this other bullshit. Let me go, man!"

Russell kept a strong grip on Eddie's shoulder with one hand while he reached for the door handle with the other. Eddie leaned forward, trying to block the door's path.

As the two men struggled, a burgundy Monte Carlo crept down the street. Rubberneckers were common enough in a situation like this, but there was something Russell didn't like about the way the scene was unfolding. Sydney was moving Eddie out of the way of the car door when the Monte Carlo's passenger window slid down and someone started shouting.

"Hey, big man!" someone shouted from the open passenger window. "Send Jimmy my regards!"

Russell looked up in time to see a bright flash erupt from the muzzle of a pistol. He let Eddie go, jumped sideways, and yelled at Sydney to get down.

Then he watched helplessly as a barrage of bullets tore into Eddie's chest and stomach just before a searing pain erupted in his own right arm.

RUSSELL DROPPED TO THE GROUND, HOPING HE'D BEEN grazed rather than hit full on. The pain was so intense he thought he might pass out, but with the shots still ringing out all he could do was focus on getting Eddie out of the line of fire.

Sydney rushed behind the car as gunfire sprayed the side of the building as well as the few cars in the lot. "Russell? Russell can you hear me? You need to get clear."

Eddie's bullet-riddled body slumped in Russell's direction, taking them both all the way to the ground. Russell could hear more shots fired behind him before a bone-jarring *thunk* as his head hit the filthy pavement. The last thing he remembered was the screech of tires as the Monte Carlo sped away—before he wondered where the hell Sydney had gotten another gun, then blacked out.

CHAPTER 34

Star Island, 1:26 p.m.

When Allen returned to the house, the interview filming had wrapped. He watched Karen snatch off her microphone, take the pins out of her hair, then storm out of the living room like a woman on a mission. He looked up when he heard Heather approach. "Thanks again for the opportunity, Mr. Warner," she said. "This should really give my career a boost."

"I'm glad it went well," Allen said.

"I was just talking to Steven over there and it sounds like he's looking forward to the game tomorrow, despite all the craziness," Heather said. "He's such a good guy . . . I hope everything works out for him."

Allen just nodded and went on his way. Steven had done great, but by the looks of things it was just a matter of time before the next shoe dropped.

KAREN THREW OPEN THE FRENCH DOORS AND STORMED into the master bedroom, furious at herself for what she'd just been part of. That whole interview was a complete mockery of emotion, right down to the phony tears that had dripped from Steve's eyes. All he'd kept saying was how sorry he was, over and over again, like it meant something. But she knew in her heart he wasn't sorry for what he did. He was just sorry he got caught.

She walked across the polished hardwood floor, picked up a Barbie doll Cassidy had left on the coffee table, and sat on the linen sofa. There was a time she'd loved this room more than any other in the house. The open airiness of it and the mesmerizing waterfront views made it the perfect place to go and relax after a long day. But now it was nothing more than a remnant of a ruined marriage.

She turned toward the closet next to the bed and noticed a Bulgari jewelry box waiting on the nightstand. She couldn't have cared less what was inside the box, but surely it was ridiculously expensive, which only made it seem like more of a clichéd gesture.

Why did men always think they could buy their way out

of trouble? As if a piece of jewelry were enough to make up for cheating, lying, and who knew what else.

She paused, wondering if Steve had ever cheated on her right there in that room. Not that it mattered now, but part of her hoped he hadn't stooped that low.

She headed into a spacious walk-in closet and came out a few moments later with a carefully selected armful of clothes. She didn't want much, but there were things she'd bought before their marriage she needed to take with her. Her heartbeat quickened when she saw Steven on the edge of the bed. He looked so tired. His back was hunched over like he had the weight of the world on him. His eyes were still red from crying.

Without a word, Karen put her clothes on the bed and began folding. Steve waved at her, hoping to draw her attention.

"What?"

He must have been taken aback by her tone. "I . . . I just wanted to say thanks for coming home and doing the interview. I know that couldn't have been easy, but it's nice having you and Cassidy back home. The place just isn't the same without you guys."

Karen didn't respond. She continued to fold her clothes without making eye contact. The sound of Steven's voice was starting to bring on a splitting headache and make her stomach feel queasy. And everything he said sounded rehearsed, made-up somehow, not at all like the real Steven.

Being here was not a good idea. It would've been so much easier to go back to the hotel and pack the bags while Steve was playing the next night.

She came out of the closet carrying more clothes and an old suitcase her mom had given her before they got married. Steven sat there looking sad, like some lost puppy. You'd think he'd take a hint.

"What are you packing for?" he asked. "You just got home."

It would be painfully obvious to anyone else what was happening, but somehow he didn't seem to get it. If it wasn't wearing a short skirt or swishing through an orange hoop, Steven seemed to be at a total loss.

"I see you didn't open the present I got for you."

Karen stuffed a few pairs of shoes into her bag. Her movements felt awkward and contrived, and she didn't like the way he was watching her. "Come on, baby, we haven't really spoken in months. Are we gonna talk or what?"

She dropped the shirt she was folding and said, "Okay, Steven, what is it you'd like to talk about? Huh?"

"How about an apology," he said. "For real, off camera, you know? I know I messed up. But I meant every word when I said how sorry I am."

"Well that just makes everything okay doesn't it? So now 'The Lord' is sorry. So now things can go back to the way they were. You've given your little tired-ass apology and bought me jewelry, so now I can come running back home and into your arms and we can live happily ever after, is that right?"

Karen picked up the shirt and started to fold it again. "This was a big mistake. I shouldn't have come back. I didn't want to come back."

"So why did you?"

"Because I got tired of being so angry at myself when you're the one I've been mad at. I didn't realize that until Allen showed up at my parents' house."

"Like I said, I know I made mistakes . . . and I really am sorry."

"Do you have any idea what you're sorry for, Steven? Tell me exactly what you're sorry for!"

He leaned closer and tried to look her in the eyes, but she turned away. "I'm sorry for Michelle. I'm sorry for putting myself in that stupid situation. I'm sorry for all the other women and everything I've put you through. How's that for starters?"

She looked at him through narrow eyes, wanting desperately to turn and walk out. "What you put me through? That's a nice way of saying it . . . when what you mean is you cheated on me every chance you had and got another woman pregnant! Do you know how that makes me feel? Do you have any idea how embarrassing that is?"

"It's been embarrassing for me, too. Haven't you been watching TV and reading the papers? It's been all over the place," Steven said. "I've got sponsors dropping me left and right over this mess. But I did everything I could to get a handle on all of this and spare you this humiliation."

"You mean you did everything you could to cover it up! And don't try to make this look like you were doing me a favor, okay? You said you did everything you could? You could've left that girl alone in the first place."

"If I could go back and change all of this, you know I would in a heartbeat. I'd give anything to make this right," Steven stood, walked to the nightstand, and picked up the box. "I was hoping this present might symbolize a fresh start. It's . . . well, open it and you'll see, but I think you'll really like it. I was actually hoping you'd wear it during the interview."

Karen slapped the box out of his hand and watched as it skittered across the floor "You really don't get it, do you?"

"I do get it and I'm sorry, Karen. What else can I say?"

"You can stop telling me you're sorry, for one thing. I know you're sorry. And I'm sorry, too, because the sad fact is, all your fame and fortune and talent doesn't mean a damn thing when it comes to what really counts."

"Baby, I can change, I promise you!"

She looked at him, letting her eyes meet his for the first time. "I wish I could believe that, Steven, I really do. But people don't ever really change, do they? I mean not really, not in the profound sort of ways that would keep a man like you from being such a miserable excuse for a husband and a father."

She watched as a look of pain settled on his face.

"It's hard to say but it's true," she said. "You've been a complete failure when it comes to me and your daughter. Do you even understand that?"

He looked at the floor, completely dejected. She wanted to feel good about getting this anger off her chest, but it was making her more miserable.

"What worries me is that when you're alone with your thoughts about this whole thing, I know you're focused on the fact you got caught and everything that's going to slip away now that you've been exposed for a liar and a cheat."

"That's part of it," Steven said after a thoughtful pause. "But that's not all of it."

"That's good because it's not just me you've betrayed. Have you ever stopped to think about what this kind of behavior means to Cassidy?" Karen said. "It'd be bad enough if she were a boy. I'd hate to have a son growing up and thinking that this is how you treat women, but she's a little girl, Steven. Think about the message you're sending about the first man she'll ever love."

"Oh come on, she's only four. She can't fully realize—"

"Don't go there, all right? You know damn well she's old enough to see things on TV and ask questions. She may not fully understand all these terrible things she's hearing about her father or what they mean, but that doesn't mean this isn't destructive."

"That's why you need to give me another chance,

Karen—to be a better father and a better husband. I promise you I can!"

Karen looked up from her hands, tears streaming down her cheeks. "Here's what I don't understand," she said as he dried her eyes. "I tried to be everything you needed. I tried to be a good wife and a good mother. Where did I go wrong? What didn't I do?"

"It wasn't you, baby. None of this had anything to do with you. This was me getting caught up in being a superstar and somehow letting myself believe the rules of life didn't apply to me. It was me being stupid and selfish was all, not anything you did wrong."

Pathetic as that sounded, at least it made a little sense. But the truth was, this is what she'd been worried about all along.

"Remember when we first met, when I told you I didn't want to date an athlete? Remember what I said about what being on the road so much of the time can do to a man, and how I never wanted to be number two to anyone?"

"Of course I do," Steven said. "And I know I made promises to you I ended up not keeping. But I tried, Karen, you know? At least I thought I was trying."

"No, Steven, you didn't. If you'd really tried, Michelle wouldn't have gotten pregnant, and she sure as hell wouldn't have been sitting courtside at the game wearing your goddamn jacket like some cheap groupie!"

"Look, I know I messed up."

"Messed up? She had better tickets than I did, and I'm married to you," she said. "I'm supposed to be your wife—your one and only—and you treated me like number two."

"You were never number two. I know that sounds crazy, but you weren't." Steven put a hand on Karen's shoulder. "I don't know how all this happened. I got caught up in the life. I got caught up with being 'The Lord' and I lost sight of Steven Lords."

"Well that's an understatement. You've changed," Karen said as she threw Steven's hand off of her. "We went from having nothing to having everything. People are running around kissing your ass. No one ever telling you when you're wrong, and you let all the money and the fame go to your head and turn you into someone I don't even recognize anymore."

"You're right, Karen. But the real me is still in there. And he's learned a lesson."

"At least in college you tried to keep the lines of communication open," Karen said. "Not only did you call, but you used to write me a journal about what you did when you and the team were on road. But all that stopped. I can barely get a phone call from you on the road, and when you are home you go out all the time with Eddie or Julian and stay out later and later. You have a family! Your ass needs to be at home."

"I know. People come up to me . . . women come up to

me . . . and I don't know what happens. I get weak. I know that's not an excuse but—"

"That's just it," Karen said. "All these people around you get you making these bad decisions . . . they don't even know the real Steven Lords and wouldn't care about him if they did. They're only after you for what they can get or what you can do for them. Wake up, Steven. Everyone around you is out for something. Allen and Eddie included. Those girls you meet out there and all those other leeches are out to get a piece of you however they can. When you let them get that access to you, you betray me and Cassidy."

"How can I make this right? What do you want me to do? I'll do anything."

"It's not about you, Steven. That's what I realized at my parents' house. The fact is, you are what you are, and I'm the one who was stupid enough to marry you. So in some ways this is really my fault."

Karen got off the bed and resumed packing. She could feel the tears coming back and her breath getting heavier.

"That's where you're wrong, Karen," she heard him say from behind her. "You aren't the problem at all. All you did was try to believe in the man you married."

He turned her around and used the back of his hand to wipe at the tears trickling down her cheeks. For a split second she let her guard down, savoring the tender gesture and the strength and softness of the hands she'd once loved touching her. But then all the anger returned. She stepped away and glared at him.

"I'm sorry, Steven. I can't do this anymore."

"Do what? What are you saying?"

"I'm saying I'll stay in town until tomorrow night. I'm going to take Cassidy to the first game of the Finals because it'd break her heart not to see you play. But after that, I'm leaving."

"Leaving? Where are you going?"

"I still have a lot of things to sort out and I can't do that here."

Steven shook his head. "You can't leave, Karen," he said. "Not now, not when what we need to do is work this out."

"Don't you dare sit there and tell me what I can't do! After everything you've put me and Cassidy through, you don't have the right to tell me a damn thing!"

"I'm not trying to tell you what to do. But now isn't a good time to be talking about separating or getting divorced. With all the media attention on me right now, your leaving will just make everything worse."

"You don't have a damn clue, you know that? If you did you'd realize I don't care about the media attention and your image and whatever the hell you think is at stake now that you've been exposed. Hell, if anything I'm glad . . . because you're a selfish bastard who deserves exactly what you're getting!"

Steven stared at the floor. "I'll quit."

"What?"

"You heard me. I'll give it all up if you stay," Steven said. "Right after the Finals. I'll announce my retirement and walk away."

Karen took a few deep breaths and turned to him. "Then you'd resent me and Cassidy for the rest of your life because you'd have nothing," she said. "Truth is, you only know who you are when you're on the court. Take that away from you and what's left?"

"I can be the man you want me to be again," Steven said, his eyes welling with tears. "I want to be that man. Just don't give up on me."

"That man is gone, and to be honest, right now I'm not sure he even existed. That's why I'm done with all of this."

She turned and, without another word, headed for Cassidy's room to start packing their daughter's things.

***

Steven lumbered back toward the bed, cursing himself for blowing the most important conversation he'd ever had in his life. He'd wanted more than anything to believe Karen was bluffing and this was all some kind of ruse to teach him a well-deserved lesson. But in his heart he knew she was serious and she really was leaving.

A light tap on the door caused Steven to sit up. It was probably Eddie, who was already late in picking him up for a shoot-around that was about the last thing on his mind.

"Come on in, Ed."

But it was Allen who opened the door and poked his head into the room. "Sorry to bother you, Steven, but I'm afraid I have some bad news."

"Christ, what now?"

"It's Eddie, Steven," Allen said. "He's been shot."

CHAPTER 35

Johnny Ray's Cafe, 2:10 p.m.

Russell cracked open his eyelids, wincing at the bright overhead lighting from what must have been the back of an ambulance. He took a moment to get his bearings as he became fully conscious and then sat up slowly, bracing for the worst.

His head hurt like hell, making it even harder to make sense of what had happened in the parking lot. He remembered watching Sydney try to get Eddie into the car, but then it was all a blur. Through the ambulance's open back door he could see several police officers trying to keep bystanders at bay, while others interviewed potential witnesses. It was good to see Sydney among the crowd, standing and looking just fine like always.

"Easy, Detective. You took quite a blow to the head," a paramedic said.

Russell inched up to the edge of the gurney. "How'd I get in the meat wagon and why are my ears ringing?"

"The EMTs put you in here, and that ringing in your ears may be a sign of a concussion. We can do some preliminary tests here but you should get to the hospital and get checked out. You also took a hit to the shoulder. Those bandages should keep it stabilized until a doctor can have a look."

"I feel fine," Russell said as he gingerly stepped down from the ambulance deck. "What happened to the other guy? Where's Eddie Brown?"

"Took some heavy fire, I'm afraid. He's alive for the moment, but barely."

Russell stood and looked over the crowd. A few reporters had ambled over to the tapeline, looking for a statement. He pretended not to hear them, thinking it best not to give an account when everything was so hazy. He stumbled toward the group of people talking to Sydney. He stood still for a moment, tried to steady himself. A trip to the hospital was probably a good idea, but there were other priorities at that moment.

Nothing seemed clear, but Syd had come up big. He was grateful she'd laid down some cover fire when things got hot, but where had her gun come from? Did she return the backup piece before the shooting or did she keep it? He shook his left leg, and to his relief his ankle holster felt lighter. So she must've kept it. It was the only explanation that made sense.

A couple of uniformed officers approached Russell, noticed him stumbling, and stood along either side of him and braced him.

"Maybe you need to sit down, Detective?"

"Thanks, guys, but I'm fine," Russell replied. "I just need to shake off a few cobwebs here. Then I'll be okay."

"We wanted to let you know that a few miles away from here, we found a car witnesses said they saw fleeing the scene," one of the officers said. "It was abandoned. Suspects fled. We have some guys trying to pull whatever we can from it, and we're canvassing the neighborhood for leads. I'm guessing the car was stolen."

"Good. If you find anything, let me know immediately."

Russell handed them each a business card with his cell number. The officers nodded and Russell continued toward Sydney, who stood next to their squad car. Even with his head still spinning to the point he was almost nauseous, he felt bad about what a big, ugly mess the situation had turned into.

"I thought you'd be on your way to the hospital," Sydney said when she saw him. "That was some fall you took once the shooting started. How's your arm?"

"Sore as hell, but my head feels worse," Russell said, looking carefully at the bullet casings. "You sure laid down some heavy fire there."

Sydney smiled. "In all the confusion, I sort of went on instinct, you know? I'm glad you're okay, though. Eddie didn't look too good when they took him out of here—a lot of blood."

"Yeah, the EMTs didn't sound too optimistic. What about you? How you doing?"

"I'm fine. I was more worried about you."

"Yeah, right," Russell said with a smirk. "But listen, I really appreciate what you did. I—"

"Save it. I was just looking out for you like I would a partner. If the roles were reversed, you'd have done the same."

"I wouldn't bet on it. I really don't like you that much," Russell said with a playful grin. "By the way, where'd you get the gun? I thought you said you weren't carrying."

"You gave me your backup piece, remember?" she said as she held up Russell's .22. "You dropped it when you hit the ground with Eddie during the shooting. It was a good thing, too. Otherwise, you'd probably be somewhere next to Eddie, fighting for your life."

Russell shrugged as he took his gun. Her account made sense, but even through the fog of his headache something still seemed off. But it didn't matter. Sydney had saved his life, and with a little luck, Eddie's too—although that seemed unlikely.

"I don't suppose you got the license plate of the car with the shooters?"

They both turned when they heard the clamoring of reporters swell. Russell groaned inwardly when he saw Captain Stewart, Chief Cavanaugh, and the rest of the suits cross the police line and head his way. His head was already throbbing and the chief was sure to want an explanation why the new lead in the case was on an operating table somewhere. Things still weren't making sense to Russell, so how was he supposed to make it make sense to Cavanaugh? Russell rubbed his head. Maybe he should've taken that ride to the hospital after all.

"You two okay?" Cavanaugh asked.

"We're fine, sir," Russell said.

Cavanaugh pointed at the bandages on Russell's arm. "What happened to you, son? Took one in the line of duty?"

"Just a nick. Nothing serious."

Chief Cavanaugh looked around. "So what happened here, then? Did this have anything to do with the suspect you were supposed to question?"

"I'm afraid so," Russell said, then gave him a quick rundown of the morning's events.

"So where's Eddie Brown now?"

"Hopefully getting right with God," Russell said. "He sustained multiple gunshot wounds and the paramedics made it sound like he's in critical condition."

"He and Russell were the victims of a drive-by shooting," Sydney added. "Seemed to be linked to the James

Cooper killing. The restaurant owner recalled two men mentioning Cooper when they approached Brown in the restaurant earlier."

"So did Brown tell you anything?"

"Directly, no. But we now know he was at the hotel that night, and we have good reason to believe he attacked Tibbs in her hotel room. Apparently, it was over some notes she'd taken for a book she and Brown were writing about Lords."

"Say what?"

"It's complicated, sir," Sydney said. "But it may all boil down to a friend trying to protect another friend from being exposed and manipulated."

"Was Lords involved?"

"According to his agent, Lords was outside the hotel waiting for Eddie to pick him up. Right now, Eddie can't refute that, so it's hearsay at this point. But we do have footage of Lords anxiously waiting for someone in front of the hotel."

"What about that security guy?"

"Russell took a handgun off of Eddie when he took him into custody," Sydney said. "Ballistics should tell us if the bullets from his gun match the ones from Cooper's head."

"So what do you think, Ms. Farrell?" the chief asked. "Does it look like we may be able to wrap this one up?"

"I remember in the reports that CSI took some prints off Tibbs's throat. It's a good possibility that those prints belong to Eddie," Sydney said. "Like I said, we may well have the murder weapon from the Cooper killing and we need ballistics to confirm what I already suspect—"

"There's no doubt Eddie was involved in these murders," Russell said. "But unless he can make some sort of miracle recovery, we may not be able to link Lords to any of them."

Chief Cavanaugh nodded. "Good work, guys. You got dealt some bad cards along the way, but both of you did a fine job here. I'll need a full report on my desk as soon as you're able. But first, I want you to go to the hospital and get that head looked at, Detective."

"I'm fine, sir. I just need a couple stitches from the EMTs and then maybe some rest. It's no big deal."

"I wasn't asking, Detective. That was an order. Ms. Farrell, make sure he goes."

Chief Cavanaugh went over to speak to the assembled media, leaving Russell holding his head. He slowly walked over to his bullet-riddled car and leaned against it. His headache hadn't let up, and the dizziness was worsening. Still, he was grateful for the chief's approval.

Sydney laid a hand on Russell's shoulder. "Why don't you go to the hospital and get yourself looked at? I can wrap up things here."

"No, I'm fine. I don't need to see a doctor."

"Yes you do, Junior. You look like hell," said Morales, who had just shown up and was now standing next to Russell and Sydney.

"Thank you. I've been trying to tell him that," Sydney

said. "See what you can do with him. I'm gonna go help the other officers."

Russell watched as Sydney walked over to speak with others on the scene. He walked behind the car, knelt down to pick up a few shell casings, and handed a couple of them to Morales.

"What's this, Junior?"

"Keep this between us, okay?" Russell handed Morales his .22 along with the small handful of casings. "See if you can have ballistics take a look at those. I'm not sure about what happened out here. Something doesn't feel right."

"What do you mean?" Morales said, a look of genuine concern on his face.

"Sydney said she used my gun to cover me and Eddie once the shooting started, but I'm not so sure that's true. So I need you to take a look at these casings and see if they came from my gun."

"Sure thing," Morales said as he waved a patrolman over. "We'll talk later."

Russell reached into his pocket for Eddie's holstered gun. "Here's the gun I got off Eddie Brown. It'll need to go to the ballistics guys as well."

"Don't worry about anything, Russell. You did a good job. I'm proud of you," Morales said. "This officer is gonna give you a ride to the hospital, okay? I'll try to come by later to check on you."

Russell leaned against the officer, who threw an arm around him and helped him to a squad car.

CHAPTER 36

Jackson Memorial Hospital, 2:40 p.m.

Allen stopped short when he saw the mayhem around Steven in the ER's waiting area. That fans would hound him for autographs in a hospital waiting room was sad, but Steven was a good sport about it like always.

Maybe Eddie had been good for something after all. At least he knew how to keep people at bay during inappropriate moments.

As security ushered the fans away, Allen took Steven's arm and escorted him down the hallway. "The nurse told me there's an office around the corner we can use to wait for Eddie while he's in surgery," he said.

"How is he?" Steven asked.

"They got him into surgery as fast as they could but I'm getting the feeling it's pretty much touch and go," Allen replied. "They won't know anything for sure until they've finished operating. But the nurse made it sound like he's lucky he even made it to the hospital."

"Anything he needs, Allen. Make sure he gets the best."

Allen held open the door for Steven, who walked in and sat behind a desk in the vacant office.

"I just can't stop thinking about who'd want to do something like this to Eddie," Steven said. "I know he can be a real ass sometimes, but this doesn't make any sense."

"It makes all the sense in the world, given the company he keeps," Allen said. "Not to mention his penchant for flying off the handle and letting his habits dictate his actions."

Allen sat in a chair on the other side of the desk. Steven leaned back in his chair with his hands over his face. The poor guy had endured a rough afternoon and it was about to get rougher. No sense trying to cover for Eddie any longer. And it was better that Steven got the full picture from him rather than hear about it on TV.

"Steven, there's something you need to know."

Steven moved his hands from his face. "What is it now?"

"I think we've both known for quite some time that Eddie's been mixed up in some real shady stuff. But now it's looking like it's worse than I thought."

"Worse how, Allen?" Steven looked at him stonily.

"It's Michelle, Steven. Eddie's the one who killed her."

"What?" Steven said, his whole body stiff with tension. "What did you just say?"

"Eddie told me the whole story. That night you went to the hotel to talk to her, he waited in the lobby and went up to her room after you left. She was mad as hell and laying it on thick, and I guess he lost it."

Steven shook his head. "This is a joke right? You're playing with me right now."

"It's no joke. He told me himself he and Michelle got into an altercation, and the next thing he knew she was on the ground."

"He lied! I asked him flat out if he did it, and he fucking lied!"

"What did you expect?" Allen said. "He told me you guys were coming from Julian's party, where it sounds like he got his hands on some pretty strong coke. He said he blacked out. You and I both know how his habits have been getting the better of him lately, and now it looks like . . ."

Allen stopped when he saw that Steven had drifted into his own world, gazing out the window and looking as shaken as Allen had ever seen anyone look.

It was almost a full minute before he said anything. "Damn, Al . . . the man's like a brother to me."

"I know that, Steven, and that's the only reason I didn't tell you sooner. Honestly, that's the only reason I didn't tell the police. But they came by when you were doing the interview, with a surveillance camera picture of him with you that night, and I couldn't protect him any longer."

Steven laid his head on top of the desk and Allen patted him on the back. "I know it's a shock. But I need you to sit up and look at me because I'm afraid there's something else you need to know about all this."

Steven slowly straightened up. "This is all my fault. Eddie told me a long time ago I should've left Michelle alone and I didn't listen. Eddie never would've done what he did if he wasn't trying to protect me."

"That's just it," Allen said. "Eddie didn't kill Michelle just to protect you, he did it to protect himself as well."

"That doesn't make any sense."

Allen looked Steven in the eye. The poor kid had endured more than anyone should have to in such a short period of time, and it was starting to show. His eyes looked puffy, and all the stress was making his face break out. Allen took a deep breath as he searched for the right words. The time had come for the last shoe to drop.

CHAPTER 37

Jackson Memorial Hospital, 8:09 a.m.
Eleven hours and twenty-one minutes until tip-off

"Yesterday police confirmed they had a new suspect in the killing of Steven Lords's alleged mistress Michelle Tibbs. Edward Brown, Lords's close friend and personal assistant, will likely be charged with the murder of Tibbs as well as that of Murcielago hotel employee James Cooper, after police found incriminating evidence at Brown's Miami Beach condo. Brown, who was a victim of a parking lot shooting at a Miami restaurant, is currently in the hospital in critical condition. Police officials haven't completely ruled out Steven Lords as a suspect, but they did say he currently is no longer a person of interest. With game one of the Finals starting tonight, that should come as good news to Lords and the team."

RUSSELL SAT UP IN HIS HOSPITAL BED, GRABBED THE REMOTE, and started flipping through the channels. It was bad enough that Eddie Brown might not survive long enough to shed any further light on Lords's involvement, but the newscast's failure to even mention the lead detective was criminal.

"Good morning, Detective Howard," a nurse said as she entered his room. "Did you sleep okay last night?"

"Not too bad," Russell replied. "Although this stay was a waste of time. All I needed was a few painkillers and I'd have been just fine."

The nurse reached for the thermometer next to Russell's bed. "Open up, please," she said as she stuck it under his tongue. "The doctor wanted to keep you for observation. You sustained a serious concussion. From what I hear, you're lucky that's all you got."

Russell opened his mouth so the nurse could remove the thermometer. He noticed a bouquet of yellow, red, and orange flowers on the table across from his bed. "Where'd those come from?" he asked.

"A very pretty young lady brought you those last night. You were so sedated you didn't even know she was here. Was that your girlfriend?"

Russell shook his head but grinned as he looked at the

flowers. He and Sydney had come a long way. There was no telling how things would've turned out in that parking lot had she not been there. It was probably crazy to think Sydney might be hiding something—the concussion playing tricks on his brain or something. But the flowers were a nice gesture.

The nurse wrapped a blood pressure cuff around Russell's arm and began pumping it up.

"Do you have any idea when can I get out of here?"

"What's the rush? You got tickets for the big game tonight or something?"

"More like a job to do," Russell said. "But I actually did score a couple of tickets. Ended up giving them away to a couple of kids."

"Well that was very nice of you," she said, smiling approvingly. "Over in the children's ward, we're turning the rec room into a little drive-in so all the kids can watch the game together."

"Really?"

"Oh sure." She kept talking animatedly while taking some notes from the screen on the monitor next to Russell's bed. "You can say what you want about Steven Lords as a husband, but the man is a real hero around here. Not only is he one of the hospital's biggest supporters, but he also visits the children's hospital on his own time during both the season and offseason. He brings presents for the kids and really spends time with them."

The nurse moved a rolling table aside as she continued to pre-examine Russell. "And it's sad, too, because the kids who are old enough to understand what he's been going through the past few days have been pretty devastated," she added. "A few even cried because they were scared for him, if you can believe that. So we got the kids together and made cards for Steven, and that helped them feel a lot better."

"That's good for the kids," Russell said, trying to keep irritation out of his voice. "But maybe it would've been better to explain to them that people aren't always who you think they are."

"Maybe," she said, returning the clipboard to its hook at the foot of the bed. "But kids have their whole lives to learn people can let you down. Why not just let them believe in someone who makes them feel good? Especially someone who makes a difference here at the hospital the way 'The Lord' does."

Russell raised an eyebrow and nodded. It was good to know Lords wasn't total scum. It took a big person to take time out to make sick kids feel good. *Bet the publicity he gets makes it all worthwhile.*

"Okay, it's been nice chatting with you," the nurse said. "The doctor should be in shortly."

Russell thanked her, and after she left he resumed his channel surfing. Station after station aired reports about Eddie's arrest, but none gave him the commendations he sought. He laid the remote on the bed. It became obvious that no one cared about the guy who got shot at trying to make the arrest everyone was talking about. They only cared about what it meant for Lords and the game tonight. Russell rested his head on his pillow and was just dozing off when he heard a familiar voice come from the television.

"Hello and welcome to *The Stat Line*. I'm your host Peter Owens. Today's show is coming at you earlier than our usual time, but I have a very exciting guest lined up for today. So stay tuned because this is an interview I'm sure you don't want to miss."

Russell sat up and grabbed the remote. He was trying to relax and wasn't in the mood to hear anything from Owens. He was about to change the channel when he saw Owens on his set, sitting next to a large man fidgeting with his hands. Russell squinted. There was something familiar about the guest, sitting there decked out in Steven Lords paraphernalia. He stared at the dark-skinned man, who had a nasty scar down the right side of his chin. As the camera closed in on Owens's guest, he flashed a big smile. His gold tooth twinkled in the lighting. Russell tilted his head to the side when the man's name splashed across the screen.

"I'm joined by a special guest who's a very close friend of Miami guard Steven Lords. Wallace Mosley, thank you for joining me today. Why don't we start with you telling us what brings you here to Miami?"

"It's been a while since I've been out here," Mosely said. "I got some cousins out this way, so I get a chance to visit with them for one thing. But the main reason I'm here is to see my man take it to L.A. tonight from the luxury box, baby."

"That's very good. Steven's taken good care of you, has he?"

"First class all the way. I got a suite in a five-star hotel overlooking the beach and luxury box seats for the game. It's been a minute since I've seen him, but my boy is taking real good care of me."

"Now, you've known Steven Lords since he was a kid. Some say you were the guy who discovered Steven Lords. How'd you two meet?"

Wallace looked into the camera before answering, discomfort obvious on his face. "It was actually at a playground in Collingswood, Tennessee. I'll never forget the first time I saw him putting in work on some of the neighborhood kids. He was young and maybe 130 pounds soaking wet, but even way back then I knew he could ball."

"Early on, what was your relationship with Steven Lords like?"

"I like to think I was a mentor to him, you know? I looked after him. Made sure the haters stayed away. I sent him to a few basketball camps too. He was like a little brother, so I tried to steer him in the right direction and make sure he was doing things the right way, on and off the court."

"I remember covering you during your college career," Owens said, a dubious look on his face. "You were a good player, but you ran into a little trouble with gambling and receiving improper benefits, didn't you? If I'm not mistaken, you were convicted of point shaving and actually did a little time for that."

"Yeah, man, things didn't work out the way I thought they should, and I did spend some time in the joint but—"

"Let me ask you this. During Lords's last year of college, he was playing a tournament game against U-Conn . . . do you remember that game?"

"Sure I do. I believe my man had twenty-six points."

"A very impressive twenty-six points as I recall," Owens said. "But it wasn't the twenty-six points that stood out for me, it was the six turnovers. Particularly the turnover late in the final seconds of the game that gave U-Conn the win."

Mosley leaned forward in his chair, body stiff with tension. "Okay, again, I'm gonna have to stop you there. I'm not here to talk about no rumors or nothin' like that. I'm just here to show love and support to my man Stevie through all these allegations and accusations. What you're talking about ain't nothin' but ancient history."

"I understand that. I was just hoping you could shed light on rumors that there was some impropriety during Steven Lords's last year in school that may have involved some—"

"You see. There you go with more of those rumors."

"I'm trying to get the facts straight. That's all. You were involved in point shaving during your collegiate career, and as you previously stated you were a mentor to him. Did you—"

"I said chill, all right? I see what this is. I see what you're about. I'm not here to help you drag my man through the mud. He's already gone through enough—"

"Mr. Mosley, I just—"

"Uh-uh! No way I'm going to sit here while you try to get something else started. I'm out!"

Wallace snatched off his microphone and stood. As he turned to walk off the set, Russell's jaw dropped. There wasn't anything familiar about Wallace Mosley the man, but there was something familiar about the jacket he wore. The Miami logo on the back was a dead giveaway, but it was the name "Lords" stitched on the front that got Russell's attention.

CHAPTER 38

After being discharged from the hospital, Russell returned to his precinct with a hundred thoughts racing through his head. There had to be more going on than met the eye. For starters, where the hell did Mosley get Steven Lords's game jacket?

By the time Russell reached his desk, the station started spinning. He leaned against the back of his chair and shut his eyes, trying to quell the nausea and dizziness. Everything still seemed cloudy, and the doctor had said to take it slow the next few days. But these next few days were too important. If he didn't get some answers, the wrong man could be facing some serious charges.

After taking a few deep breaths Russell opened his eyes and sat at his desk. He rifled through some papers until he found the hotel guest list. Somehow the name Wallace Mosley seemed familiar, and Russell nodded his head as he tapped his index finger against the list. Wallace Mosley, suite 2210—the suite right next door to Tibbs. According to his statement he'd been out partying that night and didn't know anything. Russell reached for his phone. He needed to get to the truth and as much as he hated to admit it, Owens might be the best person to start with.

He was about to dial when Morales approached his desk.

"Damn, you couldn't stop by your house to change clothes before you came in?"

"Didn't have time," Russell said. "Check this out, I was watching Owens's show and—"

"You can tell me about that later," Morales said. "I was just up front and I heard that a Rhonda Tibbs is asking to see you."

"Michelle's sister? Why would she want to see me?"

"Heck if I know. The Brown arrest has been all over the news, so maybe she wants to thank you personally. But I wanted to let you know a few things before they brought her back." Morales sifted through some papers on Russell's desk and picked up a sealed manila envelope. "Doesn't look like you read this, but you know it's the coroner's report, right?"

"I know," Russell said, mentally kicking himself for having forgotten about it. "This actually came in at the same time the tape from Owens's show arrived. But with Deputy Chief waiting, I didn't get a chance to check it out, and since we already know Tibbs died from strangulation—"

"That's what I thought too, Junior. But I got a call from the coroner this morning, who was surprised he hadn't heard back from you, given what he found out. You'd better look at the report."

Morales handed the envelope to Russell, who ripped it open. The coroner's notes were concise and to the point. There was tracheal damage indicating strangulation, but the trauma caused wasn't enough to kill her, and she had plenty of oxygen in her blood at the time of death.

The likely cause of death was head trauma—an epidural hemorrhage—from something broad and flat enough it could do major damage to the brain without leaving a mark on the exterior of the scalp. It was conceivable that could have happened if she passed out and hit her head on the floor, but at her weight that seemed unlikely.

"Jesus, Art! What if this means . . . fuck, this could change everything!"

Morales nodded, eyes wide and face serious. "I thought you'd be interested. So what now?"

Russell thought before answering. Eddie could've easily hit Michelle over the head. Judging by Art's description, he could've used her laptop before he took it. But if Eddie took the computer, why wouldn't he let Warner know? Something didn't feel right.

Was this really happening? Had his entire case and theory of the crime collapsed? Was it possible that Eddie Brown was a victim and not a perpetrator? And if so, did that mean Steven Lords was back in the hot seat?

Russell's concussion-addled brain was having trouble processing it all. All he knew was he was furious with himself for not reading the coroner's report the minute it came in.

He straightened up in his chair and looked at Morales apologetically. "Did you get a ballistics report for the bullet casings I gave you yesterday?"

"Still waiting on that, but it shouldn't take long. I did get you some information about your partner though, which I think you'll also find interesting."

Russell was about to answer when he noticed a desk sergeant approaching, escorting a woman who was the spitting image of Michelle, along with a skinny, nervous-looking man who looked none too happy to be in a police station.

"I'm sorry to interrupt you guys, but this young lady wanted to talk to Detective Howard."

"It's okay—I'll go and see if I can hunt down that ballistics report," Morales said. "I'll check back with you in a bit, but be prepared for a long day, Junior."

Morales walked away with the other officer, leaving Russell to meet with his guests. He was curious to find out what Morales had learned about Sydney, but diplomacy dictated that this come first.

"Detective Howard?" The words came out quiet, and with a light Southern drawl. Georgia, Russell guessed, or maybe Alabama. More country-sounding than Florida, but he couldn't pin it down.

Wherever she was from, it was hard not to stare at her. He couldn't believe how much she looked like her sister. They had the same smooth complexion and dark brown eyes. It was easy to see why Lords was so taken by Michelle. If she was anything like the woman standing in front of him, that woman had a special something that could make a man misbehave.

Slowly, he rose to his feet. "Yes, I'm Detective Howard. It's good to meet you, Ms. Tibbs, though I'm very sorry for the circumstances. Why don't you have a seat?"

He sat back down with his guests, smiling at the idea that Rhonda's visit may have come at an opportune time. Maybe she could shed some light on Mosley's connection to Lords.

"So what brings you by the station?"

"Me and my cousin Calvin are here to claim my sister's body and take her home," Rhonda replied. "I heard about y'all arresting Eddie for Chelle's murder and I came by to personally thank you on behalf of my family."

"You really didn't have to do that. I was just doing my job. I'm happy to bring you some kind of closure on this terrible situation."

He regretted his words as soon as he spoke. After reading

the coroner's report, they were a long way from closure. He wasn't sure how to break that to her.

"I heard Stevie will walk, but Eddie wasn't doing too good after that shooting," Rhonda said. "I don't mean to sound cold blooded or nothin', but Eddie got what he deserved. I'm just glad you didn't get hurt."

"Well, nothing too serious," Russell said as he rubbed his head. "Lords isn't off the hook yet. We have a hearsay confession from Eddie Brown, but we can't rule out the possibility Lords may have been involved. If Eddie makes any kind of recovery, then we can question him about Lords's involvement and go from there."

Russell watched as the implication settled in. They were still a long way from knowing exactly what happened. Eddie was part of it for sure, but how big a part was anyone's guess.

"How well did you know Eddie?" Russell said after a moment, directing his gaze at Calvin.

"Me and Eddie and Steve . . . we pretty much all grew up together," Calvin said. "We used to play ball on the neighborhood courts back in the day."

Russell raised an eyebrow. "Were Eddie and Steven really that close growing up?"

"They like brothers, you know? When you saw one, you saw the other," Calvin said. "Eddie always had Stevie's back, that's for sure."

"Yeah, I remember Chelle used to get mad at Stevie

because he was kickin' it more with Eddie than he did with her," Rhonda added.

"Earlier today I saw a guy on television claiming to be the guy who discovered Lords on the playground when he was a kid—"

"You talkin' 'bout Dub Mos?" Calvin asked. "Was he a tall cat and kinda built with really dark skin and a scar on his chin?"

"That's right. His name was Wallace Mosley."

"Yep, that's Dub. He was hanging around my sister a whole lot since he got out of jail," Rhonda said. "I asked her what was up between them and she said it was just business."

"So what's his deal?" Russell asked. "I saw him wearing a Miami jacket I'm pretty sure belongs to Steven. Are they still friendly?"

"Was it a black jacket with white—"

"Yeah, it was his team-issued warm-up jacket. Name on the back and everything. Have you seen it before?"

"Steven gave one to Michelle a while back," Rhonda said. "She used to wear it all the time, and one reason we're here now is that it's missing from her personal things."

"You're sure about that?"

"Positive," Rhonda said. "And there's a laptop computer that's gone missing as well. Do you have any idea what may have happened to them?"

Russell sat back in his chair. "Those items would still

be part of this investigation, so they'll be returned to you at a later time. But what I'm curious about is why a guy like Lords would be hooked up with a character like Dub. What's the connection?"

"Dub taught him how to hustle, man," Calvin said. "They used to work the dudes in the parks around town pretty good. They'd hustle cats for pick-up games and during tournaments. That was before Stevie got to be a local hero. When he started blowing up and people were packing the gym to watch his high school games, that's where they really cleaned up."

"Lords went along with that?" Russell asked.

"Stevie has it going on now, but it wasn't always like that. His moms worked two jobs and even that wasn't always enough. We'd go around to his house and sometimes the water would be off or the cable was cut off. The money was tight back then. Stevie did whatever it took to help her out."

"So how did Dub meet Lords?"

"On the basketball court," Calvin recalled. "I remember me, Stevie, Eddie, and some other fellas were shooting hoops one day. Then some dude gets real aggressive with Stevie, giving him a hard time and wanting to fight him. Dub had been watching Stevie play, and he came over and straight punked the guy. Next thing you know he gave Stevie a few dollars and from that point on, Dub put the word out that no one was to mess with Stevie."

"So Dub was a street thug that used Lords to make some money?"

"Not quite. They say Dub was a good player back in the day, and really did look out for Stevie. Sent him to camps and all that. Plus, Dub was a dude you didn't want it with," Calvin said. "We was talking about how Eddie watched Stevie's back? Fo' real, Dub protected him. Those dudes I was telling you about that hassled Stevie? They never played ball again. After Dub got one of his boys take a hammer to their shooting hands."

"So what happened between Steven and Dub then?"

Before answering, Calvin looked at Rhonda, who nodded resignedly.

"Okay, around the time Stevie got drafted, Dub got arrested for drugs. The cops had been on his ass for months and finally busted him. Word on the street was Dub thought Stevie would testify on his behalf at his trial, you know, at least as a character witness. He figured he did a lot for Stevie, and I guess he figured Stevie owed him at least that much."

"And let me guess," Russell said. "The superstar didn't want his name to be associated with a drug trial and never showed?"

"Damn straight, he didn't!" Calvin said "Hell, I don't blame him either. If I had just got drafted and making all that dough, I wouldn't have showed up either. But Dub sure as hell wasn't happy about it."

Russell nodded. "But things were okay between them, right? He may not have liked it but I'm sure Dub understood why Lords didn't show."

"I don't know, man . . . Dub pretty much lost everything when he went to jail," Calvin said. "Plus, he lost the streets after he snitched on some people to get his time cut down. So let me ask you, would you be cool with Stevie if you were in Dub's shoes?"

"Probably not," Russell tapped his finger on his desk and let the implications roll around his mind. Dub there in Miami with an ax to grind, wearing a jacket belonging to a dead woman. A totally different picture was starting to emerge and Russell didn't like it one bit.

"Detective Howard, we got a flight to catch, so we'd better get going," Rhonda said. "I just wanted to let you know that I really appreciate everything you've done. But do let me know about the rest of her stuff, okay?"

RUSSELL SPENT THE NEXT HOUR GOING THROUGH HIS notes and trying to see how the new information about Wallace Mosley fit with what he already knew. He looked up from his desk when he heard Morales approaching with a manila folder tucked under his arm.

"Shit, Junior. You look like a man with a lot on his mind."

"Talking to Tibbs's family got me thinking, is all," Russell said as he fidgeted with his playing cards.

"Well, here's more food for thought then. I just got off the phone with Greg in ballistics," Morales said, a note of urgency in his voice that Russell didn't like.

He opened the folder and took out a few sheets of paper and laid them on the desk.

"What's this?" Russell said, putting his deck of cards to the side.

"Pictures Greg faxed over. It looks like the handgun you took off of Eddie was the same one used to kill Cooper." Morales pointed at one of the images. "You see what he has circled here? The indentation left by the firing pin on the test shell casing matched the indentation on the shell casing found at Cooper's place."

"Well, that's no surprise. Eddie probably shot him to cover his tracks at the hotel."

"That's not all, though," Morales said. "If you look at these images he circled, you'll see the indentations are a perfect match."

"Don't tell me that those are the casings—"

"That's right, Junior! Those are the ones you gave me. The casings you gave me match the indentations on the casings taken from Cooper's place perfectly. They're nowhere close to matching anything that came out of your .22. Now you tell me something: how in the hell is that possible?"

An empty feeling formed in the pit of Russell's stomach, but he said nothing. Morales was clearly on the warpath and feeling like he was onto something, and that worried Russell.

"We both know you didn't tell me the whole story in having doubts about Sydney after the shooting at Johnny Ray's," Morales said. "So as soon as I saw this report from ballistics, I made that call to a contact of mine in the bureau. I think you'll find his info very interesting."

Once again Morales opened his folder and started thumbing through the pages. He stopped at a faxed report with an FBI cover sheet time-stamped from a few minutes earlier.

"Sydney Vanessa Farrell was born in Greenville, North Carolina—"

"Greenville? She said she was from Buffalo."

"Let me finish. Says here she was born in Greenville, North Carolina. Attended Winston Salem State, graduated with honors. She joined the bureau in '98, resigned six years later, and got into consulting and private investigating."

That smelled fishy to Russell. "People don't up and quit the bureau so early in their careers without good reason. So what gives?" he asked. "I'm guessing there's a reason for her early retirement?"

Morales nodded, eyes bright with excitement.

"Yeah, you might say that. I don't have a lot of details, but apparently she resigned amid allegations of impropriety stemming from an investigation of identity theft."

"No shit?"

"But wait, it gets better. It says here she was investigating a then-rookie sports agent named Allen Warner on suspicion of providing false documentation to immigrants who were in this country illegally to play baseball. That name sound familiar, Junior?"

Russell looked at his boss and smiled.

Morales nodded back, a smug look on his face. Russell knew Morales didn't get to do much real police work and couldn't blame him for enjoying helping to get a break in the case.

"That can't be a coincidence, can it?" Morales asked.

"Hardly. There are way too many things in this case that don't match up," Russell said as he stood.

"Like what?"

"I'll explain later, but right now I've got to get back over to the Murcielago. I need to get some closure and I have a feeling that's where I'm going to get it."

CHAPTER 39

Russell strode through the foyer and flashed his badge with an apologetic nod to three guests he had to cut in front of at the front desk. This trip would be the fourth he'd made since the investigation began, and with any luck this would be his last.

"Welcome to the Murcielago Hotel. How may I help you?" the desk clerk asked.

"Wallace Mosley's suite number, please," Russell said.

The clerk tapped a few keys on her computer and smiled apologetically after a glance at his badge. "I'm sorry, sir, but Mr. Mosley checked out this morning."

"Can you tell me when he checked in?"

"Six days ago."

"Did he have a reservation?"

"Yes, sir. A reservation was made for Mr. Mosley."

"Does it say who made that reservation?"

"No, I see here that the credit card used to reserve the room belonged to an Allen Warner with a request he be given suite number 2210."

Russell pounded his fist on the counter. It looked like he'd missed an opportunity to get some much-needed answers to the questions that had plagued him most of the day. He started to walk away from the desk, then paused.

"Can you call Sydney Farrell's room for me, please?"

Again the clerk punched in a few keys. "I'm sorry, but Ms. Farrell also checked out this morning."

"Did Allen Warner also make her reservation?"

"Let's see, she checked in four days ago. But I don't see a reservation for her."

Sydney and Mosley checked into the hotel two days apart. Mosley checked in a day before Tibbs was killed and Sydney a day after. It could've been a strange coincidence, but Russell didn't want to leave that to chance.

"Is there anything else I can help you with, Detective?"

"Yeah, as a matter of fact there is," Russell replied. "Is Chris here? Chris in security?"

"I believe so. Let me call the security office and—"

"That's okay. I know the way."

Russell tapped on the door before he opened it and

walked in. Chris didn't look too busy. He was kicked back with his feet up on the desk, eating a slice of pizza.

"Any chance you can cue up some surveillance footage from four nights ago?" Russell said. "I'd like to have another look at it."

"Any specific area you had in mind?"

"Not really. Let's start with the lobby and go from there."

Russell grabbed a chair and sat next to Chris so he had a good view of the main monitor. After watching several people pass by, he finally identified Sydney checking in.

"Could you fast forward it a bit?"

Chris sped up the video while Russell stared at the monitor. He still wasn't sure what he was looking for.

"Okay, let's slow it down," Russell said when he spotted Wallace Mosley walking through the lobby and proceeding out of the camera's range. He tapped the image of the figure on the screen and said, "Any ideas where that guy may have been heading?"

"He could be going into Ansovino. It's a restaurant down that corridor," Chris replied. "Let me call up another camera and we'll see."

Chris pressed a few keys and the image changed. Russell watched Dub enter the same bar Sydney had taken him to a couple of nights prior. Chris pressed a few more buttons on his keyboard, and Russell watched Dub sit at the bar and order a drink. Russell shook his head. He anticipated Wallace was there to meet someone, and he had a good idea who that someone was. As Dub sipped his drink, a woman wearing black with her hair in an all-too-familiar ponytail approached. Russell leaned closer as he waited for the events on the video to unfold.

"No sound on these feeds?" Russell asked.

"Sorry, Detective."

Russell nodded and returned his attention to the video. It was Sydney all right, and he could tell by their body language it wasn't their first meeting. They chatted for a few moments and then left the bar together without even finishing their drinks.

Chris changed the video so Russell could watch them walk through the lobby and then out to the parking lot. The time in the lower left-hand corner of the screen read 11:44 p.m. and was running properly, showing no evidence of tampering. That was about an hour before the time the medical examiner had determined James Cooper was shot.

Russell sat back in his chair, marveling at what he was seeing. A day ago he wouldn't have believed it.

A vibration in his pocket interrupted his thoughts. He pulled out his cell phone and saw a number he didn't recognize. "This is Detective Howard—who's this?"

"Hey, man, it's Darrell. Remember me from next door to Jimmy's house? You said you had some tickets for me and my boy Rodney for the game tonight. I was calling to see what's up."

"What's up is I remember you fine and I have the tickets. But the game's not until tonight."

"I know. I was just calling to make sure."

Russell got up and waved at Chris as he left the office. "Listen, I'm really busy right now but I promised you the tickets and I'll make sure you get them. Why don't you guys meet me at the station around 7:30 and we'll head over to the arena from there? Just make sure you have a ride home."

"Aight, man, we'll be there," Darrell said. "I can't wait to go check out this game!"

"You know something, Darrell? I can't either."

CHAPTER 40

Miami Coliseum
Four hours until tip-off

Steven Lords nodded at the gate attendant and turned his black Bentley Continental GT into the players' parking lot at the Miami Coliseum. The garage was almost empty, but that was normal—Steven had always made it a point to make sure he was the first player to arrive. With his custom-tailored jacket draped over his arm and iPod in hand, he proceeded to the players' entrance.

He closed his eyes and took a deep breath after he was inside. It felt good to be back in his safe haven.

He shook the hands of the locker-room attendants, who were busy getting things together before the rest of the team arrived, then hung his jacket in his stall. He reached into his pocket, took out a picture of Karen and Cassidy, pinned it inside his locker, then sat on the bench.

He sighed as he unlaced his shoes. It had been a strange few months. Leaving for games without kissing his wife and daughter goodbye had taken some getting used to, but not having Eddie around for his pregame routine and getting his meal arranged was a tough pill to swallow. Steven still couldn't get his head around the fact Eddie had sold him out. Allen was right. Drugs could make people do strange things. But the idea of his best friend dishing dirt on him to pay a drug debt was hard to fathom.

A locker-room attendant was happy to help with his meal, and after his order was in, Steven went back to getting ready for the game. He always liked to put up some shots on the game floor while there weren't many people in the arena, so he changed into warm-ups, cranked "Superstar" by Lupe Fiasco on his iPod, and let the trainers go to work taping his ankles. He stretched out on the table, closed his eyes, and envisioned what he wanted to do on the court.

Twenty minutes later he was back at his locker, savoring the aroma and comfort of his new basketball shoes as he laced them up. He always got a bit nervous before big games and he wished like crazy Eddie was there with a few of jokes to ease the tension. But that was just one more thing that would take some getting used to.

He looked up at the clock on the wall. There were still about three hours until tip-off, and that meant it was time to head out to the court. A little smile made its way onto his face. Putting up a few shots always helped work off the nervous energy.

The lights were only at half power, leaving the arena dimly lit as the cheerleading team practiced at half court. The arena speakers thumped with the sound of dance music as the girls worked through their routines. Steven grabbed a basketball from the rack and began some dribbling drills from half court to baseline and then from sideline to sideline. The ball bounced rhythmically as he switched hands dribbling, his sneakers squeaking loudly with each stop.

After he got a good feel for the ball, he took shots from different spots around the court. A ball boy saw him shooting and came out to rebound while Steven made textbook shot after shot.

He never thought about his form much during the game—out there you had to trust your stuff. But here, he thought carefully about each and every move, making sure his mechanics were perfect as he raised his arms, kept his shoulders and elbows square and in line with the basket, and released the ball at the top of his jump. He landed on the court with his hand still raised and watched the spinning ball go through the hoop.

Everything felt perfect. His mind and body were in sync. He was ready.

***

ALL THE ACTIVITY SURROUNDING THE COLISEUM MADE getting to the game a nightmare. It was getting close to tip-off and Russell and the boys were stuck in traffic while fans, scalpers, and vendors clogged the streets. Russell grinned when he saw some of the other cars trying to utilize the limited and grossly overpriced downtown parking spaces. At least he had a parking pass. The trick was getting through the throngs of people to the VIP garage.

Darrell and Rodney were both wearing Steven Lords jerseys, and as they inched their way closer, they marveled at their luck scoring tickets. "I still can't believe anyone would give away tickets to this game," Darrell was saying. "But I'm damn sure glad you did."

"If I was you I'd of taken that fine-ass lady cop you had with you," Rodney added.

Russell shook his head and smiled. He had a funny feeling she might already be at the game. He turned and looked at Darrell. "Basketball isn't really my sport, but you guys enjoy yourselves."

Once they reached the parking-lot attendant, Russell flashed the permit Dave had given him. In his peripheral vision he could see Darrell staring wide-eyed at the shiny rows of luxury SUVs and sports cars, most of which Russell was sure cost more than he made in a year.

"Man, these are some bad-ass whips in here," Darrell said. "I wonder if 'The Lord's' car is parked in here somewhere?"

The kid was right: This had to be the players' lot. Russell

managed to find a space between a Porsche 911 and a Lexus SUV, wishing he'd at least washed his crummy old Mustang sometime in the past year.

THE BOYS JUMPED OUT OF THE CAR BEFORE RUSSELL could put it in park. Rodney started toward the exit while Darrell took out his camera phone and began checking out some of the cars.

"Come on, man, hurry up!"

"Hold on—I wanna see if I can find Lords's car," Darrell said. "I want to get a picture of it and put it on my Facebook page."

Russell, who was putting on his jacket before leaving the car, lagged behind the boys. He was about to catch up to Rodney when Darrell yelled out, "Hey, Rodney, come here and check this out!"

Rodney stopped and walked over to Darrell, with Russell a step behind. Darrell stood next to a dark blue Chevy Impala. "Ain't that the car from Jimmy's house the other night?"

WITH AN HOUR UNTIL TIP-OFF, STEVEN AND SOME TEAM-mates put on their uniforms. A few of the guys had gone to the trainer for treatments but after everyone returned, Coach Hollis joined them and asked for everybody's attention as he made his way to the center of the room.

"Guys, this is it," he said as he looked at the players. "You know these past few days have really put us to the test. This team has battled through adversity better than any team I've ever been a part of, and I couldn't be any prouder of you all."

The team nodded in unison as Hollis continued. "It's been quite a journey, but through it all we've stood strong, we've persevered, and most importantly we've remained a team . . . a family. After these next four wins, we'll be champions!"

The locker room erupted with applause as Steven stood from his locker stall and walked toward Coach Hollis. He put his arm around him as he looked at his teammates.

"I just want to say thank you for all the love y'all have given me," Steven said. "It's been a terrible week, but y'all boys have had my back every step of the way and I love the hell out of y'all. If any of you ever need me for—"

"Right now we need you to go out and be Steve the muthafuckin' Lords, man," Julian said as he tucked in his jersey. "We love you too, but this ain't the time for heartfelt speeches. Save that shit for the celebration at Bicentennial Park, bro. Like Coach just said, we got four wins to get. So let's focus up and get these wins."

RUSSELL WALKED CAUTIOUSLY AROUND THE BLUE IMPALA with a Tennessee license plate. He took a deep breath as he ran his fingers through his hair. "Rodney, you're *sure* this is the car you saw the night Cooper was killed? I mean, without-a-doubt positive?"

"This is the car—I'd bet my momma's life on it. I remember that custom paint and those chrome shoes."

"Aw hell yeah," Darrell said. "I know cars and this is definitely the one. Shit, I'd even bet our tickets on it!"

Russell reached in his pocket and took out his phone. He needed a miracle before it was too late.

"Hey, Art. I'm with those kids that live next door to where James Cooper, the security tech, got killed. Sounds like they've spotted the car that was at Cooper's house the night he got shot. Do you think you could get me a search warrant so I can check it out?"

He heard shuffling in the background and then Morales answered. "I'm pretty sure I can talk Judge Baker into giving you a warrant, but it'll take a little time to get it typed up and signed."

"Like how long?"

"I don't know, couple hours, maybe. I'll have to try to track him down and I'm guessing he may be preoccupied, what with the game and all."

"I don't have a couple hours, man. I need this warrant now!"

"I'm sorry, Russell, it doesn't work that way. There are procedures. It's after eight o'clock and that's the best I can do. I don't know if you know this, but there is a

Finals game tonight and everybody's probably somewhere watching it."

"Well what am I supposed to do in the meantime, then?"

"I'll tell you what—why don't you give me the plate number and I'll run it for you and call you back?"

Russell read the letters as Darrell stood and waited. Rodney, too excited to wait, headed for the entrance.

"Got it," Morales said. "Give me a few minutes and I'll call you right back."

Russell and Darrell re-joined Rodney, and Russell walked them through the will-call doors to claim the tickets. After the boys got their passes, Russell went back to the parking garage. He had an idea who the car belonged to and was hoping for a peek inside, but the black window tint made that impossible.

Russell paced the parking lot while he waited, and it was only a moment before a security guard showed up demanding an explanation. Russell showed him his badge and explained, then called Morales's cell phone once every few minutes. Morales was putting his calls straight to voicemail, and Russell's patience was reaching its limits. Time was ticking away, and if he had any chance of getting to the bottom of all this he knew he had to act fast.

After confirming the guard wasn't looking Russell took off his jacket and wrapped it around his forearm and elbow. This wouldn't be official police procedure, but he couldn't worry about that now. He stepped back from the car and was about to put his elbow through the driver's-side window when his cell phone rang.

"Damn, Art, what took so long?" Russell said.

"I got the name of the registered owner. The car belongs to a Wallace Mosley. Does that name do anything for you?"

Russell nodded. "Yeah, I saw him on Owens's show today. He's a thug from Lords's hometown. Can you still get me that search warrant?"

"Probably, but it's gonna take a little while."

"I may not have a little while. I have a feeling that something's going down as we speak and there's no telling how long he'll be here."

"You think he's going to cut out in the middle of the game?"

"Can't rule it out."

Morales said, "You know, Russell. I'd never advise you to do anything illegal but it seems to me it'd be tough for Mr. Mosley to get too far if he had a flat tire, wouldn't it?"

Russell smiled. "You know, that's a good point. I'll keep that in mind."

"Good!" Morales said. "You do what you need to do. I'll get there as soon as I can."

STEVEN BLEW A KISS TO THE PICTURE OF HIS FAMILY AND fell into step with his teammates exiting the locker room. They heard the home crowd boo as Los Angeles took the court. As Rev concluded the prayer, Nate began the team chant.

"WE ARE?" he shouted.

"CHAMPIONS!" the team answered.

"WE WILL?

"DOMINATE!"

"WHAT TIME?"

"GAME TIME!"

An eruption of thunderous applause echoed through the arena as Steven and his teammates exited the tunnel. The energy in the place was like nothing he'd ever experienced.

His hands began to shake when he realized how many fans were proudly sporting shirts with his signature basketball crucifix logo on the front. Many even held signs saying "Praise the Lord." He smiled and waved to the crowd, savoring the support he felt from them and the sense that the city was behind him.

Cameras flashed as the team began their warm-ups. The lights were bright and the building was sold out. A palpable sense of excitement filled the air and only escalated as tip-off approached.

This was his opportunity to cut loose. To break free of all the negative publicity and turmoil and get back to something he felt at peace with: the game of basketball. Which at this moment seemed like all he had left.

***

PEOPLE SCRAMBLED FOR THEIR SEATS AS THE ARENA announcer began introductions for the visiting team. An echo of boos filled the arena as the Los Angeles players were announced and took the court. Suddenly the lights went out, sending the arena into near blackness.

Second later, cameras flashed and laser lights shot all over the arena, while the dance team shook and shimmied. A spotlight shined from the rafters onto Miami's bench. The cheering reached earsplitting levels as the booming voice over the PA announced the players. The crowd got louder and louder, peaking with the callout for Steven Lords.

The house lights came on as everyone in the building rose for the national anthem. Steven looked down at the court with his hands behind his back. He muttered a silent prayer as one of Miami's seemingly endless supply of Latina one-hit wonders sang her heart out, whipping the crowd into an all-out frenzy.

The boisterous noise swelled at the song's conclusion. Everyone was anxious to see Steven perform on the sport's biggest stage. Both starting fives took the court and exchanged handshakes. The referee took the game ball to half court as the players prepared for tip-off. It was the moment Steven had been waiting for. The butterflies were gone. The nervousness had been replaced with a calm intensity. The ball was tipped. This was his time.

CHAPTER 41

Allen sat high in his luxury suite, looking out at the thousands of fans waving white towels as the first quarter ended. It had been loud in there before, but never to the point that you could feel the walls shake. But with Miami up twenty-nine to twelve, it was no surprise the place was going nuts. Steven was dominating, destroying Los Angeles's defense to the tune of eighteen points and being an absolute madman blocking shots, rebounding, and keeping L.A. out of the paint.

Allen sat back and threw his arm over the seat next to him. It was all coming together so perfectly. "He's beautiful isn't he? His life is falling apart, his best friend's dying in the hospital, and he's still playing like the best player of our generation."

The man next to him smiled and nodded smugly, as if they were discussing his own accolades.

But Allen didn't let that bother him. He was at the threshold of not only getting Steven's lost endorsements back but also probably landing a few new ones. And this was sure to help sweeten his client list when it came to free agents and draft prospects.

He stood, walked over to the bar, and poured himself a scotch. "You see, Steven Lords is one of the greats. They don't come around very often, but he's one of them. Wouldn't you agree, Wallace?"

There was something about Wallace's expression that Allen couldn't read but knew he didn't like. Wallace seemed uncharacteristically quiet, but that was probably a blessing.

ALLEN RETURNED HIS ATTENTIONS TO THE GAME WHILE Wallace "Dub" Mosley sat close by, picking at some chicken wings while he looked around the suite. The two plasma televisions, the rows of leather chairs that overlooked the court through a retractable window, the prime location— all of this should have been his.

"Hey, Dub, are you watching this, buddy?" Allen asked. "We're not even at halftime yet and he has twenty-six points."

Dub stood and picked up the black leather case at his side. Allen was as relaxed as he'd ever seen him, but this was no time for pleasantries. Up until now everyone in the room had cashed in big time on the phenomenon that was Steven Lords. Now it was Dub's turn.

"I knew what kind of player he was when I found him playing in the park thirteen years ago," Dub said. "Obviously you knew what you were getting when you took him away and got him to sign with you."

Allen turned to look at Dub, face tight with sudden irritation. "Are we really going to rehash all of this now? That was seven years ago, Wallace. C'mon, man, let it go!"

Dub was going to do just that but Allen, on his third drink, kept talking.

"What were you gonna do with him, anyway? Have him shedding points for his entire career? Maybe hustle some nickel bags after he got caught?"

Allen smiled smugly and then took a long drink before continuing. "Just look at all those number 14 jerseys out there. Look at the Steven Lords crucifix T-shirts. You might have found him, sure, and more power to you for recognizing his *obvious* talent. But I'm the one who made him an icon!"

Dub swallowed hard and took a few breaths to keep his irritation in check. The more Allen talked, the more he wanted to get paid and get out. He'd rather watch the game from the nosebleeds than listen to this arrogant prick.

"I had a lot more to do with Stevie's coming up," Dub said. "Who fronted the cash to send him to camps and get him on the best AAU teams? It was me, homie. I did that. I taught him how to step up his game, and you had no right to tell him to leave me hanging after everything I did for him."

Allen waved a hand dismissively. "Come on, man, stop with that, would you?" We both know your trial wasn't good for his image. You'd have done the exact same thing if you were in my shoes—at least if you had a lick of sense, you would have."

"What, have my boy stab me in the back like that?" Dub said. "I'm sitting on trial looking at some serious time, and I couldn't even get Stevie on the damn phone because you had his numbers changed!"

"You were bad for business, Wallace. And it's not like you didn't make a nice little profit from your investment along the way. You managed to hustle yourself up some nice payday, not to mention the six figures you got for delivering Steven to good ol' Coach Maddox."

"That's beside the point."

"No that is the point. I . . ." Allen turned his head just in time to see Steven leap for an errant alley-oop pass from Kyle that anyone else on the team would have let go by. "Did you see that? Did you see that move?"

Allen paused when his cell phone started ringing.

Dub put his case on the floor as he sat back in his chair. Who the hell was Allen to criticize somebody for hustling a dollar or two off Stevie? He frowned as he looked at the Hublot watch on Allen's wrist. He was damn sure getting his, and he'd never even invested a single dollar into the man, so to hell with him.

Allen laughed as he put his phone back into his pocket. "That was Frank Powell from ConAgra. Says he wanted to let us know they're open to resigning Steven to a new endorsement deal. See, I knew they'd be back. They always love a winner."

"I'm happy for you. Now can we get down to our deal?" Dub put the case on the arm between his seat and Allen's and looked him in the eye.

"All in due time, Wallace. This is a big night for all of us. Why don't you sit back and enjoy the show?"

"You weren't exactly patient when you asked me to get this book back, were you?"

"And you didn't exactly hesitate when you told me what it would cost me," Allen said. "Now if you don't mind, I'd like to see some of this game. We'll get to it in a bit."

Dub took his case back to the bar. He could feel his impatience grow with each passing minute. By this point his payday was assured, but it was hard to relax. He tried to focus on the game but found his gaze drifting to Allen's companion, who seemed to get better and better looking each time he saw her.

"Hey, how about me and you take a little cruise out to Jamaica once this is all over and talk about the future?" Dub said, nodding suggestively. "I like the way you handle yourself with a gun, and I think me and you can do some great things together."

He watched Sydney turn from her perch next to the window overlooking the arena and join him next to the food table. Man, she was pretty!

"Why don't you put it in park, tough guy?" she said. "It'll take a lot more than what Allen's paying you to get me to spend another minute with you once this thing is done."

"You say that now," he said, flashing his best smile. "But I can be very persuasive."

"Let's get something straight. If you were on fire, I wouldn't spit on you to put you out, okay?

Dub laughed. "Girl, you still mad about that parking lot thing?"

"That little stunt nearly got me killed. Not to mention blowing the lid off our arrangement here. I still don't know what the hell you were thinking."

"I told you that was my call," Allen said, after getting up from his seat and putting his glass on the bar. "None of us wanted you to get hurt. Eddie was getting to be a liability and we'd come too far to let him screw everything up."

"But couldn't you find another way to take care of him?"

Allen shrugged. "Once you told me about the problem James Cooper was having," he paused and cut his eyes to Dub. "Well let's just say it was too good an opportunity to pass up. A lot less heat if the cops think it's gang-related, or some kind of beef over drugs, don't you think?"

"Maybe," Sydney said. "But you could've told me

something ahead of time! This job wasn't supposed to be dangerous. Wasn't that what you promised me?"

"I promised you a lot of things, and I made good on most of them. You're being exceptionally well compensated for your services, for one. And some things, as you well know, are out of our control sometimes."

"What's *that* supposed to mean?"

Dub watched both of them closely. Why all the tension all of a sudden?

"Let's not overthink things, all right? I'm sorry about what happened at Johnny Ray's, but let's try and relax, okay?"

Dub watched as Allen put his arm around Sydney and gently pulled her closer. She stiffened when he tried to kiss her on the cheek, so he let go and turned his gaze back to Dub, who looked at him as if to say *let's get on with it.*

Allen finally took a hint. "Draw those blinds, would you, Syd? It looks like our friend Mr. Mosley here is anxious to conclude our business."

After everyone was seated, Dub joined them and pulled a black Toshiba laptop from its case and put it on the bar.

"This is it, Al. This is what all this shit was about," Dub said. "Eddie may have messed things up at the hotel, but being next door made it much easier for me to go in and do what I had to do. So . . . you got my money?"

"Oh, I have your money," Allen said. "Unlike Michelle, I honor my agreements. One million dollars sitting in a

Grand Cayman account. To give you access to it, I just have to make sure the merchandise is good." Allen looked at Sydney. "Could you check it out and make sure our friend has what we need?"

Sydney flipped the screen up and pressed the power button, but nothing happened. She pressed it again, but got the same result.

"What's wrong with this?" she asked. "Is the battery dead or something?"

"I cracked it," Dub said. He lifted the laptop up to show Sydney the slight crack in the base. "But if you plug it in it should work okay."

"Christ, is that Michelle's hair?" Allen asked.

"'Fraid so," Dub replied. "Considering the shape Eddie left her in, I thought it was more humane to end her suffering. Plus, the bitch had it coming for trying to play me. I hope we won't have that same problem."

Sydney looked down at the crack in the laptop, which indeed had a few strands of hair stuck in it. She looked at Dub and asked, "Do you have the adapter?"

"Should be in the case."

It was, and it only took a moment to boot the computer. She glanced at Allen, who was relieved at seeing the power light come on.

"I think the file you're looking for is a Word file labeled 'Stevie baby'," Dub said. "That's the whole book."

Sydney opened a Microsoft Word file and scrolled through

it quickly. "It looks like this could be it. You guys have been busy, too. The document is over three hundred pages."

Allen reached into his pocket, pulled out a cell phone, and tossed it to Dub.

"What the hell is this?"

"Money talks, my friend. There's one number programmed in that phone," Allen said. "Why don't you dial it up?"

Dub didn't hesitate. He pressed send and placed the phone to his ear, his hands slightly shaking. He'd been waiting for this moment for months, and in some ways it had felt like a lifetime. To think he was seconds away from becoming a bona fide millionaire . . .

He listened as the automated voice informed him he'd reached Cayman National Bank. Before the voice could ask for a pass code Allen said, "33235410." When prompted, Dub typed in the code and listened to the electronic balance.

"I included a little extra for your help with James Cooper and our friend Eddie," Allen said. "I trust I won't have to worry about you uttering a single other word about Steven Lords or what happened here?"

"I'm out of the book-writing business for good," Dub said with a smile. "I may try my hand at being a sports agent, seeing how it's treated you well."

"It has indeed, my friend," Allen stood and took a bottle of champagne from the refrigerator. "This calls for a little toast," he said as he popped the cork and filled three glasses.

Dub joined Allen at the bar, still reveling from shock. After years of hustling and crime and dirty dealing, he was finally getting paid. And with the ugliness of all this finally behind him, he felt something take root in his chest that he hadn't experienced in ages. His future actually seemed bright.

"Sydney, you did a terrific job with the police," Allen said, holding up his glass. "Here's to new beginnings, bigger opportunities, and better paydays."

The trio clanked their glasses together. Dub was about to take a sip of his champagne when he heard a gentle tap on the door.

CHAPTER 42

Russell didn't wait for an answer before cracking open the door and peeking at what was going on inside. He would have liked to be surprised that the first thing he saw was his so-called partner drinking champagne with a cold-blooded murderer and the man who put him up to it. He'd misjudged her as badly as he'd misjudged Steven Lords. He couldn't bring Michelle or James Cooper back, but if he played his cards right now there would be justice. He'd just have to put on the performance of a lifetime.

The tension on Syd's face, icy stares, and silence spoke volumes as he walked into the room.

"Am I interrupting something?" he asked, smiling thinly at Syd.

"Russell? What are you doing here?"

Allen put his hand gently on top of hers. "Actually, we were in the middle of celebrating Steven's potentially record-breaking performance," Allen replied. "So if you wouldn't mind—"

"Staying? Oh I'd be happy to," Russell said. "Thanks for the invite." He walked casually into the suite and joined everyone else at the bar. "Fancy seeing *you* here," he said, looking at Sydney.

She was about to respond when Russell noticed Allen squeezing her hand. "Can I offer you a drink, Detective?" Allen asked, his tone guarded.

"No thanks, I'm still on duty," Russell smirked at Sydney, whose steely eyes were locked on him. She was trying to look cool and maybe even intimidating. But it was all for show. She was definitely freaked out. The goose bumps on her arms gave her away.

"I've got to say, guys, I'm a bit offended I didn't get an invite your little party here. But I see Sydney got hers," Russell said with a smile. "Or is that Syd? That is what you called her at Lords's house, right? Her friends call her Syd. How's your dad doing out in Greenville, by the way? Maybe you should tell him I said hello."

She looked away.

"We're all friends here, Detective Howard," Allen said as he patted Sydney's hand. "We're all here basking in the triumph of another close friend of ours. I'd be remiss if I didn't thank you for your hard work in getting him exonerated. This wouldn't be possible if it wasn't for you and your department."

"No thanks needed. I was just doing my job," Russell said. "But you should probably thank Syd. I'm sure she was worth every penny you're paying her and more."

He watched as Sydney whispered something to Allen, who nodded but said nothing in return. Mosley hadn't said a word but didn't look happy to see Russell either.

The blinds were closed and the TVs were muted, so aside from the hum of the A/C all he could hear was the muted ebb and swell of crowd noise from the other side of the thick glass. Russell made a show of looking around carefully as if trying to make sense of what was going on, then smiled when he saw a black laptop computer lying on the coffee table.

He turned his attention back to Dub, who was looking around the room nervously.

"Please excuse my manners, Detective. I forgot to introduce you," Allen said. "Detective Howard, I'd like you to meet—"

"Wallace Mosley," Russell said. "Or better yet Dub Mos."

Allen squinted. "So, you two know each other?"

"No, I've never had the pleasure, but I know of him. In fact, I saw him on Owens's show this morning."

Allen looked at Dub. "You were on Owens's show?"

"Yeah, I ran into him when I was over at Joe's Stone Crab. He remembered me from my college playing days and he asked me to do an appearance."

Allen rolled his eyes. "Owens is nothing more than a

bottom-feeding lowlife. He tries to twist everything you say and turn it against you—"

"Oh, don't worry about that," Russell interjected. "Dub was a good boy, left the set before he could get you into any trouble. I had to call Owens to find out everything Wallace wouldn't say on the show, and boy, did he give me an earful."

"Really?" Allen said. "I can only imagine what wild stories Owens could have told you."

Russell smiled affably, as if making cocktail chitchat. Syd looked miserable.

"Well, you don't have to imagine. Let's start with the point shaving," Russell said. "Seven years back during the NCAA tournament. Turns out that Owens and Dub go back to Dub's college-playing days. And believe it or not, Dub— being the upstanding citizen he is—did a little point shaving in college, and it actually got him kicked off his team."

"What's that got to do with Steven?"

"Why don't you tell me, Allen? Surely you're well aware of the speculations about Steven's point shaving back when he was in college."

Russell paused and looked hard into Allen's blank stare.

"Owens said he'd tried several times to get someone on the record about it but everybody had developed a sudden case of amnesia. But I remember that game vividly. You see, my dad was a gambler and that put a real strain on Mom. Like any good son, I wanted to help out. I'm sure Steven

Lords could appreciate that. I borrowed money from some guys and put a pretty hefty bet on Lords's team, not only to win but also to beat the spread."

Sydney rolled her eyes. "Russell, nobody wants to hear some pathetic gambler's tale about how they lost their nut on a bet," she said. "Why don't you just—"

"Fourth quarter, tie score. Final seconds of the game UConn goes into a half-court trap that catches Lords just past half court. It was a weak double team. In fact, I'd seen him split better traps than that all season long. But that time he didn't split it. He dribbled the ball off of his foot and UConn picked it up. A stupid foul on a made three-pointer and the made free throw afterward meant UConn beat the spread and cost me some serious money. Money I couldn't pay back."

"I'm sorry to hear about your bad luck," Allen said. "But you should know by now that you can't believe anything that comes out of Peter Owens's mouth. Hell, as far as I'm concerned that's just another story he's been trying to concoct to make himself look like a credible reporter. There's no evidence of Steven—"

"Spare me the bullshit, will you? I know ol' Dub here took advantage of Lords, who only went along with the point shaving to help his mother," Russell said. "I'll admit I was dead wrong about Lords. Sure he's a lousy husband, but a guy who sacrifices his time to help sick kids and a struggling mother isn't all bad. I can respect that."

Russell stopped for a moment and looked at Dub. "Michelle must have gone to you when Lords broke things off with her because she knew you had an ax to grind and had enough dirt on him to help her bury him. That right, Dub?"

Dub said nothing.

"So the way I figure it, somewhere along the way Allen here convinced you the loyal thing to do would be to clean off the dirt you helped shovel on Lords's image by getting back the book you were helping her write. Then voilà, his accuser winds up dead along with at least one other victim, and here the three of you are having a little victory party while Steven's best friend fights for his life in the ICU."

Allen's laugh came out hard and brittle. "That's quite a story, Detective. If police work doesn't pan out for you, you could have a great career as a writer. Hell, you're better than Owens."

Russell fixed his eyes on Dub, who was somehow able to muster a smile. His gold tooth shined from between his lips. His eyes weren't shifting like they were before.

"You know, when I was here a few days ago to talk to Steven, I found out something interesting. Did you know the team issues new warm-up jackets every year?"

"Well, that's very interesting, but what's that got to do with anything?" Allen said.

"I'm getting to that," Russell said. "When I was in the hospital I tuned in to Owens's show, and I saw our man

Wallace here wearing this season's Miami warm-up jacket, with Lords's name on it."

"So what, dawg?" Dub said. "I got that jacket from a shop in my hometown. They have all kinds of Steven Lords shit back there. Everybody's proud of the homegrown hero, you know?"

"Oh, I'm sure they are. Only problem is, you can't get that jacket in stores. Player-issued jackets are the only ones that have the players' names on the front. The jackets in stores don't. So . . . why don't you tell me how you really got that jacket?"

Dub took his arm off the backrest and sat up. Breathing heavily, he looked at Allen and Sydney sitting calmly on the sofa.

"It was a gift," Allen interjected. "I got the jacket from Steven and gave it to Wallace here as a peace offering, if you will. Wallace and Steven had been so close for so long, I thought it was a shame their relationship soured over some . . . misunderstandings."

"Here I was thinking that jacket may have been the same jacket Steven gave to Michelle," Russell said. "That seemed like a good possibility because I know for a fact she had it with her when she came to Miami."

He paused, eyes locked on Allen. "You know what else is interesting, though? She was also carrying a black Toshiba laptop. Just like that one on the table, actually."

"I don't know anything about Michelle's jacket," Allen

said. "Maybe she sent it to the hotel laundry to be dry-cleaned. I'm sure it'll turn up."

"Oh, I'm sure it will," Russell said. "But now that I think of it, this computer is a real mystery. One minute it's in her room. Next thing we know Michelle is dead and her computer disappears, only to turn up—"

"Sorry, Russell. This one here is mine," Sydney snapped. She pressed a few keys and turned the laptop around. "We were checking out Steven's new shoe commercial."

Russell looked at the streaming video on the screen. These guys had an answer for everything. He sat back and looked at Sydney.

"Well you're just full of surprises aren't you?"

"What's that supposed to mean?"

"First, your choice in laptops. Yours is the same size, shape, color, brand—heck, probably even the same model—as the one that disappeared from the victim of a crime you were investigating," Russell said, eyes wide with feigned amazement. "That's really quite a coincidence.

"But what really amazes me is your choice in guns, Sydney. I mean what are the odds you would use the same type of gun Eddie Brown carried?"

Sydney straightened, bristling and looking impatient. "I don't know what you're getting at, Russell, but I'm getting tired of your games. What are you doing here anyway?"

Russell smiled. "Just wrapping up a few loose ends. You see, I picked up a few shell casings from the parking lot after the shooting and had the boys in the lab take a look at them. Would you like to know what they discovered?"

"Oh please, tell me. I'm on the edge of my seat with anticipation."

"The indentations made by the gun matched the ones from the shells we found at James Cooper's place. Can you believe that?"

"So what? You had Eddie's gun. Why are you even bringing this up?"

"Because the cases didn't come from Eddie's gun," Russell said. "They came from *your* gun. The one I saw you firing when all hell broke loose outside Johnny Ray's."

Sydney raised her eyebrows. "Are you sure about that?"

"I'm positive. I had Eddie's gun on me when the shooting started," Russell said.

"Christ, Russell, I saw your medical charts when I went to see you. You suffered a grade two concussion. That comes with some memory loss," Sydney said. "So let me ask you: Are you sure I had the same handgun Eddie did?"

Russell constricted his brow. "I see what you're trying to do, but it won't work. I saw you shooting and—"

"You saw me shooting. Hell yes, I was shooting. I saved your life and you're welcome, by the way. But you can't be sure what I was shooting. I may have been shooting that .22 you gave me."

"So how'd the shells wind up on the ground?"

"That's not my job to explain, Detective. The burden

of proof is on you in this little fantasy scenario you've concocted."

Russell sat motionless.

"Are there any other ideas or theories you'd like to run by us?" Sydney said. "If not, could you please leave so we can finish enjoying the game?"

With nothing left to say, Russell stood. The smirks on their faces tore through him like surgical blades. There had to be something else he hadn't tried. There must've been something he could use to get leverage on one of them.

CHAPTER 43

Russell was brushing crumbs off his pants when he felt something in his pocket. He smiled at the realization of what it was: a shell casing he'd found outside at Johnny Ray's.

He stopped, turned, and sat back down in a chair next to Sydney, casing gripped in his hand.

"Just one more question," he said.

"Will you knock this off, Russell?" Sydney said. "Face it, it's over."

"Not so fast," Russell said. "Do you remember those kids I gave my tickets to, the ones who lived next door to James Cooper? Well, I drove them to the arena tonight, and on our way in one of them identified the car that was at Cooper's house the night he was killed."

"Is that right?"

Russell glanced over at Mosley, whose smile slowly disappeared from his face. "That *is* right. So naturally I ran the plates. Needless to say, I was more than a little surprised to find the car belongs to your new friend Dub here."

"So what, Russell?" Sydney said. "Those boys said all sorts of cars were in and out of that place all the time."

"That was true. But I when searched that car I found something really interesting."

Russell unclenched his fist and placed the shell casing next to the laptop on the table.

"What's that?" Sydney asked. "Don't tell me you're going to try to bluff me with some bullshit like this. You really are a gambler, aren't you?"

"I think you know exactly what it is," Russell said. "Because you're probably the one who put it there."

"What?"

"That's right. It's a shell casing. The very same one you put under the driver's seat of Dub's car."

Mosley stood. "What do you mean, you found that under the driver's seat? What the hell is going on here?"

"Calm down, Wallace. I worked his case. He doesn't have anything," Sydney said.

"Maybe not when it comes to you or Allen—at least not yet. But I got everything I need on Dub here. I've got two witnesses who can ID his car, plus a shell casing I'm quite sure will match the gun used to kill Cooper."

"Wait a minute, man! What the hell do you mean you have everything you need on me? Somebody better tell this man something!" Dub said. "This is some bullshit."

"He's just fishing and looking pretty pathetic in the process," Sydney said. "If you got that from his car, where's your search warrant? You can't execute a search like that without a warrant."

"Are you willing to risk that, Dub? I mean, you've had brushes with cops. You know how it works, what we can get away with when we know someone's guilty."

Russell could see the panic setting in. Dub was looking all over the place, ignoring Allen's and Sydney's pleas to calm down. "I saw the surveillance video from the hotel the night Cooper was killed. I saw you and Sydney leave the hotel together," he added.

"What does that prove? Leaving the hotel together is hardly a crime. You've got nothing. The case is closed, Russell. Everybody knows it was Eddie. It's over," Sydney said. "Wallace, don't listen to any of it. He's just trying to play you against us. It's the oldest trick in the book, like something out of a bad cop movie."

"Then what happened?" Russell asked Dub. "Did you distract Cooper while Sydney came in through the back door and shot him? What happened to the shell casing? There were two shots and we only recovered one casing. Did you see Sydney pick up the other one? I can tell you, it wasn't at the scene. I didn't find it. The CSIs didn't find it.

But it turned up in your car, under your seat. How do *you* think it got there?"

"Wallace, don't be a fool," Allen said. "Think about it. None of what he's saying makes sense."

"He's just trying to scare you," Sydney added. "He didn't find anything in your car because there was nothing to find. Just stay cool, all right?"

"Stay cool with the fact that you both used this man to do your dirty work? Don't take the fall for them, Wallace. Tell me how it happened. They paid you to kill Michelle and they used you to get Cooper."

Small beads of sweat began to trickle from Dub's forehead as he shifted back and forth while he listened.

"They set Eddie up!" Russell said. "He was Lords's best friend and they set him up. What the hell do you think they'll do to you, huh? You're just another loose end they need to tie up. They paid you to kill a pregnant woman, and now they're trying to frame you for the murder of James Cooper like they framed Eddie. And if you let them get away with this, I can guarantee you'll never see the light of day again," Russell said. "They'll shoot you full of so much electricity that you'll smell like crisp applewood bacon. Then what are you gonna do with all that money I'm guessing Allen paid you?"

Russell stood, letting his voice get louder with intensity. "You think these bastards care? Eddie thought so, and that got him a one-way ticket into the ICU. I can tell you right now there won't be any hospital bed for you. There's gonna be a pine box, and all Allen and Sydney will say is, 'So long, Dub, thanks for being our little bitch!'"

Taking his eyes off Dub's, even for a split second, turned out to be a mistake. Dub was a lot faster than he looked and he sprang from his defiant, angry posture, knocking Russell over the chair he'd vacated. As his forehead hit the floor a bright burst of light exploded behind his eyes, followed by a flood of excruciating pain. Russell somehow stayed conscious and watched as Allen and Sydney jumped to their feet. But he could do no more than curl into a defensive posture as Dub pummeled him in the head.

"I ain't nobody's bitch, you hear me? You hear me!"

Dub wasn't sure why Russell suddenly went limp. He started stirring again after a few seconds, but not before Dub got a look at a .22 handgun in his ankle holster peeking out from his pantleg. Without a second thought Dub delivered a swift kick to Russell's midsection and bent over to grab the firearm.

"This has all just gone to hell now!" Allen shouted. "You've really fucked this situation up, you know that? I had it all planned out and it was all going the way it was supposed to before you decided to assault a cop and all but confess to his claims."

"Did that plan include setting me up?" Wallace turned and pointed the gun at Allen. "You've cut me out before. Were you trying to pull that shit again?"

"Are you out of your mind?" Sydney said. "Are you fucking crazy?"

"Shut up, bitch! Did you and your boyfriend here think y'all were just gonna set me up? Did you really think it was gonna go down like that? I told y'all I ain't the one for that shit. I told that bitch Michelle the same thing and you see where it got her!"

"Nobody was trying to set you up, Wallace. Russell was lying, plain and simple. I never left a shell casing in your car, you idiot!"

"You better watch who you're calling an idiot," Dub said, turning the gun on Sydney.

"Put the gun down, Wallace. Let's work this out," Allen said.

"Work this out?" Dub said, now turning the gun on Allen. "You think you can talk your way out of this, Allen? You think you can set me up like a chump and negotiate your way out of this?"

"Wallace, stop it!" It was Sydney, who had started toward him, eyes blazing.

"No you stop it!" When she kept approaching, Dub pointed the gun at Sydney's stomach and pulled the trigger.

***

SYDNEY FELT A WHITE-HOT PAIN IN HER GUT. HER MOUTH flooded with saliva, followed by an intense urge to vomit. Her stomach hurt so much she thought she'd pass out, but as she fell to the floor she managed to muster the strength to put pressure on her abdomen in hopes of stopping the bleeding.

"What the hell is wrong with you?" Allen shouted, tears in his eyes as he wadded up his jacket.

"This is how you treat me?" she heard Dub say. "I take care of Michelle for you just like I promised. Then I helped Sydney with James Cooper. Then I find some boys to take care of Eddie for you and you think you can play me like some sucker? Is that what you thought?"

"Nobody was trying to set you up!" Allen said. Sydney could feel him pushing hard on her stomach with his coat, but everything was getting warmer and in a few seconds she felt herself slip into unconsciousness.

RUSSELL SAT UP, HIS MIND REELING FROM THE SCENE THAT had played out in front of him. The sharp report of the gunshot had brought him to, and while his head hurt like crazy he had no problem making sense of what happened. His bluff had worked but then backfired. Now Sydney had a bullet in her gut and there was no telling what Dub would do if he didn't tell him the truth. Or even if he did.

"He's right, Dub," Russell said, struggling to his feet.

"Allen didn't set you up—I did. That was a shell casing I took from the parking lot shooting. But make no mistake, this thing is over. Don't make it any worse. Just put the gun down."

The door banged open and the room flooded with police and arena security. Several officers already had their guns drawn, which meant someone must have heard the shot, even above all the crowd noise.

"We need medical help in here right away!" Russell said.

"Drop the gun!" a cop ordered.

Mosley had his gun trained on Allen but was staring wide-eyed at the policemen closest to him.

"You've got to listen to them, Mosley," Russell said. "There's nowhere for you to go. You need to give it up now."

Mosley's gaze shifted from the police to Russell and then to Allen, who was frantically trying to keep pressure on Sydney's stomach. His jacket was soaked and a dark pool of blood was growing on the floor under her.

"I really fucked this up, didn't I?" Dub said, his voice suddenly hollow and monotone. Russell watched as Dub turned the gun away from Allen and toward his own head.

"Don't do that, son," a voice said behind them. Russell turned to see an older unarmed policeman slowly walking to where Mosley stood. "That's not the answer. Just put the gun down and no one else needs to get hurt. Do you understand?"

Meanwhile Sydney had lifted her head and after a flash of

eye contact with Russell yelled, "Hey, Wallace, you know only punk bitches kill themselves, right?"

Wallace turned to Sydney, giving Russell the opportunity he needed. He jumped to his feet, closed the space between them in two quick steps, and tackled Mosley from behind, knocking him to the floor and sending the gun skittering underneath the sofa.

It only took a second for Russell to get his service revolver from its holster and plant its barrel against the base of Mosley's skull. "It's over, do you understand me?"

THINGS MOVED FAST AS THE POLICE HANDCUFFED MOSLEY and read him his rights while two EMTs put Sydney on a stretcher. After directing one of the officers to arrest Allen Warner for conspiracy to commit murder, Russell stopped the gurney at the door and looked into Sydney's half-open eyes. She looked weak but still conscious and she met his gaze with woozy indifference.

"So was it worth it?" he asked quietly.

The question was directed at Sydney, but Allen, who had his hands behind his back and was being handcuffed, answered instead.

"You know, most agents would give anything to have a client who could do what Steven did on and off the court. What happened here was just—"

"I wasn't talking to you," Russell said. "But you know what,

Allen? I'm sure you'll find some way to twist all this nonsense in your own mind to make it out like you were doing the right thing, looking after the interests of your client.

"But at the end of the day you're just a greedy scumbag who did nothing but betray your client in the worst kind of way. You're a criminal. And I'm going to make sure you get *exactly* what you deserve."

Allen glared at him. He was being led toward the door when Russell heard some commotion in the hallway and then saw Art Morales pushing through the growing crowd of onlookers and into the suite.

"Well I guess you won't be needing this," Morales said, holding up an envelope. "Here I go moving heaven and earth to get you your warrant, and now I find out there's been a shooting and we've got two suspects in custody. So why don't you tell me what the hell happened?"

"It's a long story," Russell said, smiling at the prospect that the case was finally closed. "Give me until tomorrow and I'll explain everything in my report."

"Hey, Russell, you look like hell. You should get yourself checked out." Morales said. "Where are you going?"

"In case you haven't realized, there's a game going on tonight," Russell said. "I'm going to watch Steven Lords bring a title to Miami."

EPILOGUE

There were no bright lights or news cameramen standing outside when Steven pulled up to his house, only lonely silence. He couldn't remember his house ever looking so dark.

He'd thought about checking into a hotel, but given his previous experiences that was out of the question. Still, the house looked so much emptier when he knew no one would be coming to the door to meet him. Steven pressed a button in his car to turn on some interior house lights. Sitting out in the driveway wasn't going to make walking in any easier, and wishful thinking wasn't about to bring anyone back.

He got out of his car and grabbed his bags from the backseat. Eddie used to help him get his things inside a lot of the time, especially after big games, but those days had come and gone. It was still hard to believe everything that had gone down—supposedly for the sake of preserving his image, but in reality because of all-out greed.

He'd only had a brief chance to talk with Detective Russell after the game, but it was long enough to get the picture. He couldn't help wondering if Allen had lost his mind at some point along the way or if he'd been corrupt all along.

As Steven set his bags on the front porch to unlock the door, he felt the weight of the realization that nothing would ever be the same again. His wife and daughter were gone. His agent's actions had left two people dead and his best friend clinging to life in the ICU. All because he had been stupid and selfish enough to need saving from himself.

AFTER STEVEN STEPPED INSIDE, HE PUT HIS BASEBALL CAP and keys on the foyer table and dropped his bags on the floor. The silence was deafening as he limped upstairs.

The cheers from that night's victory were a distant memory, as was the fleeting sense of elation he felt at helping his team take game one. In its place was a crushing sense of guilt and profound sadness unlike anything he'd ever experienced.

On his way to his bedroom he stepped over a toy Cassidy must have dropped in the hallway. He doubled back and bent down to pick it up. It was Whoopi, Cassidy's pink stuffed rhinoceros he had bought for her the year prior, when they went to Animal Kingdom. Steven smiled when he remembered Cassie had named it Whoopi because she and her mom watched *The View* almost every morning. He limped into her bedroom with it and turned on the bedside table lamp. Looking at her tiny canopy reminded him of when he would come home after a game and put her to bed. Cassidy always hated to go to sleep without saying her prayers with him. Steven was about to lay Whoopi on the bookshelf when he decided to hold on to it. He turned off the light, closed the door, and continued to limp down the hall to his bedroom.

He sat on the edge of the bed and laid Whoopi next to him. He carefully took off his shoes and looked at his swollen ankle. He knew he should've made an ice bag when he was in the kitchen. If Karen were there, she would've put a cold pack in the freezer for him or ran him a hot shower for his aching muscles. Steven looked at Whoopi and wondered how Cassie was doing without her toy. He took out his cell phone and called Karen. Even though she was upset, he was hoping he could at least talk to his daughter. Steven rolled his eyes when her voicemail picked up.

"Hey, babe, it's me. I found Whoopi in the hallway and I know how much Cassidy loves it. Why don't you call me and I'll bring it to you, or you can come over and pick it up? I'll talk to you later. Love you."

He put his phone down and picked up the television remote. He smiled as he leaned against his pillows and cued up Sports Center. It was unlikely Karen would call back, so

Steven didn't see the point in fighting off sleep. It had been a long night and he could feel his eyes starting to get heavy. He reached for Cassidy's toy and held it closer to him as he started to fall asleep. There was nobody there to tell him goodnight as he lay in his huge bed alone.

But then the phone rang . . .

ACKNOWLEDGMENTS

THANK GOD FOR THE TALENT, THE PATIENCE, AND THE endurance to see this venture through to the end. Thank you to my mother, Barbara J. Monds, and my father, Willie M. Turner, for all your wisdom and support. Thanks to Jennifer Jones for the inspiration. To all my friends, there are too many of you to list by name, I greatly appreciate all the support. And a special thanks to Ross Browne and his staff at the Editorial Department. Thank you for taking a chance on a bunch of words written on a pile of papers.

ABOUT THE AUTHOR

BILLY TURNER is a graduate of St. Thomas University with a BBA in Sports Administration. He has worked extensively with the NBA's Miami Heat along with the CBA, NFL, and several other sports organizations. *Personal Foul* is his first novel.

Made in the USA
San Bernardino, CA
09 March 2015